Like a man and a maid in love for the first time, they helped each other dress, with Will touching, kissing, laughing with Elodie as she donned her simple maid's gown. He knew once they reached Paris she would try to slip away from him, but he felt too light and euphoric to worry about it. Happiness was fizzing in his chest like a freshly opened bottle of champagne.

He'd had many an adventure...but never one like this. Never with a woman who was a companion as uncomplaining as a man, as resourceful as any of the riding officers with whom he'd crept through the Spanish and Portuguese wilderness, working with partisans and disrupting the French.

Their liaison was too fragile to last, but for now he'd be like his Elodie and suck every iota of joy from an already glorious day that promised, once he'd taken care of provisions for the morrow and found her a room with a bed, to become even more wonderful.

He twined his fingers in hers as they went back to their horses. 'How glad I am to be out of those monk's robes! I've been dying to touch you as we travel.'

'Good thing,' she agreed. 'Since you're grinning like a farmer who's just out-bargained a travelling tinker. I doubt anyone could look at us now and not know we are lovers.'

He stopped   d?'

'No I'm   ther, Will

RANSLEIGH ROGUES

Where these notorious rakes go,
scandal always follows…

Max, Will, Alastair and Dominic Ransleigh—
cousins, friends…and the most wickedly attractive
men in Regency London. Between war, betrayal
and scandal, love has never featured in
the Ransleighs' destinies—until now!

Don't miss this enthralling quartet from Julia Justiss.

It started with Max's story in
THE RAKE TO RUIN HER
March 2013

Now follow Will's story in
THE RAKE TO REDEEM HER
April 2013

Look for Alastair and Dominic's adventures
coming 2014

THE RAKE TO REDEEM HER

Julia Justiss

First published in Great Britain 2013
by Mills & Boon, an imprint of Harlequin (UK) Limited.
Harlequin (UK) Limited, Eton House, 18-24 Paradise Road,
Richmond, Surrey TW9 1SR

© Janet Justiss 2013

ISBN: 978 0 263 89821 7

Harlequin (UK) policy is to use papers that are natural, renewable and recyclable products and made from wood grown in sustainable forests. The logging and manufacturing process conform to the legal environmental regulations of the country of origin.

Printed and bound in Spain
by Blackprint CPI, Barcelona

Julia Justiss wrote her first plot ideas for a Nancy Drew novel in the back of her third-grade notebook, and has been writing ever since. After such journalistic adventures as publishing poetry and editing an American Embassy newsletter she returned to her first love: writing fiction. Her Regency historical novels have been winners or finalists in the Romance Writers of America's Golden Heart™, *RT Book Reviews* Best First Historical, Golden Quill, National Readers' Choice and Daphne du Maurier contests. She lives with her husband, three children and two dogs in rural east Texas, where she also teaches high school French. For current news and contests, please visit her website at www.juliajustiss.com

Novels by the same author:

THE WEDDING GAMBLE
THE PROPER WIFE
MY LADY'S TRUST
MY LADY'S PLEASURE
MY LADY'S HONOUR
A SCANDALOUS PROPOSAL
SEDUCTIVE STRANGER
THE COURTESAN
THE THREE GIFTS
   (part of *A Regency Lords & Ladies Christmas* anthology)
THE UNTAMED HEIRESS
ROGUE'S LADY
CHRISTMAS WEDDING WISH
   (part of *Regency Candlelit Christmas* anthology)
THE SMUGGLER AND THE SOCIETY BRIDE*
A MOST UNCONVENTIONAL MATCH
WICKED WAGER
FROM WAIF TO GENTLEMAN'S WIFE
SOCIETY'S MOST DISREPUTABLE GENTLEMAN
THE RAKE TO RUIN HER†

Silk & Scandal Regency mini-series
†*Ransleigh Rogues*

AUTHOR NOTE

Sometimes a minor character grabs your imagination and won't let go, intriguing you so much that you know you will have to uncover the rest of her story. Such was the case with the mysterious Madame Lefevre, the woman who lured Max Ransleigh into friendship at the Congress of Vienna in order to set up an assassination attempt on Lord Wellington in the first book of *The Ransleigh Rogues* mini-series, THE RAKE TO RUIN HER.

Where had she come from? What drove her to participate in the plot? What happened to her afterwards? As I explored the answers to those questions I discovered a unique and intriguing woman—a French emigrée whose family was destroyed by the Revolution, a survivor dragged along by the turbulent historical forces that catapulted France in one generation from monarchy to republic to empire and back. Taught by remorseless circumstance to depend only on herself, Elodie trusts no one and expects nothing.

Who could I pair with such a resourceful and determined heroine? Though I'd originally intended a different story for him, only one man could match her: Will Ransleigh, Max's illegitimate cousin. Cast into the London slums on the death of his mother, a clergyman's daughter seduced and abandoned by Max's uncle, Will survived by his wits on the streets for six years before Max's father plucked him from Seven Dials and sent him to his country estate, instructing Max and his cousins to make a proper Ransleigh out of this gutter rat.

I hope you will enjoy Will and Elodie's story.

I love to hear from readers! Find me at my website, www.juliajustiss.com, for excerpts, updates and background bits about my books, on Facebook at www.facebook.com/juliajustiss and on Twitter @juliajustiss

Chapter One

◆◆◆◆◆◆◆

Barton Abbey—late spring, 1816

'I wager *I* could find her.' Smouldering with anger against the woman who had destroyed his cousin Max's diplomatic career, Will Ransleigh accepted a glass of brandy from his host.

'Welcome back to England,' Alastair Ransleigh said, saluting Will with his own glass before motioning him to an armchair. 'Far be it from me to bet against "Wagering Will", who never met a game of chance he couldn't win. But why do you think *you* could find her, when Max, with all his official contacts, could not?'

'I never had much use for *officials*,' Will observed with a grimace. 'Would have transported me for stealing a loaf of bread to feed myself and my starving mates.'

'You've cleaned up so well, I sometimes forget you were once gallows-bait,' Alastair said with a grin. 'But to be fair, where would one expect to look? Madame Lefevre was cousin and hostess to Thierry St Arnaud, one of Prince Talleyrand's top aides in the French delegation at the Congress of Vienna. The family's quite old and well known, even if they did turn out to be Bonapartists.'

'That may be. But it's those in the serving class who really know what goes on: maids, valets, cooks, grooms, hotel employees, servants at the Hoffburg, keepers of public houses. I'll use them to track Madame Lefevre.'

'When I visited Max at his wife's farm, he insisted he was content there.' Alastair laughed. 'He even claimed training horses is rather like diplomacy: one must coax rather than coerce. Except that horses don't lie and their memories are short, so they don't hold your mistakes against you.'

'Just like Max to make light of it. But all of us—you, me, Dom—knew from our youth that Max was destined to be one of England's foremost politicians—Prime Minister, even!

Would he choose training horses over a brilliant government career, if he *truly* had a choice? I don't believe it.'

'I was suspicious, too, at first,' Alastair admitted. 'Max, who never showed any interest in a woman who wasn't both beautiful and accomplished, happily wedding a little nobody who prefers rusticating in Kent to London society? But I ended up liking Caro. She rides better than I do—an admission I make most unwillingly—and breeds top-notch horseflesh on that farm in Kent. She's quite impressive—which is saying something, given my generally low opinion of womankind.' He paused, a bleakness passing over his face.

He's still not over her, Will thought, once again consigning to eternal hellfire the woman who'd broken her engagement and Alastair's heart.

His fury reviving against the latest female to harm one of his Ransleigh Rogue cousins, he continued, 'The very idea is ridiculous— Max, involved in a plot to assassinate Wellington? I'd have thought his valour at Waterloo put a stop to that nonsense.'

Alastair sighed. 'The hard truth is that the attempt in Vienna embarrassed both the

French, who were negotiating as allies at the time, and our own forces, who didn't winkle out the conspiracy. Now that Bonaparte's put away at St Helena for good, neither side wanted to rake up old scandals.'

'Couldn't his father do anything? He's practically run the Lords for years.'

'The Earl of Swynford preferred not to champion his son and risk further damaging his political standing, already weakened by Max's "lapse in judgement",' Alastair said drily.

'So he abandoned him. Bastard!' Will added a colourful curse from his days on the London streets. 'Just like my dear uncle never to let his family's needs get in the way of his political aspirations. Makes me glad I was born on the wrong side of the blanket.'

Alastair shook his head, his expression bitter. 'Whoever set up the Vienna scheme was clever, I'll give them that. There'd be no approach more likely to elicit Max's response than to dangle before him some helpless woman in need of assistance.'

'He always had a soft spot for the poor and downtrodden,' Will agreed. 'His treatment of me being a prime example. We need to get

Madame Lefevre back to England! Let *her* explain how she invented some sad tale to delay Max's rendezvous with Wellington, leaving the commander waiting alone, vulnerable to attack. Surely that would clear Max of blame, since no man who calls himself a gentleman would have refused a lady begging for his help. He found no trace of St Arnaud, either, while in Vienna?'

'It appears he emigrated to the Americas. It's uncertain whether Madame Lefevre accompanied him. If you do mean to search, it won't be easy. It's been more than a year since the attempt.'

Will shrugged. 'An attack on the man who led all of Europe against Napoleon? People will remember that.'

Alastair opened his mouth as if to speak, then hesitated.

'What?' Will asked.

'Don't jump all over me for asking, but can you afford such a mission? The blunt you'll get from selling out will last a while, but rather than haring off to the Continent, don't you need to look for some occupation? Unless... did the earl come through and—?'

Will waved Alastair to silence. 'No, the earl

did not. You didn't really expect our uncle to settle an allowance on me, did you?'

'Well, he did promise, after you managed to scrape together the funds to buy your own commission, that if you made good in the army, he'd see you were settled afterward in a style befitting a Ransleigh.'

Will laughed. 'I imagine he expected me to either be killed or cashiered out. And, no, I've no intention of going to him, cap in hand, to remind him of his pledge, so save your breath.'

'Then what will you do?'

'There are some possibilities. Before I pursue them, though, I'll see Max reinstated to his former position. I've got sufficient blunt for the journey with enough extra to gild the right hands, if necessary.'

'I'll come with you. "Ransleigh Rogues for ever", after all.'

'No, you won't. Wait, hear me out,' he said, forestalling Alastair's protest. 'If I needed a sabre-wielding Hussar to ride beside me into a fight, there's no man I'd rather have. But for this journey…'

Looking his cousin up and down, he grinned. 'In your voice, your manner, even your walk, there's no hiding that you're Alastair Ransleigh of Barton Abbey, nephew of an earl, wealthy owner of vast property. I'll need to travel as a man nobody notices and the alley rats would sniff you out in an instant.'

'You're the nephew of an earl yourself,' Alastair pointed out.

'Perhaps, but thanks to my dear father abandoning my mother, unwed and increasing, in the back streets of London, I had the benefit of six years' education in survival. I know how thieves, Captain Sharps and cutthroats operate.'

'But these will be Austrian thieves, Captain Sharps and cutthroats. And you don't speak German.'

Will shrugged. 'Thievery is thievery and you'd be surprised at my many talents. The army had more uses for me after Waterloo than simply letting me hang about the hospital, watching over Dom's recovery.'

'He's healed now, hasn't he?' Alastair asked, diverted by Will's mention of the fourth cousin in their Ransleigh Rogues' gallery. 'Has he... recovered?'

Will recalled the desolate look in Dom's one remaining eye. 'Dandy Dominick', he'd been called, the handsomest man in the regiment.

Besting them all at riding, hunting, shooting—and charming the ladies.

His face scarred, one arm gone, his physical prowess diminished, Dom would have to come to terms with much more than his injuries, Will knew. 'Not yet. Once I got him safely back to England, he told me I'd wetnursed him long enough and kicked me out. So I might as well go to Vienna.'

Alastair frowned. 'I still don't like you going there alone. Max said the authorities in Vienna strongly discouraged him from investigating the matter. You'll get no help from them. It could even be dangerous.'

'Dangerous?' Will rose and made a circuit of the room. 'Do you remember the first summer we were all together at Swynford Court?' he asked abruptly, looking back at Alastair. 'The lawyer who found me in Seven Dials had just turned me over to the earl, who, assured I was truly his brother's child, dumped me in the country. Telling you, Max and Dom to make something of me, or else. I was…rather unlikeable.'

Alastair laughed. 'An understatement! Surly, filthy, cursing everyone you encountered in barely comprehensible cant!'

'After two weeks, you and Dom were ready to drown me in the lake. But Max wouldn't give up. One night he caught me alone in the stables. I tried every dirty trick I knew, but he still beat the stuffing out of me. Then, cool as you please, he told me my behaviour had to change. That I was his cousin and a Ransleigh, and he was counting on me to learn to act like one. I didn't make it easy, but he kept goading, coaxing, working on me, like water dripping on stone, until he finally convinced me there could be advantages to becoming more than the leader of thieves in a rookery. Max knew that if I didn't change, when the earl returned at the end of the summer, blood kin or not, he would toss me back into the streets.'

Will stared past Alastair out the library window, seeing not the verdant pastures of Barton Abbey, but the narrow, noisome alleys of Seven Dials. 'If he had, I'd probably be dead now. So I owe Max. For my life. For giving me the closest, most loyal friends and cousins any man could wish for. I swear on whatever honour I possess that I won't take up my own life again until I see his name cleared. Until he has the choice, if he truly wishes, to become the great political leader we all know he should be.'

After studying him for a moment, Alastair nodded. 'Very well. If there's anything I can do, you'll let me know, won't you? If Max hadn't led you and Dom after me into the army, I might not have survived, either. For months after Di—' he halted, having almost said the forbidden name. 'Well, I didn't much care whether I lived or died.'

Will wondered if sometimes, Alastair still didn't much care.

'I might need some help on the official front when it comes time to get the wench into England.'

'She may balk at returning. After all, if she proves herself a spy, the gallows await.'

'I can be…persuasive.'

Alastair chuckled. 'I don't want to know. When do you propose to leave?'

'Tomorrow.'

'But you have just got back! Mama expects you to stay at least a week and Max will want to see you.'

Will shook his head. 'Your mama's being kind and Max would only try to dissuade me. Better I don't see him until…after. If he asks, tell him the army still has business for me on the Continent. Besides, you were right; it's been more than a year. No sense waiting for memories to fade any more than they already have.'

'Do keep me posted. It might take some time to ride to your rescue.'

'Tonight, all I'll need rescue from is too much brandy. Unlikely, as you're being entirely too stingy with it.'

Laughing, Alastair retrieved the bottle and refilled their glasses. 'Ransleigh Rogues for ever!'

'Ransleigh Rogues,' Will replied, clinking his glass with Alastair's.

Chapter Two

~~~~~~~~~~~~~~~~~~~~

Vienna, Austria—six weeks later

Elodie Lefevre shifted her chair into the beam of afternoon sunlight spilling through the window. Taking up her needlework again, she breathed in the soft scent of the late-blooming daffodils she'd planted last autumn in the tiny courtyard garden below. Nodding violas added their sweet fragrance as well.

She paused a moment, letting the calm and beauty seep into her soul, soothing the restless anxiety that lurked always just below the surface. By this evening, she would have this consignment of embroidery finished. Clara would come by with dinner, bringing a new load of embroidery and payment for completing the last.

Against all the odds, she had survived. Despite the constant imperative gnawing within her to get back to Paris, she must remain patient and continue working, hoarding her slowly increasing store of coins. Perhaps late this year, she would finally have enough saved to return…and search for Philippe.

A wave of longing gripped her as her mind caressed his beloved image—the black curls falling over his brow, the dark, ever-curious, intelligent eyes, the driving energy that propelled him. Was he still in Paris? How had he changed in the nearly eighteen months since she'd left?

Would he recognise her? She glanced at herself in the mirror opposite. She was thinner, of course, after her long recovery, but except for her crooked fingers, most of the injuries didn't show. Her blue eyes were shadowed, perhaps, and long hours indoors had dulled the gold highlights the sun had once burnished in her soft brown hair, but otherwise, she thought she looked much the same.

Suddenly, something—a faint stir of the air, a flicker of light—seized her attention. Instantly alert, moving only her eyes, she discovered the source: a barely perceptible movement in the uppermost corner of the mirror, which reflected both her image and the adjacent window that also overlooked the courtyard.

Scarcely breathing, she shifted her head a tiny bit to the right. Yes, someone was there—a man, perched soundlessly on the narrow balcony beside the window, watching her, all but the top of his tawny head and his eyes hidden behind the wall and the vines crawling up it. Had she not chanced to look into the mirror at that precise instant, she would never have seen him move into position.

From the elevation of his head, he must be tall, and agile, to have scaled the wall so soundlessly. The minuscule amount of him she could see gave her no hint whether he was thin or powerfully built. Whether he was armed, and if so, with what.

Not that the knowledge would do her much good. All she had to defend herself was her sewing scissors; her small pistol was hidden in her reticule in the wardrobe and her knife, in the drawer of the bedside table.

But as seconds passed and he remained motionless, she let out the breath she'd been holding. The afternoon light was bright; he could clearly see she was alone. If he'd meant to attack her, surely he would have made a move by now.

Who was he, then? Not one of the men who'd been watching the apartment from the corner ever since Clara brought her here. No one had bothered her since the foiled attack; so small and damaged a fish as herself, she thought, was of little interest, especially after Napoleon's exile at St Helena put an end once and for all to dreams of a French empire.

Elodie kept her gaze riveted on the mirror as several more seconds dragged on. Despite her near-certainty the stranger did not mean her any immediate harm, her nerves—and a rising anger—finally prompted her to speak.

'*Monsieur*, if you are not going to shoot me, why not come inside and tell me what you want?'

The watching eyes widened with surprise, then in one fluid motion the stranger swung himself through the window to land lightly before her. With a flourish, he swept her a bow. 'Madame Lefevre, I presume?'

Elodie caught her breath, overwhelmed by the sheer masculine power of the man now straightening to his full height. If he meant to harm her, she was in very bad trouble indeed.

He must be English. No other men moved with such arrogance, as if they owned the earth by right. He loomed over her, tall and whipcord-lean. There was no mistaking the hard strength of the arms and shoulders that had levered him so effortlessly up to the balcony and swung him practically into her lap.

His clothes were unremarkable: loose-fitting coat, trousers and scuffed boots that might have been worn by any tradesman or clerk toiling away in the vast city.

But his face—angular jaw, chiselled cheekbones, slightly crooked nose, sensual mouth and the arresting turquoise blue of his eyes— would capture the attention of any woman who chanced to look at him. Certainly it captured hers, so completely that she momentarily forgot the potential danger he posed.

He smiled at her scrutiny, which might have embarrassed her, had she not been suddenly jolted by a sense of *déjà vu*. 'Do I know you?' she asked, struggling to work out why he seemed so familiar. 'Have we met?'

The smile faded and his eyes went cold. 'No, *madame*. You don't know me, but I believe you knew my kinsman all too well. Max Ransleigh.'

Max. His image flashed into her mind: same height and build, thick, wavy golden hair, crystal-blue eyes. An air of command tempered by a kindness and courtesy that had warmed her heart then—and made it twist again now with regret as she recalled him.

The afternoon sun touched this man's tawny hair with tints of auburn; rather than clear blue, his eyes were the hue of the Mediterranean off St Tropez. But beyond that, the two men were remarkably similar. 'You are Max's brother?'

'His cousin. Will Ransleigh.'

'He is well, I trust? I was sorry to have done him…a disservice. I hoped, with Napoleon escaping from Elba so soon after the event in Vienna, that his position had not been too adversely affected.'

He raised one eyebrow, his expression sardonic. Her momentary bedazzlement abruptly vanished as her senses returned to full alert. This man did not mean her well.

'I regret to inform you that your tender hopes were not realised. As you, the cousin of a diplomat, surely know, the "event" that embroiled him in the near-assassination of his commander ruined his career. He was recalled in disgrace and only the outbreak of war allowed him a chance to redeem himself on the field of battle.'

'I understand the carnage was terrible at Waterloo.'

'It was. But even his valour there was not enough to restore his career, which was destroyed by his association with you.'

'I am sorry for it.' And she was. But given the stakes, if she had it all to do over again, she would do nothing differently.

'You are *sorry*? How charming!' he replied, his tone as sardonic as his expression.

Her anger flared again. At men, who used women as pawns to their own purposes. At a woman's always-powerless position in their games. What matter if this man did not believe her? She would not give him the satisfaction of protesting.

As she remained silent, he said, 'Then you will be delighted to know I intend to offer you a chance to make amends. Since you don't appear to be prospering here...' he swept a hand around to indicate the small room, with its worn carpet and shabby furnishing '...I see no reason why you shouldn't agree to leave for England immediately.'

'England?' she echoed, surprised. 'Why should I do that?'

'I'm going to escort you back to London, where we will call on the Foreign Office. There you will explain exactly how you entrapped my cousin in this scheme, manoeuvring him into doing no more than any other gentleman would have done. Demonstrating that he was blameless in not anticipating the assassination attempt, and any fault should be assigned to the intelligence services whose job it was to sniff out such things.'

Her mind racing, Elodie weighed the options. Her hopes rose crazily as she recognised that travelling to London, as this man apparently had the means to do, would get her a deal closer to France, and immediately—not next autumn or in another year, which was as soon as she'd dared hope her slowly accumulating resources would allow.

But even with King Louis on France's throne and the two nations officially at peace, as a French citizen she was still vulnerable. If she testified to involvement in an attempt on the life of the great English hero Lord Wellington, saviour of Europe and victor of Waterloo, she could well be imprisoned. Maybe even executed.

Unless she escaped on the way. Ransleigh would likely want to journey by sea, which would make the chances of eluding him before arrival in England very difficult. Unless…

'I will go with you, but only if we stop first in Paris.' Paris, a city she knew like the lines on her palm. Paris, where only a moment's inattention would allow her to slip away into a warren of medieval alleyways so dense and winding, he would never be able to trail her.

Where, after waiting a safe interval, she could hunt for Philippe.

He made a show of looking about the room, which lacked the presence of a footman or even a maid to lend her assistance. 'I don't think you're in much of a position to dictate terms. And I have no interest in visiting Paris.'

'A mistake, Monsieur Ransleigh. It is a beautiful city.'

'So it is, but unimportant to me at present.'

She shrugged. 'To you, perhaps, but not to me. Unless we go first to Paris, I will not go with you.'

His eyes darkened, unmistakable menace in their depths. 'I can compel you.'

She nodded. 'You could drug me, I suppose. Gag, bind and smuggle me aboard a ship in Trieste. But nothing can compel me to deliver to the London authorities the sort of testimony you wish, unless I myself choose to do so.'

Fury flashed in those blue eyes and his jaw clenched. If his cousin's career had truly been ruined by her actions, he had cause to be angry.

Just as she'd had no choice about involving Max in the plot.

'I could simply kill you now,' he murmured, stepping closer. 'Your life for the life you ruined.' He placed his hands around her neck.

She froze, her heartbeat stampeding. Had she survived so much, only for it all to end now? His hands, warm against the chill of her neck, were large and undoubtedly strong. One quick twist and it would be over.

But despite the hostility of his action, as the seconds ticked away with his fingers encircling her neck, some instinct told her that he didn't truly mean to hurt her.

As her fear subsided to a manageable level, she grasped his hands with a calm she was far from feeling. To her great relief, he let her pull them away from her neck, confirming her assessment.

'Paris first, then London. I will wait in the garden for your decision.'

Though her heart pounded so hard that she was dizzy, Elodie made herself rise and walk with unhurried steps from the room. Not for her life would she let him see how vulnerable she felt. Never again would any man make her afraid.

Why should they? She had nothing left to lose.

Out of his sight, she clutched the stair rail to keep from falling as she descended, then stumbled out the back door to the bench at the centre of the garden. She grabbed the edge with trembling fingers and sat down hard, gulping in a shuddering breath of jonquil-scented air.

Eyes narrowed, Will watched Elodie Lefevre cross the room with quiet elegance and disappear down the stairwell.

Devil's teeth! She was nothing like what he'd expected.

He'd come to Vienna prepared to find a seductive siren, who traded upon her beauty to entice while at the same time playing the frightened innocent. Luring in Max, for whom protecting a woman was a duty engraved upon his very soul.

Elodie Lefevre was attractive, certainly, but hers was a quiet beauty. Sombrely dressed and keeping herself in the background, as he'd learned she always did, she'd have attracted little notice among the crowd of fashionable, aristocratic lovelies who'd fluttered like exotic butterflies through the balls and salons of the Congress of Vienna.

She had courage, too. After her first indrawn breath of alarm, she'd not flinched when he clamped his fingers around her throat.

Not that he'd had any intention of actually harming her, of course. But he'd hoped that his display of anger and a threat of violence might make her panic and capitulate before reinforcements could arrive.

If she had any.

He frowned. It had taken a month of thorough, patient tracking to find her, but the closer he got, the more puzzled and curious he became about the woman who'd just coolly descended to the garden. As if strange men vaulted into her rooms and threatened her life every day.

Maybe they did. For, until she'd confirmed her identity, he'd been nearly convinced the woman he'd located couldn't be the Elodie Lefevre he sought.

Why was the cousin of a wealthy diplomat living in shabby rooms in a decaying, unfashionable section of Vienna?

Why did she inhabit those rooms alone—lacking, from the information he'd charmed out of the landlady, even a maid?

Why did it appear she eked out a living doing embroidery work for a fashionable dressmaker whom Madame Lefevre, as hostess to one of the Congress of Vienna's most well-placed diplomats, would have visited as a customer?

But neither could he deny the facts that had led him, piecing together each small bit of testimony gathered from maids, porters, hotel managers, street vendors, seamstresses, merchants and dry-good dealers, from the elegant hotel suite she'd presided over for St Arnaud to these modest rooms off a Vienna back alley.

St Arnaud himself had disappeared the night of the failed assassination. Will didn't understand why someone clever enough to have concocted such a scheme would have been so careless about ensuring his cousin's safety.

And how had she sensed Will's presence on the balcony? He knew for certain he'd made no sound as he carefully scaled the wall from the courtyard to the ledge outside her window. Either she was incredibly prescient, or he'd badly lost his touch, and he didn't think it was the latter.

Her awareness impressed him even more than her courage, sparking an admiration he had no wish to feel.

Any more than he'd wanted the reaction triggered when he'd placed his hands around her neck. The softness of her skin, the faint scent of lavender teasing his nostrils, sent a fierce desire surging through him, as abrupt and immediate as the leap of her pulse under his thumbs.

Finding himself attracted to Elodie Lefevre was a complication he didn't need. What he did need were answers to all the questions he had about her.

Such as why it was so important for her to get to Paris.

A quick examination of her room told him nothing; the hired furniture, sewing supplies and few basic necessities could have been any-one's. She seemed to possess nothing that gave any clue to the character of the woman who'd lived here, as he'd learned, for more than a year, alone but for the daily visits of her for-mer maid.

He'd just have to go question the woman herself. He suspected she would be as vigilant at keeping her secrets as she was at catching out uninvited visitors to her rooms.

To achieve his aims, he needed to master both those secrets—and her. Turning on his heel, he headed for the garden.

Chapter Three

Will found Madame Lefevre picking spent blooms from the border of lavender surrounding a central planting of tall yellow flowers.

Hearing him approach, she looked back over her shoulder. 'Well?'

He waited, but she added nothing to that single word—neither pleading nor explanation nor entreaty. Once again, he was struck by her calm, an odd quality of stillness overlaid with a touch of melancholy.

Men awaiting battle would envy that sang-froid. Or did she not truly realise how vulnerable she was?

'For a woman who's just had her life threatened, you seem remarkably tranquil.'

She shrugged. 'Nothing I say or do will

change what you have decided. If it is to kill me, I am not strong or skilled enough to prevent you. Struggling and pleading are so…undignified. And if I am to die, I would rather spend my last moments enjoying the beauty of my garden.'

So she did understand the gravity of her position. Yet the calm remained.

As a man who'd earned much of his blunt by his wits, Will had played cards with masters of the game, men who didn't show by the twitch of an eyelid whether they held a winning or losing hand. Madame Lefevre could hold her own with the best of them. He'd never met a woman so difficult to read.

She was like a puzzle spread out in a jumble of pieces. The more he learned about her, the stronger his desire to fit them all together.

Delaying answering her question so he might examine that puzzle further, he said, 'The garden is lovely. So serene, and those yellow flowers are so fragrant. Did you plant it?'

She lifted a brow, as if wondering why he'd abruptly veered from threatening her to talking about plants. 'The daffodils, you mean.' Her lips barely curved in amusement, she looked at him quizzically. 'You grew up in the city, Monsieur Ransleigh, no?'

'Commonplace, are they?' A reluctant, answering smile tugged at his lips. 'Yes, I'm a city lad. But you, obviously, were country bred.'

'Lovely flowers can be found in either place,' she countered.

'Your English is very good, with only a trace of an accent. Where did you learn it?'

She waved a careless hand. 'These last few years, English has been spoken everywhere.'

She'd grown up in the country, then, he surmised from her evasions, probably at an estate with a knowledgeable gardener—and an English governess.

'How did you come to be your cousin's hostess in Vienna?'

'He never married. A diplomat at his level has many social duties.'

Surprised at getting a direct answer this time, he pressed, 'He did not need you to perform those "duties" after Vienna?'

'Men's needs change. So, *monsieur*, do you accept my bargain or not?'

Aha, he thought, gratified. Though she gave no outward sign of anxiety—trembling fingers, fidgeting hands, restless movement—the abrupt return to the topic at hand showed she wasn't as calm as she was trying to appear.

'Yes,' he replied, deciding upon the moment. At least seeming to agree to her demand was essential. It would be a good deal easier to spirit her out of Vienna if she went willingly.

He was still somewhat surprised she would consent to accompany him upon any terms. Unless...

'Don't think you can escape me in Paris,' he warned. 'I'll be with you every moment, like crust on bread.'

'Ah, warm French bread! I cannot wait to taste some.'

She licked her lips. The gesture sent a bolt of lust straight to his loins. Something of his reaction must have showed in his face, for her eyes widened and she smiled knowingly.

He might not be able to prevent his body's response, but he could certainly control his actions, he thought, disgruntled. If anyone was going to play the seduction card in this little game, it would be him—if and when he wished to.

'How did you, cousin to Thierry St Arnaud, come to be here alone?' he asked, steering the discussion back where he wanted it. 'Why did he not take you with him when he fled Vienna?'

'Nothing—and no one—mattered to my cousin but restoring Napoleon to the throne of France. When the attempt failed, his only thought was to escape before the Austrian authorities discovered his connection to the plot, so he might plot anew. Since I was no longer of any use to him, he was done with me.'

It seemed St Arnaud had about as much family loyalty as Will's uncle. But still, self-absorbed as the earl might be, Will knew if anyone bearing Ransleigh blood were in difficulties, the earl would send assistance.

What sort of man would not do that for his own cousin?

Putting aside that question for the moment, Will said, 'Were you equally fervent to see Napoleon restored as emperor?'

'To wash France free of the stain of aristocracy, Napoleon spilled the blood of his own people…and then created an aristocracy of his own. All I know of politics is the guillotine's blade was followed by the emperor's wars. I doubt the fields of Europe will dry in our lifetime.'

'So why did you help St Arnaud?'

'You think he gave me a choice?'

Surprised, he stared at her, assessing. She met his gaze squarely, faint colour stirring in her cheeks at his scrutiny.

A man who would abandon his own cousin probably hadn't been too dainty in coercing her co-operation. Had he hurt her?

Even as the question formed, as if guessing his thoughts, she lowered her gaze and tucked her left hand under her skirt.

An unpleasant suspicion coalescing in his head, Will stepped closer and seized her hand. She resisted, then gasped as he jerked it into the waning sunlight.

Two of the fingers were slightly bent, the knuckles still swollen, as if the bones had been broken and healed badly. 'An example of your cousin's persuasion?' he asked roughly, shocked and disgusted. A man who would attack a woman was beneath contempt.

She pulled her hand back, rubbing the wrist. 'An accident, *monsieur*.'

Will didn't understand why she would protect St Arnaud, if he truly had coerced her participation, then abandoned her. He didn't want to feel the niggle of sympathy stirring within him, had that really been her predicament.

Whatever her reasons, she was still the woman who'd ruined Max's career.

'You'd have me believe you were an innocent pawn, forced by St Arnaud to do his bidding, then discarded when you were no longer of use?'

She smiled sweetly. 'Used, just as you plan to use me, you mean?'

Stung, his anger flared hotter. Plague take her, *he* wasn't her bloody relation, responsible for her safety and well-being. If he used her, it was only what she deserved for entrapping Max.

'Why is it so important for you to go to Paris?' he asked instead.

'It's a family matter. You, who have come all this way and worked so diligently on your cousin's behalf, should appreciate that. Take me to Paris and I will go with you to England. I'll not go otherwise—no matter what…persuasion you employ.'

He stared into her eyes, assessing the strength of her conviction. She'd rightly said he couldn't force or threaten her into testifying. Indeed, even the appearance of coercion would discredit what she said.

He hoped upon the journey to somehow charm or trick her out of going to Paris. But unless he came up with a way to do so, he might end up having to stop there first.

Although one should always have a long-term strategy, all that mattered at the moment was playing the next card. First, he must get her out of Vienna.

'It doesn't appear you have much to pack. I should like to leave in two days' time.'

'How do you mean to spirit me away? Though the watchers have not yet interfered with my movements, I've not attempted to leave the city.'

Having drunk a tankard with the keeper of the public house on the corner, Will had already discovered the house was being watched, but he hadn't expected a woman, diplomat's cousin or no, to have noticed. Once again, surprise and reluctant admiration rippled through him. 'You're aware of the guard, then?'

She gave him an exasperated look, as if he were treating her like an idiot. '*Bien sûr* I'm aware! Although as I said, rightfully judging that I pose no threat, they've done nothing but observe. But since I have recovered enough to—' She halted a moment, then continued, 'There have always been watchers.'

Recovered enough. He wasn't sure he wanted to know from what. Shaking off the thought, he said, 'Do you know who they are?'

'Austrians, I expect. Clara has flirted with some of them, and from their speech they appear to be local lads. Not English. Nor French. Talleyrand has enough agents in keeping, he can learn, I expect, whatever he wishes from the Austrians.'

Will nodded. That judgement confirmed what the publican had told him. Local men, hired out of the army by government officials, would be easier for him to evade than Foreign Office professionals. During the two days he was allotting *madame* to settle her things, he'd observe the guard's routine, then choose the best time and manner in which to make off with her—in case the authorities should object to her departure.

'Are you thinking to have me pay off the landlady and simply stroll out the front door, valise in hand?' *madame* asked, interrupting his thoughts.

'You'd prefer to escape out a window at midnight?' he asked, amused.

'The balcony worked well enough for you,' she retorted. 'It might be wise to anticipate opposition. I should probably go in disguise, so that neither the landlady nor the guards at the corner immediately realise I've departed.'

Though by now he shouldn't be surprised by anything she said, Will found himself raising an eyebrow. 'Leave in disguise? Interesting education the French give their diplomatic hostesses.'

'France has been at war for longer than we both have been alive, *monsieur*,' she shot back. 'People from every level of society have learned tricks to survive.'

It appeared she had, at any rate. If being abandoned by her cousin in a foreign capital were any indication, she had needed to.

'What do you suggest?'

'That we leave in mid-afternoon, when streets busy with vehicles, vendors and pedestrians will distract the guards and make them less vigilant. You could meet my friend, Clara, at a posting inn not far from these rooms. Bring men's clothing that she can conceal beneath the embroidery in her basket. She will escort you up, telling the landlady, if you encounter her, that you are her brother. You will then exit by the balcony while I, wearing the clothing you provide, will walk out with Clara.'

Her suggestion was so outrageous, Will was hard put not to laugh. 'I've no problem exiting by way of the balcony, but do you really think you could pass as a man?'

'I'm tall for a woman. As long as I don't encounter Frau Gruener, who knows me well, it should work. She almost always takes her rest of an afternoon between two and four, by the way. Those watching at the corner, if they notice us at all, will merely see Clara leaving the building, as she went in, with a man. Once we are away from the watchers, I leave it to you—who did so good a job locating me—to manage the rest.'

Intrigued by *madame*'s unexpected talent for subterfuge, he had to admit that the plan had merit. 'It might work. As long as you can walk in men's clothing without it being immediately obvious that you're a woman.'

She smiled grimly. 'You might be surprised at my talents. I'm more concerned about you remaining for more than a few hours in this

vicinity without attracting attention. You are…
rather distinctive.'

'You don't think *I* can pass unnoticed, if I
choose?'

'Your clothing is unremarkable, but you,
monsieur, are not.' She looked him up and
down, her gaze coming to rest on his face.
'Both that golden hair—and your features—
are far too striking.'

He couldn't help feeling a purely male satisfaction that she found him so notable. As he
held her gaze, smiling faintly, a surge of sensual energy pulsed between them, as powerful as if she'd actually touched him. From the
gasp she uttered and her widened eyes, Will
knew she'd felt it, too.

Hell and damn. Bad enough that he'd been
immediately attracted to her. If he excited her
lust as well…

It would complicate things, certainly. On the
other hand, as long as he kept his head, if not
his body, focused on his objective, he might
be able to use that attraction later. Seducing
her to achieve his aims would be much more
pleasant for them both than outright coercion.

Filing that possibility away, he forced himself to look away, breaking the connection.

'I'm a dab hand at disguises myself. I'll not accompany your friend as her brother, but as her old uncle, who wears spectacles and has something of a limp. The gout, you know.'

Tilting her head, she studied him. 'Truly, you are Max Ransleigh's cousin?'

He couldn't fault her scepticism; no more than she could Will imagine Max sneaking on to a balcony, breaking into a woman's rooms, threatening her, or disguising himself as an old man.

'I'm from the wrong side of the blanket, so I come by my disreputable ways honestly.'

'Ah, I see. Very well, Clara will meet you at three of the afternoon, two days from now at the Lark and Plough, on Dusseldorfer Strasse. She'll look for a bent old man with spectacles and a cane.' She offered her hand.

'Honour among thieves?' Amused anew, he took her hand to shake it…and a zing of connection flowed immediately through her fingers to his.

Her face colouring, she snatched her hand back. No longer annoyed by the hardening of his loins, Will was beginning to find the possibility of seduction more enticing than regrettable.

'Three o'clock, then.' As she nodded and turned to go back into the house, he said, 'By the way, *madame*, I will be watching. If any tall young man with a feminine air exits your lodgings in the interim, I will notice.'

She lifted her chin. 'Why should I try to elude you? I *want* to return to Paris and you will help me do so. Until then, *monsieur*.'

Before she could walk away, a woman's voice emanating from the second floor called out, '*Madame*, where are you?'

'Get back!' she whispered, pushing him into the shadows beneath the balcony.

'That's Clara, isn't it? The maid who helped you?' Will asked in an undertone as footsteps sounded on the balcony overhead.

'Ah, there you are, in the garden,' came the voice. 'Shall I bring your dinner down there?'

'No, I'll be right up,' *madame* called back.

She pivoted to face Will. 'As soon as you hear me above, go back over the wall the way you came. I will do as you ask; there's no need for you to harass Clara.'

'What makes you think I haven't already... harassed her?'

Her eyes widened with alarm before she steadied herself, no doubt realising that if he *had* accosted the maid, she would have probably arrived frightened and frantic, rather than calmly calling her mistress to supper. Still, even now it might be worth following the maid home and seeing if he could dredge out of her any additional information about her mistress.

As if she could read his thoughts, *madame* said fiercely, 'If any harm comes to Clara, I will *kill* you.'

Amused at her audacity in daring to threaten him—this slender woman who must weigh barely more than a child and possessed neither strength nor any weapon—Will grinned. 'You could try.'

Her gaze hardened. 'You have no idea what I am capable of, *monsieur*.' Showing him her back, she paced into her lodgings, a wisp of lavender scent lingering in her wake.

Chapter Four

Her heart beating hard, feeling as weak as if she'd run a mile through the twisting Vienna streets, Elodie hurried up the stairway to her rooms. Having placed her basket on a table, Clara was looking at the embroidery Elodie had just completed.

'Ah, *madame*, this is the prettiest yet! The colour's lovely, and the bird so vivid, one almost thinks it will fly off the gown.' Looking up at Elodie, the maid nodded approvingly. 'You've got some colour back in your face. A stroll in the fresh air agreed with you. You must do it more often.'

Elodie wasn't about to reveal that it wasn't the garden air that had brought a flush to her

cheeks, but an infuriating, dictatorial, dangerous man.

His touch had almost scalded her. It had
been many years since she'd sought or experienced such a physical response. The sensation carried her back to the early days of her
love for her late husband, when a mere glance
from him could set her body afire.

She shook the memory away before sadness
could follow in its wake. Given her reaction to
him, travelling in Will Ransleigh's company
might be more hazardous to her well-being
than she'd first thought. But she could worry
about that later; now, she had more immediate matters to address.

'I've brought you a good dinner,' the maid
said as she bustled about, putting plates and
silverware on the table and lighting candles.
'Frau Luvens made meat pie and some of her
apple strudel. You will do it justice now, won't
you?'

To her surprise, for the first time in a long
time, Elodie found the idea of food appealing.
The knowledge that at last, at last, she would
be able to stop marking time and get back to
Paris, was reviving her vanished appetite. 'You
won't have to coax me tonight; it sounds deli-

cious. You are joining me, aren't you? You can tell me all the news.'

While Clara rambled on about her day and her work at the grand hotel where she'd taken employment after her mistress had recovered enough to be left on her own, Elodie edged to the window. Though from this angle, she couldn't see all the way under the balcony, her surreptitious inspection of the garden indicated that Monsieur Ransleigh had indeed departed.

By now, Clara had the covers off the dishes and was waving her to the small table. 'Come, eat before the meat pies get cold. Gruber gave me some extra bread from the hotel kitchen. I'm so glad to see your appetite returning! Just in time, as we'll be able to afford meat more often. Madame Lebruge was so complimentary about your work on the last consignment of embroidery, I told her the next lot would be ten schillings more the piece. She didn't even protest! I should have asked for twenty.'

Elodie seated herself and waited while the maid attacked her meat pie. 'I won't be doing another lot. I'm leaving Vienna.'

Clara's hands stilled and she looked up, wiping savoury juice from her chin. 'Leaving?

How? I thought you said it would be months before you could save enough to travel.'

'My plans have changed.' Omitting any mention of threats or the edgy undercurrent between herself and the man, Elodie told Clara about Will Ransleigh's visit and offer to escort her to Paris.

She should have known the maid would be suspicious. 'But can you trust this man, *madame*? How do you know he truly is Monsieur Max Ransleigh's cousin?'

'When you see him, you'll understand; the resemblance between the two men is striking.'

'Why would he wish to do you the favour of taking you to Paris?'

'Because I am to do him a favour in return. I promised I would go to England and testify about how I embroiled his cousin in St Arnaud's plot.'

'*Gott im Himmel, madame!* Is that wise? Is it safe?'

Though she was nearly certain Ransleigh was gone, a well-developed instinct for caution impelled her to lean close and drop her voice to a whisper. 'I have no intention of actually going to London. Once we get to Paris, I shall elude him.'

Clara clapped her hands. 'Ah, yes, and I am sure you shall, now that you've finally recovered your strength! But…should I not go with you as far as Paris? I do not like the idea of you travelling alone with this man about whom we know so little.'

'Thank you, dear friend, but you should stay here. Vienna is your home. You've already done more for me than I ever expected, more than I can ever repay.'

The maid waved a hand dismissively. 'How could I do less, when you were so kind to me? Taking on an untried girl as your dresser, you who had to appear with the cream of society before all Vienna! Nor could I have obtained my present position without all I learned serving you.'

'You've returned many times over any favour I did you.'

'In any case, my lady, you shouldn't travel alone.'

'That might be true…if I were travelling as a "lady". But I shall not be, nor is the journey likely to be comfortable. Perhaps not even safe. I don't know if the watchers will be pleased when they discover I've left Vienna and you've already faced enough danger for me. I must go alone.'

'You are certain?' the maid asked, studying her face.

'Yes,' she replied, clasping Clara's hand. Even if she'd planned to travel as a lady of substance, she wouldn't have allowed Clara to accompany her. Escaping swiftly, drawing out of Vienna whatever forces still kept surveillance over her, was the best way to ensure the safety of the woman who had taken her in and nursed her back to health after she'd been brutalised and abandoned.

'So, no more embroidery,' Elodie said. 'But I'm not completely without resources yet.' Rising, she went to the linen press and extracted two bundles neatly wrapped in muslin. Bringing them to Clara, she said, 'The first is a ball gown I never had a chance to wear; it should fetch a good price. The other is the fanciest of my dinner gowns; I've already re-embroidered it and changed the trimming, so Madame Lebruge should be able easily to resell that as well.'

'Shouldn't you have the money, *madame*? Especially if you mean to travel. I could take these to her tomorrow. She's been so pleased with all the other gowns you've done, I'm sure I could press her for a truly handsome sum.'

'Press her as hard as you like, but keep the money for yourself. It's little enough beside my debt to you. I've something else, too.'

Reaching down to flip up the bottom of her sewing apron, Elodie picked the seam open and extracted a pair of ear-rings. Small diamonds twinkled in the light of the candles. 'Take these. Sell them if you like, or keep them…as a remembrance of our friendship.'

'*Madame*, you mustn't! They're too fine! Besides, you might need to sell them yourself, once you get to Paris.'

'I have a few other pieces left.' Elodie smiled. 'One can't say much good of St Arnaud, but he never begrudged me the funds to dress the part of his hostess. I can't imagine how I would have survived this year without the jewels and finery we were able to sell.'

The maid spat out a German curse on St Arnaud's head. 'If he'd not been in such a rush to leave Vienna and save his own neck, he would probably have taken them.'

Elodie shrugged. 'Well, I am thankful to

have had them, whatever the reason. Now, let me tell you how my departure has been arranged.'

Half an hour later, fully apprised of who she was to meet, when and where, Clara hugged her and walked out. An unnerving silence settled in the rooms after her footsteps faded.

Though she supposed there was no need to work on the gowns the maid had left, from force of habit, Elodie took the top one from the basket and fetched her embroidery silks.

Along with the sale of some gems, the gowns she'd worn as St Arnaud's hostess, re-embroidered and sold back to the shop from which she'd originally purchased them, had supported her for six months. At that point Madame Lebruge, pleased with the elegance and inventiveness of her work, sent new gowns from her shop for Elodie to embellish.

Letting her fingers form the familiar stitches calmed her as she reviewed what had transpired in the last few hours. Clara was right to be suspicious; she had no way of knowing for sure that Will Ransleigh would actually take her to Paris, rather than murdering her in some alley.

But if he'd wanted to dispose of her, he could have already done so. Nor could one fail to note the fervour in his eyes when he talked of righting the wrong she'd done his cousin. She believed he meant to take her to London—and that she'd convinced him she'd not go there unless they went to Paris first.

She smiled; he'd immediately suspected she meant to escape him there. Just because he was Max Ransleigh's cousin, and therefore nephew to an earl, it would not do to underestimate his resourcefulness, or think him hopelessly out of his element in the meaner streets of Paris. He'd tracked her down here, most certainly without assistance from any of the authorities. He'd not been shocked or appalled by her idea of escaping in disguise, only concerned that she couldn't carry off the deception. He'd then proposed an even cleverer disguise, suggesting he was as familiar as she was with subterfuge.

Perhaps he worked for the Foreign Office, as Max had, only in a more clandestine role. Or maybe he was just a rogue, as the unpredictability and sense of danger that hung about him seemed to suggest.

He'd been born on the wrong side of the blanket, he'd said. Perhaps, instead of growing up in the ease of an earl's establishment, he'd had to scrabble for a living, moving from place to place, much as she had. That would explain his housebreaker's skill at scaling balconies and invading rooms.

The notion struck her that they might have much in common.

Swiftly she dismissed that ridiculous thought. She sincerely doubted that *he* had ever had his very life depend on the success of the disguise he employed. Nor should she forget that he'd sought her out for a single purpose, one that left no room for any concern about *her* wellbeing. Still, depending on what happened in Paris, she might consider going to London as she'd promised.

She would give much to right the wrong she'd been forced to do Max Ransleigh. After studying the background of all of the Duke of Wellington's aides, St Arnaud had determined Max's well-documented weakness for and courtesy towards women made him the best prospect among those with immediate access to Wellington to be of use in his plot. He'd ordered her to establish a relationship with Max, gain his sympathy and learn his movements, so he might be used as a decoy when the time was right.

She'd been instructed to offer him her body if necessary, but it hadn't been. Not that she found Max unappealing as a lover, but having learned he'd already taken one of the most elegant courtesans in Vienna as his mistress, she judged him unlikely to be tempted by a tall, brown-haired woman of no outstanding beauty.

His attentions to her had been initially just the courtesies any diplomat would offer his occasional hostess. Until one day, when she'd been sporting a bruised face and shoulder, and he'd figured out that St Arnaud must have abused her.

She'd told him nothing, of course, but from that moment, his attitude had grown fiercely protective. Rather ironic, she thought, that it had been St Arnaud's foul temper and vindictive spirit, rather than her charms, that had drawn Max closer to her.

In fact, she'd be willing to bet, had the moment not occurred for St Arnaud to spring his plot, Max would have tried to work out an honourable way for her to escape her cousin.

But the moment did occur. As little choice

as she'd had in the matter, it still pained her to recall it.

The night of the attack had begun with an afternoon like any other at the Congress, until Max had casually mentioned that he might be late arriving to the Austrian ambassador's ball that evening, since he was to confer briefly in private with the Duke before accompanying him to the festivities. It was the work of a moment for Elodie to inveigle from him in which anteroom that meeting was to take place, the work of another that night to intercept Max in the hallway before he went in.

She waylaid him with a plea that he assist her on some trumped-up matter that would call down on her the wrath of her cousin, should she fail to speedily accomplish it. Despite his concern for her welfare, so great was his impatience to meet his commander, who had a well-known intolerance for tardiness, that she was able to delay him only a few minutes.

It was long enough. St Arnaud's assassin found his target alone, unguarded, and only Wellington's own battle-won sixth sense in dodging away an instant before the stranger bursting into the room fired his weapon, had averted tragedy.

To the Duke, anyway. Captured almost immediately, the failed assassin withstood questioning only briefly before revealing St Arnaud's, and therefore her own, connection to the plot. Assuming the worst, St Arnaud had dealt with her and fled. She'd been in no condition afterwards to discover what had happened to Max; she assumed that, disgraced and reprimanded, he'd been sent back to England.

Dear, courteous Max. Perhaps the kindest man she'd ever known, she thought, conjuring up with a sigh the image of his face. Odd, though, that while he was certainly handsome, she hadn't felt for him the same immediate, powerful surge of desire inspired by his cousin Will.

An attraction so strong it had dazzled her into forgetting, for the first few moments, that he'd invaded her rooms. So strong that, though he'd coerced and threatened her, she felt it still.

It had also been evident, even in his ill-fitting breeches, that the lust he inspired in her was mutual. Elodie felt another flush of heat, just thinking of that sleek hardness, pressing against his trouser front.

Such a response, she suddenly realised, might be useful later, when she needed to escape him. A well-pleasured man would be languid, less than vigilant. And pleasuring Will Ransleigh would be no hardship.

Eluding him in Paris, however, would be another challenge entirely.

Chapter Five

Loitering at the corner, hidden from view by the shadow of an overhanging balcony, and cap well down over the golden hair Madame Lefevre had found so distinctive, Will watched the guard posted at the opposite end of the alley. He'd grab some dinner and return to remain here through the night, noting how many kept watch and when they changed. Although he'd agreed with *madame*'s suggestion that she leave in full daylight, it would be wise to know how many men had been employed to observe her—and might be sent in pursuit when they discovered she'd fled.

He shook his head again over her unexpected talent for intrigue.

Before seeking his dinner, he would question *madame*'s friend Clara. He'd not bothered the girl before, having worked out where *madame* had gone to ground without having to accost the maid. Although the person who'd protected *madame* would likely be the most reluctant to give him any information, after an interview that had given rise to more questions than it answered, it was worth the attempt to extract from the girl anything that might shed more light on the mystery that was Madame Lefevre.

A woman who thus far hadn't behaved as he would have expected of an aristocratic French-woman who'd served as hostess to the most important leaders of European society.

Now that he'd confirmed that the woman he'd found was in fact Madame Lefevre, it was time to re-examine his initial assumptions about her.

The speed with which she'd come up with the suggestion that she escape in disguise—masculine disguise, at that—seemed to indicate she'd donned such a costume before. Recalling the grim expression on her face, Will thought it hadn't been in some amateur theatrical performance for amusement of friends.

'France has been at war longer than we've

been alive...' Had her family been caught up in the slaughter leading from monarchy to republic to empire and back? It seemed likely.

He wished now he'd paused in London to plumb for more detail about the St Arnaud family. Thierry St Arnaud's employer, Prince Talleyrand, possessed an exceptional skill for survival, having served as Foreign Minister of France during the Republic, Consulate, Empire and now the Restoration. At the Congress of Vienna, the Prince had even managed the unlikely feat of persuading Britain and Austria that France, a country those two allies had fought for more than twenty years, should become their partner against Russia and Prussia.

What remarkable tricks of invention had the St Arnaud clan performed to retain lands and titles through the bloodbath of revolution and empire?

Perhaps, rather than spending her girlhood tucked away at some genteel country estate, *madame*'s aristocratic family, like so many others, had been forced to escape the guillotine's blade. They might even have fled to England; the British crown had supported a large *émigré* community. That would explain her excellent, almost accentless speech.

Or perhaps she was such a mistress of invention because she was one of Talleyrand's agents. His gut churned at that unpleasant possibility.

But though Will wouldn't totally discount the idea, Talleyrand was known to be an exacting master. It wouldn't be like the prince to leave a loose end—like a former agent—flapping alone in the Viennese breeze for over a year; Madame Lefevre would likely have been eliminated or spirited away long since.

Still, it wouldn't be amiss to behave around her as if she had a professional's expertise.

He smiled. That would make the matching of wits all the sweeter. And if the opportunity arose to intertwine bodies as well, that would be the sweetest yet.

But enough of carnal thoughts. He couldn't afford to let lust and curiosity make him forget his goal, or lure him into being less than vigilant. He was certain she intended to try to escape him during their journey, and he'd need to be on his best game to ensure she did not.

As he reached that conclusion, Clara exited *madame*'s lodgings. Keeping into the shadow of the buildings, Will followed her.

To his good fortune, since the onset of evening and the thinning crowds would make it harder to trail her unobserved, the maid headed for the neighbouring market. He shadowed her as she snapped up the last of the day's bread, cheese and apples at bargain prices from vendors eager to close up for the night.

The Viennese were a prosperous lot, he noted as he trailed a few stalls behind her, and remarkably careless with their purses. Had he a mind to, he could have snatched half a dozen as he strolled along.

Unable to resist the temptation to test his skill and thinking it might make a good introduction, Will nipped from behind the maid to snag her coin purse while she lingered by the last stall, bidding farewell to the vendor and rearranging the purchases in her market basket.

He followed her from the market until she reached a mostly deserted stretch of street, where the buildings' overhanging second storeys created a shadowy recess. Picking up his pace, Will strode past her and then turned, herding her towards the wall. With a deep bow, he held out the coin purse.

'Excuse me, miss, I believe you dropped this.'

With a gasp, she shrank back, then halted.

'Why…it is my purse! I was sure I put it back into my reticule! How can I thank you, Herr…' Belatedly looking up, she got a glimpse of his face. 'You!'

Will bowed again. 'Will Ransleigh, at your service, miss.'

Alarm battled anger in her face. 'I should call the authorities and have you arrested for theft!'

He raised an eyebrow. 'How could you do that, when I've just returned your purse? If officials in Vienna arrest every fellow who follows a pretty girl, the jails would be full to overflowing. I mean you no harm.'

She sniffed. 'I note you don't deny you took it! But seeing as how you could have just as easily knocked me over the head as given it back, I suppose I'll not scream the houses down—for the moment. What do you want?'

'I intend to help your mistress leave the city.'

She looked him up and down, her expression wary. 'I warned her not to trust you. Oh, I don't doubt you'll help her, all right—to do what *you* want her to. Just like that worthless cousin of hers.'

Remembering *madame*'s bent and swollen

fingers, Will felt a surge of dislike. If he ever encountered Thierry St Arnaud, he'd force the man to test his strength against a more fitting adversary. 'He intimidated her, didn't he?'

'Bastard.' The maid spat on cobblestones. 'I only saw him strike her twice, but she almost always had bruises. I'll not hurt her more by telling you anything.'

'I appreciate your loyalty. But whatever you can tell me—about her relationship with St Arnaud or my cousin—will help me protect her on the journey. I can do a better job if I'm aware of potential threats before they happen. If I know who's been watching her, and why.'

Her expression clouded, telling Will she worried about her mistress, too. 'Herr Ransleigh, your cousin, was an honourable man,' she said after a moment. 'You promise to keep her safe?'

'I promise.' To his surprise, Will found he meant it.

Clara studied him, obviously still reluctant. 'You want her to stay safe, too, don't you?' he coaxed. 'How about I tell you what I know and you just confirm it?'

After considering another moment, the maid nodded.

'You've been with your mistress more than a year. She engaged you when she first arrived in Vienna—September 1814, wasn't it?'

Clara nodded.

'That last night, before her cousin fled the city, he...hurt her.'

Tears came to the girl's eyes. 'Yes,' she whispered.

'Badly?' Will pressed, keeping a tight rein over his rising temper, almost certain now he knew what she would tell him.

'She was unconscious when I found her. Her ribs broken for sure, and her arm and hand bent and twisted. Didn't come back to herself for more than a day, and for the first month, I wasn't sure she would survive. Bastard!' the maid burst out again. 'Blaming her for the failure of his foolish plan! Or maybe just taking it out on her that it failed. He was that kind.'

'You took her from the hotel to rooms at a boarding house and nursed her. Then, once she'd recovered sufficiently, you moved her to the lodgings here,' Will summed up the trail his search had taken him on.

'By then, she said she was recovered enough to work. I'd sold jewels for her those first few months, until her bad hand healed enough for

her to use the fingers. She started doing embroidery then.'

'And there were watchers, each place you
stayed with her?'

'I guess there were, though I didn't notice
them until she pointed them out after she got
better. I was frightened, but what could they
want with her? After a few months, I got used
to them hanging about.'

'Viennese lads, they were.'

'Yes. I spoke to some of them, trying to see
if I could find out anything, but they seemed
to know only that a local man hired them. I'm
certain someone more important was behind
it, but I don't know who.'

Will filed that observation away. 'Why is
she so insistent on returning to Paris?'

'Her family's there, I expect. She never spoke
about herself, nor was she the sort who thought
only of her own comfort. Waiting for her at the
dressmakers or at those grand balls, I heard
other maids talking about their ladies. *Madame*
wasn't like most of them, always difficult and
demanding. She was kind. She noticed people
and their troubles.'

Her eyes far away, Clara smiled. 'One night,
Klaus the footman had a terrible head cold,

hardly able to breathe, poor man. *Madame* only passed by him in the hall on her way to a reception, but first thing the next morning, she had me fetch herbs and made him a tisane. Not that she made a great fuss about doing so, playing Lady Bountiful. No, she just turned it over to the butler and told him to make sure Klaus drank it.'

'Did you ever wonder why she'd not brought her own maid to Vienna?'

Clara shrugged. 'Maybe the woman didn't want to travel so far. Maybe she couldn't afford to bring her. I don't think she had any coin of her own. St Arnaud paid my wages, all the bills for jewels, gowns and the household expenses, but he gave her no pin money at all. She didn't have even a few schillings to buy ices when we were out.'

So, as she'd claimed, Will noted, *madame had* been entirely dependent on St Arnaud. 'She never spoke of any other relations?'

'No. But if they were all like St Arnaud, I understand why she wouldn't.' The maid stopped abruptly, wrinkling her brow. 'There was one person she mentioned. Several times, when I'd given her laudanum for the pain after

St Arnaud had struck her, she murmured a name as she dozed. Philippe.'

Surprise and something barbed and sharp stung him in the gut. Impatiently he dismissed it. 'Husband…brother…lover?'

'Not her husband—St Arnaud said he'd died in the wars. I did once ask her who "Philippe" was, but she just smiled and made no answer, and I didn't want to press. She sounded… longing. Maybe he's someone she wanted to marry, that her cousin had refused; I can see him sending away anyone he didn't think grand enough for the St Arnauds. Maybe St Arnaud promised if she helped him in Vienna, he would let her marry the man. I know he had some sort of power to force her to do his will.'

For some reason he'd rather not examine, Will didn't like the idea of Madame Lefevre pining for a Parisian lover. Shaking his head to rid himself of the image, he said, '*Madame*'s dependence on St Arnaud for food, clothing, housing and position would have been enough to coerce her co-operation.'

'No, it was more than that,' Clara insisted. 'Not that she didn't appreciate fine silks and pretty gems—who would not? But when she had to, she sold them without any sign of regret. She seemed quite content to live simply, not missing in the least the grand society for whom she used to play hostess. All she spoke about was earning enough coin to return to Paris.'

Not wishing to hear any more speculation about the mysterious "Philippe", Will changed direction. 'She's had no contact with St Arnaud since the night of the attack, then?'

The maid shuddered. 'Better that he believe she died of her injuries. She came close enough.'

'St Arnaud emigrated to the Caribbean afterwards.'

'That, I can't say. I only know he left Vienna that night. If there's any justice in the world, someone somewhere caught him and he's rotting in prison.'

Clara looked up, meeting his gaze squarely. 'If God has any mercy, once she's done what you want, you'll let her go back to Paris. To this Philippe, whoever he is. After all she's suffered, losing her husband, enduring St Arnaud's abuse, she deserves some happiness.'

Will wasn't about to assure the maid he'd send *madame* back—to Paris or her 'Philippe'—

until he'd finished with her. And resolved what had already flared between them.

Instead, he pulled out a coin. 'Thank you, Clara. I appreciate—'

'No need for that,' the maid interrupted, waving the money away. 'Use it to keep her safe. You will watch out for her, won't you? I know if someone wished her ill, they could have moved against her any time this last year. But still…I worry. She's such a gentle soul, too innocent for this world, perhaps.'

Will remembered the woman in the garden, quietly picking spent blooms from her flowers while a stranger decided whether or not to wring her neck. She was more *resigned* than gentle or innocent, he thought. As if life had treated her so harshly, she simply accepted evil and injustice, feeling there was little she could do to protect herself from it.

Since his earliest days on the streets, Will had faced down bullies and fought to right wrongs when he found them. Picturing that calm face bent over the blooms and the brutal hand St Arnaud had raised against it, Will felt a surge of protectiveness he didn't want to feel.

No point getting all worked up over her little tragedy; if she'd ended up abused, she'd played her role with full knowledge of the possible consequences, he reminded himself. Unlike Max, who'd been lured in unawares and betrayed by his own nobility.

And of course the maid thought her a heroine. If she could take in Max, who was nobody's fool, it would have been child's play for her to win over a simple, barely educated girl who depended on her for employment.

Suppressing the last of his sympathy towards Madame Lefevre, he nodded a dismissal to her maid. 'I'll meet you at the inn in two days.'

Clara nodded. 'The old man's disguise—you're sure you can carry it off?'

'Can she carry off hers?'

'She can do whatever she must. She already has. Good-night, sir.' With an answering nod, the girl walked into the gathering night.

Will turned back towards the inn where he planned to procure dinner, mulling over what he'd learned from Clara.

According to the maid, *madame* had been brought, without other money or resources, to Vienna and forced to do St Arnaud's bidding. She cared little about wealth or high position.

Her sole ambition was to return to Paris…and 'Philippe'.

She can do whatever she must, the maid had said. Apparently, betraying Max Ransleigh had been one of those things. Eluding Will and cheating Max of the vindication due him might be another.

She was surely counting on trying to escape him, if not on the road, then once they arrived in Paris. He'd need to remain vigilant to make sure she did not.

From the maid's reactions, it seemed even she feared the watchers might not be pleased to have her mistress leave Vienna. Madame Lefevre might well have other enemies in addition to the angry cousin of the man she'd ruined.

Her masculine disguise, which he'd first accepted almost as a jest, now looked like a prudent precaution.

For a moment, he envisioned *madame*'s slender body encased in breeches that outlined her legs, curved over thigh and calf, displayed the turn of an ankle. His mouth watered and his body hardened.

But he couldn't allow lustful thoughts to distract him—yet. His sole focus now must be on getting her safely to Paris. Because until they reached London, he meant to ensure no one *else* harmed her.

Chapter Six

Late in the afternoon two days later, garbed in the clothing of an old gentleman, wearing spectacles so thick she could hardly see and leaning heavily on a cane, Elodie let Clara help her into the taproom of a modest inn on the western outskirts of Vienna. As the innkeeper bustled over to welcome them, Will Ransleigh strode in.

'Uncle Fritz, so glad you could join me! The trip from Linz was not too tiring, I trust?'

In a voice pitched as low as she could make it, Elodie replied, 'Tolerable, my boy.'

'Good. Herr Schultz,' he addressed the innkeeper, 'bring some refreshment to our room, please. Josephine, let's help our uncle up.'

With Clara at one arm and Will Ransleigh at the other, Elodie slowly shuffled up the stairs.

Not until she'd entered the sitting room Ransleigh had hired and heard the door shut behind her did she breathe a sigh of relief. The first step of her escape had proceeded without a hitch. Exultation and a rising excitement sent her spirits soaring.

As she sank into a chair and pulled off the distorting spectacles, she looked up to see Will Ransleigh's expression warm with a smile of genuine approval that gratified her even as her stomach fluttered in response. His expression serious, he was arresting, but with that smile—oh, my! How did any woman resist him?

'Bravo, *madame*. I had grave doubts, but I have to admit, you made a wonderfully credible old man.'

'You made a rather fine old gentleman yourself,' she said, smiling back at him. 'I wouldn't have recognised you if you'd not arrived with Clara. You were a wizard with the blacking as well, going from white-powdered hair to brunette faster than I could don the clothing you provided. Now I see you've transformed yourself yet again.'

Though he'd kept his hair darkened with

blacking, he'd changed from the modest working-man's attire he'd worn the day he climbed up her balcony into gentleman's garb, well cut and of quality material, but not so elegant or fashionable as to attract undue notice.

Still, the close-fitting jacket emphasised the breadth of shoulders and the snug pantaloons displayed muscled thighs. If he'd appeared powerfully, dangerously masculine in his drab clerk's disguise, the effect was magnified several times over in dress that better revealed his strength and physique.

His potent masculine allure ambushed Elodie anew, intensifying the flutter in her stomach and igniting a heated tremor below. She found herself wondering how it would feel to run her fingers along those muscled arms and thighs, over the taut abdomen…and lower. While her lips explored his jaw and cheekbones, the line of brow over those vivid turquoise eyes…

Realising she was staring, she hastily turned her gaze away.

Not fast enough that he didn't notice her preoccupation, though. A satisfied gleam in his eye, he said, 'I hope you approve of the latest transformation.'

'You're looking very fine, sir, and don't you know it,' Clara interposed tartly. 'Ah, mistress, didn't you make a marvellous old gent! I believe we could have met Frau Gruener herself on the stairs without her being the wiser.'

'It's just as well we didn't. I'm no Mrs Siddons,' Elodie said, arching to stretch out a back cramped from bending over a cane during their long, dawdling transit.

'What do you know of Mrs Siddons?' Will asked, giving her a suspicious look.

Cursing her slip, Elodie said, 'Only that she was much praised by the English during theatrical entertainments at the Congress, who claimed no Viennese actress could compare. With your expertise in disguises, I begin to believe you've trod the boards yourself. Is that how you found this moustache?' Stripping off the length of fuzzy wool, she rubbed her lip. 'It itched terribly, making me sneeze so hard, I feared it would fall off.'

'My apologies for the deficiencies in your costume,' he replied sardonically. 'I shall try to do better next time.'

'See that you do,' she flashed back, relieved

to have detoured him from any further probing about her familiarity with the English stage.

'I don't wonder your back is tired,' Clara said. 'I don't know this quarter of Vienna and you could hardly see behind those spectacles. The transit seemed to take so long, once or twice I feared we might be lost.'

'No danger of that; I shadowed you all the way and would have set you straight if you'd strayed,' Ransleigh said. 'I also wanted to make sure you were not followed.'

Reassured by his thoroughness, Elodie said, 'We weren't, were we?'

'No. It was a good plan you came up with.'

Elodie felt a flush of warmth at his avowal and chastised herself. She wasn't a giddy girl, to be gratified by a handsome man's approval. She needed to remember the purpose for which he'd arranged this escape—that hadn't been done for *her* benefit.

Despite that acknowledgment, some of the warmth remained.

A knock sounded at the door and Elodie turned away, averting her now moustache-less face until the servant bringing in the refreshments had deposited the tray and bowed himself back out.

'Shall we dine?' Ransleigh invited. 'The inn is said to set a good table.'

Elodie shook her head wonderingly. 'Just how do you manage to discover such things?'

He gave her an enigmatic smile. 'I'm a man of many talents.'

'So I am discovering.' She wished she could resist being impressed by his mastery of detail, but fairness wouldn't allow it.

'*Fraulein*, will you join us before you leave?'

At the maid's nod, they seated themselves around the table. Since their previous exchanges had been limited to threats on her life and plans for escaping Vienna, Elodie wondered whether—and about what—Ransleigh would talk during the meal.

Somewhat to her surprise, he kept up a flow of conversation, discussing the sights of Vienna and asking Clara about her experiences with the notables she'd encountered during the Congress.

Will Ransleigh truly was a man of many talents. He seemed as comfortable drawing out a lady's maid as he might be entertaining a titled lady in his uncle the earl's drawing room. If he did, in fact, frequent the earl's drawing room.

He claimed he'd been born on the wrong

side of the blanket, but his speech and manners were those of the aristocracy. Where was he in his true element? she wondered. Skulking around the modest neighbourhoods of a great city, chatting up maids and innkeepers, or dancing at balls among the wealthy and powerful?

Or in both?

He was still an enigma. And since she was forced to place her safety in his hands, at least until Paris, that troubled her.

Their meal concluded, Clara rose. 'I'd best be getting home. It will be dark soon and I don't know these streets.'

'I'll escort you,' Ransleigh said.

'I'd not put you to the trouble,' Clara protested.

'Of course he will,' Elodie interrupted, relieved by the offer and determined to have him honour it. 'I'd like him to accompany you all the way home…and make sure there's no unexpected company to welcome you,' she added, voicing the uneasiness that had grown since she'd successfully escaped her lodgings.

'Your mistress is right. Though I don't think her flight has yet been discovered, we should take precautions,' Ransleigh said. 'Once whoever has set a guard realises she has left the city, they'll probably come straight to you.'

Dismay flooded her. All her attention consumed by the magnificent prospect of returning to Paris, Elodie hadn't imagined that possibility. Turning to Ransleigh, she said anxiously, 'Should we take Clara with us, for her own safety?'

'I don't think she needs to leave, though she might well be questioned. If we're lucky, not until we're well away. She can then tell them truthfully that a certain Will Ransleigh urged you to accompany him to London and met you at this inn, but how or with whom you left it and in which direction, she has no idea. After all, if they want anyone, it's you, not her.'

'Are you sure? I'd thought my leaving, drawing after me whatever threat might still remain, would keep her safe. But what if I'm wrong?' Elodie turned to Clara, still torn. 'If anyone harmed you—'

'Don't distress yourself, *madame*,' Ransleigh interrupted. 'I've already engaged a man to watch over the *fraulein* until he's sure she's in no further danger. A solid lad, a former

Austrian soldier I knew from the army. He's waiting below to help me escort her home.'

'Thank you, sir.' Clara dipped Ransleigh a curtsy—the first sign of respect she'd accorded him. 'I never expected such a thing, but I can't deny it makes me feel easier.'

Surprised, touched and humbled, Elodie felt like curtsying, too. *She* should have realised it was necessary to guarantee Clara's safety after their departure. Instead, this man she'd viewed as concerned only with achieving his own purposes had had the forethought—and compassion—to arrange it.

In her experience, aristocrats such as St Arnaud viewed servants as objects put on earth to provide for their comfort, like horses or linens or furniture. Her cousin would never have seen Clara as a *person*, or concerned himself with her welfare.

Ransleigh had not only anticipated the possible danger, he'd arranged to protect Clara after their departure, when the maid was of no further use to him.

She couldn't prevent her opinion of his character from rising a notch higher.

Still, she mustn't let herself be lured into trusting in his thoroughness, competence and compassion—qualities that attracted her almost as much as his physical allure. They were still a long way from Paris.

Before Elodie could sort out her tangled thoughts, Clara had wrapped herself in her cloak. Elodie's previous high spirits vanished as she faced parting for ever from the last, best friend she possessed.

'I suppose this is farewell, *madame*,' Clara said, a brave smile on her face. 'I wish you a safe journey—and joy, when you get to Paris at last!'

Unable to summon words, Elodie hugged her. The maid hugged her back fiercely, blinking away tears when at last Elodie released her. 'I'll try to send word after I'm settled.'

'Good. I'd like to know that you were home—and *safe*,' she added, that last with a meaningful look at Ransleigh.

'Shall we go, *fraulein*?' Ransleigh asked.

Smiling, Clara gave her a curtsy. 'Goodbye, *madame*. May the blessed angels watch over you.'

'And you, my dear friend,' Elodie replied.

'After you, *fraulein*,' Ransleigh prompted gently as they both stood there, frozen. 'Your soldier awaits.'

Nodding agreement, Clara stepped towards the door, then halted to look at him searchingly. 'Maybe I was wrong. Maybe *madame* should trust you.'

Much as she told herself that after a lifetime of partings and loss, she should be used to it, Elodie felt a painful squeezing in her chest as she listened to their footsteps echo on the stairs. When the last sound faded, she ran to the window.

Peeping around the curtain, so as to be hidden from the view of anyone who might look up from the street, she watched three figures emerge from the inn: Ransleigh, Clara and a burly man who looked like a prizefighter. As they set off through the darkness, the thought struck her that Ransleigh, moving with the fluid, powerful stride of a predator on the prowl, seemed the more dangerous of the two men.

Elodie's spirits sagged even lower as she watched Clara disappear into the darkness. The maid had been her friend, companion and saviour for more than a year.

Now, she'd be alone with Ransleigh. For better or worse.

She got herself this far, she'd make it the rest

of the way, she told herself bracingly. And at the end of this journey…was Philippe.

With that rallying thought, she settled in to wait for Ransleigh's return.

Chapter Seven

The maid conveyed safely to her lodging where, fortunately, there had been no one waiting to intercept her, Will left Heinrich on watch and headed back to the inn. Their room above the entry was dark when he glanced up at the window before entering.

He'd already paid the proprietor, explaining he planned an early departure. In truth, he intended for them to leave Vienna during the blackest part of the night. Since it appeared *madame* was already asleep, he'd slip in quietly, letting her get as much rest as she could before what would be an arduous journey.

Taking care to make no sound that might attract the attention of the innkeeper serving customers in the taproom beyond, he crossed the entry and silently ascended the stairs. As he eased through the door into their room, the dim outline of something by the far wall had him reaching for his knife, until he realised what he'd sensed more than seen in the darkness was Madame Lefevre.

'I thought you'd be resting,' he said, closing the door quietly behind him.

'I couldn't sleep until I knew our plans. And I wanted to thank you for seeing to Clara's safety. That was generous of you...and unexpected. I'm very grateful.'

'She being an innocent in all this, I'd not want to be responsible for causing her any harm.'

Harm coming to *madame* he had less of a problem with, he thought. But if she were threatened, it would be after conviction for crimes committed, her punishment determined by the rule of law, not by an attack in some back alley.

Crossing to the window, he made sure the curtains were securely drawn. Lighting a taper, he said, 'I think we can chance one candle.'

As it flared to life, he saw Elodie Lefevre, still in old man's attire, seated in the corner next to the window—her back to the wall, beside the quickest exit from the inn. The very spot he would have chosen, were he required to wait alone in this room, unsure of what danger might threaten.

While he wondered whether she'd seated herself there by design or accident, she said, 'What have you planned for tomorrow?'

'Actually, I've planned for tonight. As soon as all is quiet downstairs and in the street, we will slip out by the kitchen door into the mews. I checked last night; no one keeps watch there. We'll be out of the city and along the road to Linz well before daylight.'

Madame nodded. 'The sooner we begin, the sooner we arrive.'

'When he travelled from Paris to Vienna for the Congress, Wellington made it in just ten days…but he only slept four hours a night. Though I don't mean to dawdle, I'm allowing a bit longer.'

'I'm ready to travel as quickly as you wish. Much as I enjoyed limping on my cane, though, I think another change of costume would be wise.'

Will had a strong sense that this wasn't the first time Elodie Lefevre had fled from pursuit. Had the Revolution forced her family out of France? She would have been scarcely more than a babe during the Terror.

Quelling for now the urge to question her further, he said, 'What do you have in mind?'

'If anyone interrogates the innkeeper, they'll be looking for a young gentleman accompanied by an older man. If that trail goes cold, they would probably next seek a man and a woman posing as a married couple or lovers or siblings or cousins. Whatever explanation we used, if I travel as a female with no maid and only a single male companion, we'll attract notice, making it much more likely that innkeepers and stable boys and barmaids at taverns and posting inns will remember us.'

'What makes you think we'll be stopping at taverns or posting inns?' he asked, teasing her to cover his surprise about her knowledge of the realities of travel. Had she spent her whole life eluding pursuers?

Ignoring the remark, she continued, 'We could pose as an older woman and her maid, but it's still unusual for women to travel without a male escort, to say nothing of the difficulty of your being convincing in either role for any length of time. So I think our best alternative would be for you to remain as you are, a young gentleman, and I will travel as your valet. Men travel the posting roads all the time; you'd be just one more of many and no one pays attention to servants.'

Her scheme for leaving her lodgings had been good; this one was even better. Trying to suppress the admiration he didn't wish to feel, Will said, 'You think you could play the role of valet better than I could that of an old woman?'

She nodded. 'Much more easily. As I said, a woman of any age travelling would excite curiosity, while a valet would be virtually invisible. Whether we stay at an inn—or under a tree or in a hedgerow,' she added with a quirk of a smile at him. 'And if we need to make a hasty exit, it will be much easier if I'm not encumbered by skirts.'

Will couldn't imagine any of the aristocratic ladies of his acquaintance—Alastair's mother or sisters, for example—inventing so unorthodox a scheme or proposing it in such a straightforward, unemotional manner. 'Why do I have the feeling you've done this before?'

A faraway look came into her eyes, and for a long moment, while he hung on her answer, she remained silent. 'I've had to come up with…contrivances upon occasion,' she said at last.

Which told him nothing. *Where have you been and what have you done?* Will wondered. 'You're a most unusual woman, Madame Lefevre.'

She gave him a faint smile, but said only, 'These old man's garments will suffice until we can procure others. I've kept two gowns in my portmanteau, in case I might need them before we arrive at Paris. Have you a route in mind?'

Will stifled a pang of disappointment that she'd not responded to his compliment by telling him more about her life. His curiosity fanned ever hotter by each new revelation, he was by now eager to discover what events had shaped her.

Maybe along the way, he'd figure it out, find a way to fit the puzzle pieces together. Or, even better, maybe along the way he'd lure her into trusting him enough to volunteer the information.

It would only be prudent to arm himself with as much knowledge about her as possible. As long as he kept in mind that anything she revealed might contain more craftiness than truth.

'Have *you* a route in mind? Your suggestions thus far have been excellent.'

She dropped her gaze and, though he couldn't tell for sure in the dim candlelight, he thought she flushed. 'Thank you,' she said gruffly. 'I've only travelled this way once, when I accompanied St Arnaud, so I don't know the road. It would be wise, I think, to keep as much as possible to the larger cities, where one gentleman will hardly be noticed among the host of travellers. Have you the means to hire horses? It would make the journey faster.'

'A gentleman travelling with his valet would more likely travel by coach.'

'Not if the valet were a bruising rider. The further and faster from Vienna we travel, the safer we'll be from pursuit.'

Will wasn't so sure. If Talleyrand were keeping tabs on *madame*, they would be more vulnerable the closer they got to Paris. But he didn't want to voice that fact, adding more anxiety to what must already be a difficult situation, with her poised to assume yet another false identity. Despite the maid's assertion that she could do 'whatever she had to', he didn't want to push her too hard and risk having her fall apart.

'Very well; I'll travel as a young gentleman. "Monsieur LeClair", shall we say? And you will be my valet, "Pierre".'

'"LeClair"?' she repeated, a slow smile lighting her face. 'Very good, considering nothing about this journey is "clear" or straightforward!'

The honest delight on her face, so strikingly different from the expressionless calm with which she usually concealed her feelings, struck Will near his breastbone with the force of a blow. Warmth blossomed in its wake. Damn and blast, he didn't want to start…liking her!

While he wrestled with his reaction, she continued, 'I'm pleased you approve my plan.'

'For the time being, subject to change as I feel necessary,' he cautioned, pulling himself back together. 'I've got horses waiting at an inn on the edge of Vienna. With hard travel, we may reach the outskirts of Linz by late tomorrow.'

'Excellent. You are very thorough, *monsieur*,' she said approvingly. 'Anything else I should know?'

'No, Pierre; we'd better get a few hours' sleep. I'll rouse you when it's time. You use the bed.'

'Oh, no, *monsieur*, that would never do. Your valet should occupy a pallet at the foot of the bed. I've left the wig and cane over there—' she indicated the dining table '—for you to return to your store of trickeries.'

Flinging the blanket she'd held in her lap over her shoulders, she crossed to the bed and settled herself on the floor by the footboard— back to the wall, with a clear view of both the window and the door, he noted. '*Bonsoir*, Monsieur LeClair.'

'*Bonsoir*, Pierre.'

She closed her eyes. Within a few moments, the even sound of her breathing indicated she must have fallen asleep.

Will should sleep, too. He had only a few hours before he needed to be up, all his wits about him, ready to spirit them out of the inn unobserved or to improvise some sleight of hand, should that be necessary for them to escape pursuit. But as he blew out the candle and lay down on the bed, Will found slumber elusive.

Partly, it was his ever-deepening curiosity

about Elodie Lefevre. What remarkable experiences had shaped this woman who noticed watchers at her corner, came up with plans for escape and evasion and talked of disguises as casually as another woman might discuss attending the theatre or purchasing a bonnet?

When he compared her reactions to the emotion-driven behaviour of the women he'd known, he was struck again by her calm. After leaving the only friend she knew, about to creep away with a virtual stranger in the middle of the night, she'd displayed no more than a natural sadness at parting from the maid. There'd been no panic, no fretting over whether she was doing the right thing. No worrying over her ability to carry out her part in the deception, no endless questioning over what was to happen next and—praise Heaven!—no tears. She hadn't even called down evil upon his head for forcing her into this.

Instead, she'd made a single terse compliment about his thoroughness.

'You truly are an amazing woman, Elodie Lefevre,' he told her sleeping form. *But I'd be an idiot to trust you.*

She had paid him one other compliment in

their short acquaintance—she'd called him 'striking'.

For the last few hours, the urgency of getting her out of her lodgings and the necessity of planning their escape had helped him dam up his strong physical response to her. But in the darkness, safe for the moment and all plans in place, that one memory was enough to send desire flooding over the barriers.

Despite the contrivance of having her travel as his 'valet', with her bundled at his feet, her soft breaths filling the silence and the subtle scent of lavender beguiling his nose, it was impossible for him to think of Elodie Lefevre as anything other than a woman. A woman made even more alluring by her unique, exceptional abilities.

A woman he wanted.

He stifled a groan as, despite his fatigue, his body hardened. His mind might be urging him to review each detail of their upcoming journey, but his body was recalling the softness of her neck under his fingers, the surge of connection between them when she took his hand.

Damn and blast, what had begun as a grim mission to vindicate Max had become a challenge that filled him with unanticipated excitement. He relished the idea of being on the road with her, overcoming whatever dangers arose, discovering bit by bit more pieces to the puzzle that was Elodie. At the same time, he must maintain a delicate balance between his growing fascination and the necessity to stay vigilant, lest she lull him into complacency and play him for a fool.

And then there was lust. With an anticipation so intense it ought to alarm him, he looked forward to sharing a room with her at the posting inns—and all the enticing possibilities for seduction that offered.

But when he recalled the disguises they'd agreed upon, he had to stifle a laugh. She could have contrived no better way to keep his amorous impulses at bay. They could hardly travel unnoticed if he was seen to be openly lusting after his valet!

He'd just have to get her back into maiden's attire as soon as possible.

Chapter Eight

Five days later, in a small inn south of Stuttgart along the road to Paris, Elodie loitered in a dim, smoky corner of the taproom, mug of ale in hand. Will sat at a table in the centre, gaming with a disparate group of fellow travellers.

Wearing gentleman's attire, the only disguise he employed was hair-blacking, there being nothing he could do beyond keeping his face downcast to camouflage those remarkable eyes. He lounged with cravat askew, long legs outstretched in an indolent pose, as he held the cards before him.

To a casual observer, he appeared to be just another young man who'd decided to go adventuring now that Napoleon's wars no longer threatened the Continent. A younger son of good family, probably, well born but not important or wealthy enough to require an entourage. A young man seemingly indifferent to his comfort—and that of his humble valet, since he'd chosen to ride on this journey, rather than spend the additional blunt necessary to hire a carriage.

It was an image he'd calculated with care. But Elodie, now better attuned, knew that despite his lazy stance, Will keenly observed every detail of the men in the room and the inn itself, always assessing possible threats, ready to make a quick exit in case of danger. Much as she herself did.

From the beginning of their odyssey, she'd watched him intently, at first apprehensive, since she'd had to commit her safety into his hands. By now she'd relaxed a bit, appreciating the high level of alertness he maintained—with remarkably little sleep—and the care he took to evaluate their surroundings and the people with whom they came into contact.

For as long as she could remember, *she'd* been the one who had to be vigilant to protect herself and those she loved. How much easier it was for a man, who could interact with innkeepers and barmaids and grooms and tradesmen virtually unnoticed, as a woman could not. She'd even allowed—if only to herself— that his skill at disguise, invention and evasion equalled her own.

She was beginning to believe that Will Ransleigh would get her safely to Paris after all.

Though she must never forget he was expending all that effort for his own purposes.

Over the last few days, they'd worked out a routine, riding hard by day, not choosing an inn for the night until well after dark, by which time she was so weary she almost fell out of the saddle. In the early dawn, Will would arrange fresh horses and buy food to carry with them for the next day, and they'd take their meals by the roadside.

She smiled into the darkness. Breaking their fast in the open might have been a dreary, rushed affair, but in Ransleigh's company, the meals had assumed almost a picnic atmosphere. She had to admit she was intrigued by him. Though she herself said little, with a bit of prompting, she'd persuaded him to regale her with tales of his many adventures.

He was a marvellous storyteller, his vivid descriptions making her feel she was reliving the episodes with him. He had her laughing at his account of dismal billets and narrow escapes from marauders on the Peninsula, the comic ballet of Brussels packed to the gills with foreigners. Unknowing, he fed her starved soul with details of the Paris he'd explored before Napoleon slipped his leash at Elba and plunged France back into war.

Notably missing among his tales, however, was any mention of his origins. Which was only fair, since she'd divulged absolutely nothing about herself. But she'd grown increasingly curious to know more about the man, as the relationship of captor and—though willing—captive subtly began to alter, until it now verged dangerously close to camaraderie.

Which was perhaps the point of his tall tales. Perhaps he was trying to earn her trust, beguile her into thinking of him as a friend, a companion…a lover?

Tightness coiled in her belly and she blessed again the disguise that required them to stay at arm's length during the day, the arduous long rides that made her fall asleep almost instantly when she could finally rest for the night.

Otherwise, the two of them alone in the secret darkness… She didn't think she could have resisted the temptation to taste those sculpted lips that she watched, fascinated, as he spun his tales, acutely conscious of his sheer masculine power and the fierce pull of attraction between them. Resisted the desire to run her fingers down the muscled thighs she watched day after day control his mount with effortless precision. Denied herself the chance to explore the naked torso of which she caught only teasing glimpses when he pulled off his shirt to wash in the early mornings.

Did he wait to do that until he knew she was awake, deliberately tempting her?

Over the years, she'd used her body when necessary and, more often, had it used without her consent. It had been a very long time since she'd *wanted* a man.

But she wanted Will Ransleigh. In his smoky gaze when no one was watching them, in the lingering caress of fingers on her arm or hand the few times touching her had been necessary, she knew he wanted her, too.

The day of reckoning was coming when that mutual desire would no longer have to be denied. Heaven help her, how she *burned* for it!

But that time wasn't here…yet. They were still too far from Paris. And she was still too far from deciding just how—and when—she would seduce Will Ransleigh.

Tonight, announcing he needed to replenish their funds with a little gaming, Will had insisted, despite her fatigue, that she remain in the taproom and linger in the shadows. So she would be close at hand, in case they needed to leave the inn in a hurry.

She'd forced herself to stay awake by watching the game, counting cards and points. She'd been annoyed to discover she must admire Will Ransleigh's prowess at cards, too.

With the same precision he analysed rooms and roads, he surveyed his opponents with that deceptively disinterested, downcast gaze. Having watched the game for several hours, Elodie was convinced he'd worked out just how much he could win from each opponent without straining their purses enough to provoke a belligerent response and just how much overall so as not to have his skill excite comment. He bolstered her belief by deliberately losing a hand from time to time and by his occasional crows of triumph when he won, as if winning were a surprise. Whereas, she was certain he could have fleeced all his opponents, had he chosen to.

Clara had told her how he'd lifted her purse at the market.

Would he have the skill to fleece her, when the time came? Smiling faintly, she thought of Will removing the rough, scratchy man's garb, covering her mouth with his, her body with his, parting her legs to bare to his touch and possession that hottest, most needy place…

The cold splash of ale on her knee jerked her back to awareness. Lost in sensual imagining, she'd drifted off and nearly dropped her mug. Alarmed to have come close to creating a commotion that would have attracted unwelcome attention, she looked up to find Will staring at her.

Elodie froze; not wishing to bring her to anyone's notice, Will never looked directly at her when in company.

'Pierre, take yourself up to the room before you shatter the mug—or spill any more of that good ale! I can wash up and remove my own coat tonight.'

A quick nod punctuated the command. Too weary to object, Elodie walked quietly out, hearing as she closed the door Will tell the others, 'Doesn't have the stamina of youth, poor Pierre. Old family retainer, you know.'

A murmur of commiseration followed her up the stairs. Old family retainer indeed, she thought indignantly, recognising the subtle taunt. The day was coming, Monsieur Ransleigh would soon discover, when she would be neither 'old' nor slavishly obedient.

Their room tonight was on the top floor. She paused after climbing to the first-floor landing, which boasted a window overlooking the street. Weary though she was, the star-spangled sky called out for admiration.

Just a few days' journey ahead, Paris beckoned. And somewhere within that teeming city, she urgently hoped, was Philippe.

Longing for him swelled within her, the ache sharper than usual. She'd been away so long, she was as apprehensive as she was excited to arrive at last and discover whether the long months of hope were justified. Whether she could find him and make him hers again.

She immediately banished a soul-chilling fear that she might fail. Of course she would succeed, she reassured herself. They belonged together. No amount of time or separation could change that.

With a sigh, she trudged up the final set of stairs, the starlight from the window below fading as she ascended. Five steps down into the darkness of the hallway, she was grabbed roughly from behind. The hard chill of a blade pressed against her neck.

'Come with me quietly, madam,' a voice murmured, 'or your next move will be your last.'

Elodie tensed, her heartbeat skyrocketing. After an instant, though, she forced back the panic, emptying herself of everything but the need to calculate the physical advantage of the man detaining her and the meaning of his words.

Though he'd spoken in French, his accent was English; he knew she was not Ransleigh's valet, which meant he must have tracked them from Vienna. Would he kill her, or just threaten her to force her co-operation?

'Don't hurt me, sir!' she said, putting some of the alarm she'd suppressed into a voice pitched as low as she could make it. 'You're mistaken; I'm Monsieur LeClair's valet, Pierre.'

'No, you are Elodie Lefevre, implicated in the plot to assassinate Lord Wellington in Vienna last year,' the voice replied. 'You're going to descend these stairs with me to the back entrance. Now.'

Her mind tumbling over itself, looking for some means to escape, Elodie let the man push her ahead of him to the landing, stumbling as much as she dared to delay their progress. 'You are wrong, *monsieur*!' she whispered urgently. 'Speak to my master, he can straighten this out!'

A short laugh huffed against her ear. 'I mean to speak to him. After I take care of you.'

'Take care of me? What do you—?'

'Silence!' the man hissed in her ear. 'Speak again and I'll shut you up permanently.'

The assailant knew what he was doing; he kept her arms pinned behind her as he shuffled her forwards, and the blade at her throat never wavered. Could she stumble, catch her foot under his boot and use his own weight to knock him down the stairs, ducking out of the way before he cut her throat?

Probably not. Dragging her feet from step to step, muscles tensed and body poised to flee at the first opportunity, Elodie let her captor push her down the stairs and turn her towards the back exit leading to the stables.

Once outside, she would have more room to manoeuvre. Her assailant knew she was a woman; perhaps she could pretend to faint.

Just a moment's opportunity and, thankfully free of encumbering skirts, she could take to her heels.

Her assailant unlatched the door and thrust her into the deserted stable yard. Knowing this would probably be her best chance, she'd gathered herself to make a break when, out of the stillness, came the unmistakable metallic click of a pistol being cocked.

Her assailant heard it, too, and halted. From deep within the shadows by the wall, Will said, 'Put down the knife, or I'll blow your head off. At this distance, I can't miss.'

'I can cut her throat before you can fire.'

'Perhaps.' A glimmer of humour coloured his voice. 'But you would still be dead, so what would it matter? *Monsieur*, you will oblige me by giving over the knife and keeping your hands well in front of you. Then you will accompany me and my much-maligned valet up to our room.'

When the man holding her hesitated, Will sighed. 'Do not try me, sirrah. I'm not at all averse to decorating this wall with your brains.'

With a reluctant laugh, the man surrendered

his knife. Taking it, Will said, 'Pierre, search his pockets.'

Weak-kneed with relief, Elodie turned to face her attacker. She had no idea how Will had discovered them, but she'd never in her life been so relieved to see anyone.

While Will kept his pistol trained on the man, Elodie hurriedly rifled the man's great-coat, removing a pistol from each pocket and holding them up. 'That's all.'

'Good. Pierre, you go first and make sure no one else is about. Sound an all clear and we'll follow you.'

A few moments later, Will herded her erstwhile attacker into their top-floor bedchamber. After pushing him into a chair, he quickly bound the man's wrists behind him, then motioned her to light a candle.

As soon as he held it close enough to make out the attacker's features, his expression turned from angry to incredulous. 'George Armitage! What the deuce are you doing here?'

'Trying to keep you from catching a bullet or being fitted for the hangman's necktie,' Armitage replied.

While Elodie tried to figure out what was going on, Will said drily, 'Your concern would overwhelm me...if you hadn't been trying to carve up my valet. If I unbind you, do I have your word as an officer you'll not threaten him again or try to escape?'

'You do,' Armitage said.

'Pierre, pour some wine,' Will directed as he set about removing the ropes.

'No need to maintain the fiction; I know he's no lad,' Armitage said.

'But the rest of the inn doesn't need to know. What are you doing here, skulking about and attacking harmless servants? Last time we talked, you were about to leave Paris with your regiment, bound for London.'

'So I was, and did. Sold out and went back to the estate, but as Papa has no intention of turning over the reins any time soon, it was bloody boring. I took myself off to London and lounged about the club, losing at cards and vying for the favours of various actresses until Locksley—you remember him, lieutenant in the 95th—talked me into joining the Foreign Office. Thought it might provide some of the excitement I'd missed since leaving the army.'

'But how did you end up here?'

'You were seen leaving England, bound for Vienna, barely two weeks after returning from

Brussels. Knowing what had happened to your cousin Max, it wasn't difficult to figure out what you meant to do.'

'And the Foreign Office was so displeased by that, they sent a bloodhound after me?'

'Though the officials weren't too concerned when Max tried to track down Madame Lefevre, some who knew you felt you might be better at ferreting her out. I can't believe you weren't aware that no one, neither the English, nor the French, nor the Austrians, *wished* her to be found. So when I discovered they meant to send someone to stop you, I volunteered. Fellow officer and all—didn't want to see you come to harm.'

'I suppose I owe you thanks, then. I must say, though your tracking skills are acceptable, if tonight was an example of how you plan an ambush, your Foreign Office career is likely to come to a quick and violent end.'

Ignoring that jibe, Armitage continued, 'The Foreign Office just wants you back in England, out of this, but there are others with less charitable intentions. Once *madame* scarpered, according to my superiors in Vienna, several agents set out after her.'

Will's amused expression sobered. 'Who?'

'They didn't say. Could be French agents, or maybe the same Bonapartists who embroiled St Arnaud, angry the plot didn't succeed and eager to punish those who failed. I don't suppose I could persuade you to abandon plans of bringing the lady back to England?'

As Will shook his head, George sighed. 'Knowing your aim was to restore Max's reputation, I didn't think so. Now that I've warned you, if you're not prepared to listen to reason, you're on your own.'

'What will you do now? Honour among old soldiers notwithstanding, I don't imagine your superiors would be pleased to learn we had a pleasant chat and you let me go.'

'No, I'll tell them I tracked you to the inn, but you'd left before I arrived.'

'You think they'll believe that?' Will laughed. 'I repeat my advice about seeking another career.'

Armitage waved a careless hand. 'If they do give me the sack, I'll find something else to do. I can always retire in disgrace on Papa's land and die of boredom. What of you? Not knowing who else may be trailing you or how close they are, you'll leave at once, I expect?'

Will frowned—his expression mirroring

Elodie's concern as she followed the conversation, too alarmed by Armitage's news to object to being treated as if she were a piece of the furniture.

As the months after the assassination attempt had passed without incident, her worry that someone besides St Arnaud wished her dead had slowly dissipated. In time, she'd even found the presence of the guards keeping watch over her lodgings comforting. Discovering that she was being followed by some anonymous someone had just shattered that peace of mind.

'As soon as it's light enough to see,' Will was saying.

'Let's drink a bottle, then, to friendship and the regiment. Who knows when we'll meet again?'

Will nodded. 'I considered knocking you out before we left, to give you a more believable excuse for not apprehending me, but you could say instead that I drugged you. Much less painful.'

Armitage grinned. 'Much more civilised.'

Will gestured to Elodie. 'Fetch more wine from the saddlebags, Pierre. Then get some rest.'

Chapter Nine

~~~~~~~~~~~~~~~~~~~~

They had left Armitage, who imbibed the majority of the wine, sleeping off his efforts at conviviality. During their hurried preparations to depart and the hard ride that followed, they had not had—or made—time to discuss the events of the previous night.

Not until after mid-afternoon the next day did Ransleigh signal them to a stop. As he led their mounts into the shade of some tall trees, within sight of the main road, but far enough away that they'd not eat the dust of passing carriages with their bread, Elodie wondered if he would speak of it now.

She shivered, still feeling the sting at her neck where the blade had nicked her.

What would George Armitage have done

with her, if Will Ransleigh hadn't come to her rescue? He'd wanted to save his army comrade from Foreign Office scrutiny, possible danger—and from her. She warranted no such protection.

No one, neither the English, nor the French, nor the Austrians, wished her to be found, he'd said.

Unease clenched in her belly. Who was tracking her? Not since the earliest days after the attack in Vienna had she felt so vulnerable.

After extracting bread, cheese and wine from the saddlebags, Will parcelled out portions and they settled to eat, making stools and a table out of a fallen log.

Setting down his wine, Will turned to her, his eyes sparkling as they always did when he was about to spin another tale. But whatever he saw on her face made the gleam fade.

'You're wondering who else is out there and if last night's attack is only the first,' he said abruptly.

She nodded, then felt a tingle of shock that he had read so much in her face. Had she been that unguarded?

Or had he just learned her expressions too well?

Pushing back that alarming thought, she replied simply, 'Yes. And I should thank you for rescuing me. How did you know I was in danger, by the way?'

'I heard the two of you on the stairs as I left the taproom. Since there was only one logical way for your attacker to smuggle you out and you were very cleverly delaying him, it was easy enough to slip out the front and await you in the stable yard.'

Despite his dismissive words, Elodie knew the successful intervention had required skill and timing. Putting a hand to the scratch at her throat, she said, 'Anyway, thank you. I don't know what he would have done, if you'd not intercepted us.'

Will shrugged. 'Since it was George, probably just tied you up while he tried to talk me into turning you over to the local authorities and heading back to England.'

Elodie had a sudden, terrifying vision of being cast off penniless and friendless, under very real threat of imprisonment. Thank heaven Will Ransleigh was so dedicated to his cousin! 'I'm grateful for your help. But what of those who might be more dangerous?'

'From what George told us, everyone from

the Austrians to the British Foreign Office knows we're headed for Paris. After failing to stop us, George will have to report where he discovered us and the identities under which we were travelling.'

'Time for a new disguise, then?' She sighed. 'They'll still be looking for two lone travellers, whatever new appearance we assume. If we could somehow merge with a group, it would be easier to continue unremarked.'

'I'm thinking it might be better to head south and take a less direct route. They'll be watching for us on the major posting roads now.'

'They'll be watching for us to arrive in Paris, too, however long it takes,' she pointed out.

'True, but after another week, when they could reasonably expect us to turn up on our present course, they'll be less vigilant. There must be hundreds of people entering Paris every day. The guards can't scrutinise every one of them...especially if we enter in the early morning, with the rush of farmers bringing goods to market.'

She smiled, trying to envision Will Ransleigh in a farmer's smock, driving a herd of pigs. He'd probably do it expertly and look dashing. 'After we travel south, should we purchase some livestock?'

'Yes, valet Pierre should probably become farmwife Paulette.' From the saddlebag, he extracted a map and consulted it. 'If we turn due south towards Bavaria, skirt around the edges of Switzerland and proceed from Strasbourg towards Nancy, we could head west straight to Paris.'

She shook her head. A map! She tapped the saddlebag. 'Hair-blacking, spectacles, canes, wigs—I almost expect there's a flock of chickens hidden in there, too. Is there anything you do not carry in that bag of deception?'

He grinned. 'I like to be prepared.' The smile fading, he continued, 'We shouldn't underestimate the pursuers. The other parties to the affair seem to want to forget it happened, so the most serious threat might be posed by St Arnaud's confederates. He can't have been working alone; if his partners discovered that, contrary to what St Arnaud assured them, you'd not been silenced, they might want to correct his lapse.'

'Quite possibly,' she agreed. The thought was dismaying, but it was useless to panic. It was hardly the first time her life had been in danger. If they *were* being trailed by forces who wanted to eliminate her, there was nothing she could do but take all reasonable precautions—and keep going.

'Well, today seems the very breath of early summer, with wildflowers blooming under a gentle sun and the sky blue as the Mediterranean. This bread is fresh and crusty, the cheese piquant, the ham savoury, and the wine delicious. I don't intend to allow whoever might be out there to steal my enjoyment of it. So, tell me another story.'

Instead of obliging, Ransleigh remained silent, studying her. 'You are remarkable, you know,' he said after a moment.

'Remarkable?' she echoed, raising an eyebrow.

'You've been threatened by me, forced to leave your only friend, hauled out of Vienna, attacked at midnight at knifepoint and acknowledged that everyone from the British Foreign Office to Bonapartist agents may be looking to snuff you out. Yet all you ask of life, of me, is a story.'

She shook her head, a little mystified by his intensity. 'All we can ever ask of life is the joy of this moment. There are no promises about the next.'

'The joy of this moment,' he repeated. 'Ah, *yes.*' Before she could imagine what he meant to do, he reached over, tipped back her hat and kissed her.

Elodie couldn't have stopped him if Talley-rand himself were holding a pistol on them. For days, she'd been unable to tear her eyes from the play of those lips as he spun his tales…from imagining how they'd feel and taste pressed against hers.

Their touch was hard, demanding, flavored of the wine he'd drunk. The taste of him in-toxicated her, as if she'd drained the whole of the wineskin. She heard small mewing noises of encouragement and was shocked to realise they came from her, while, driven by a hunger long denied, she wrapped her arms around his shoulders and plastered herself against him.

His tongue probed her lips, opening her, and plunged deep. It chased hers in fiery dance, then encircled and suckled, pulling her deeper, unleashing a maelstrom of desire so intense her sole imperative was to have all of him.

She fumbled at the waistband of her trou-sers, desperate to open herself to the sleek hardness pressed against her, to feel it invade her body as his tongue had conquered her mouth.

Suddenly, in a shock of cold air, he pushed her away. In a tumult of clashing sensations—desperate need, impatience to continue, dismay that he had stopped—she finally heard it: the clatter of jangling harness, a murmur of voices as travellers approached down the road.

At least she had the solace of knowing he felt the same desire and disappointment. As he backed away, he grabbed her chin and, one last time, his mouth captured hers. Then, before refastening the single button she'd managed to unloose in her trouser flap, he slid a hand through the opening and stroked his fingers swiftly across the hot waiting flesh.

Just that glancing touch to the sensitive nub jolted through her like a lightning bolt, the sensation so powerful that, had it lasted a touch longer, she would have reached her release.

When had she last felt that joy? Had she ever felt it so intensely?

Gasping, disoriented, Elodie tried to settle her agitated senses as travellers came into view on the road beyond. Soon, a group of friars with cart and cattle slowly lumbered past.

'Would that I could get away with kissing my soon-to-be-former valet one last time,' Ransleigh murmured against her ear, the warmth of his breath setting her still-acutely sensitive body pulsing again. 'But you wished for a group to travel with and I think the Lord just answered that prayer. Given how we were engaged as they arrived, you can't say the Almighty doesn't have a sense of humour.'

Trying to quell the desire still raging through him, Will concentrated on regulating his breathing as he and Madame Lefevre watched the monks plod past.

As soon as the dust settled, she turned back to him. 'Travelling under the protection of the good friars is tempting, but we'd be rather conspicuous, don't you think? Unless you have robes, hoods, sandals and rope belts hidden in that bag.'

'Not yet, but I will. By the quantity of cattle and the amount of goods in the wagon, this group must have been to the farmers' market at Sonnenburg. Moving as slowly as they are, they probably spent the night at the religious guesthouse we passed at mid-morning. You stay here; I'll ride back and obtain what we need to become "Brother Pierre" and "Brother LeClair".'

'That's outrageous!'

'What, you don't think you can pass as a monk?'

'No! Well, yes, but lying to a priest? A whole group of priests?'

She looked so aghast, he had to laugh. 'Ah, so you do possess some scruples! I, alas, have none. Come now, think of it as...divine intervention sent to protect you. It would be a wonderful disguise, you must admit. We could travel south to wherever they are going, spend a few days at their monastery and then head for Paris. Absolutely no one would think to look for us dressed as monks.'

She nodded reluctantly. 'That's true enough.'

'If it chafes your conscience so badly to dissemble to the holy brothers, you could confess the deception before we leave. Besides, even if we admit we are in disguise, have not religious houses for millennia offered sanctuary to those in danger?'

Since she didn't immediately lodge another protest, Will knew she was weakening. Though he thought it a brilliant plan, her concession was all he needed.

'I suppose so,' she admitted at last. 'But how do you plan to obtain the supplies? The guest-house isn't a clothing shop.'

'I'm sure the friars have a few robes and vestments they can spare. I'll tell the abbot there was a fire at my monastery that destroyed some of the brothers' robes and, as penance for some misdeed, I pledged to replace them. If I let him charge twice what they are worth, I'm sure I can persuade him to sell me a few.'

Frowning, *madame* wrapped her arms around her head. At Will's raised eyebrow, she said, 'I shield myself from the lightning bolt the *bon Dieu* will surely send to punish your sacrilege.'

Will chuckled. 'Never mind the good Lord, just protect yourself from view by passing travellers. It shouldn't take me more than an hour to reach the guesthouse. I'll have us out-fitted and on our way to catch up with the friars before nightfall.'

As promised, after a glib explanation and a generous donation, Will returned to *madame*'s hiding place two hours later with the necessary robes, hoods, belts and shoes. After giv-

ing her some privacy to change into the latest
disguise—and trying very hard to avoid the
further sacrilege of imagining her naked—he
stowed the rest of their provisions and clothing in the saddlebags.

A few moments later, she returned, face
lowered beneath the shadowing hood, hands
clasped together in her sleeves in a prayerful
attitude, looking the very picture of a humble
friar.

'What an excellent Brother Pierre you
make!' he marvelled. 'If I didn't know your
identity, I would absolutely believe you a man
of God.'

She shuddered. 'Please, don't tempt the
Lord's wrath again by claiming that! Since
Armitage knows our current aliases, we
should complete the blasphemy by changing
names. Shall I be "Brother Innocent" and you,
"Brother Francis"?'

'Of Assisi?' he asked with a grin, following her thoughts.

'Yes. A sinner and voluptuary before he
came to the Lord. Perhaps the so-divine aura
of the name will stick,' she replied tartly. 'I intend to protect what's left of my immortal soul

by swearing a vow of silence. You will have to spin this web of lies by yourself.'

Throwing herself up on to her mount, she rode off. He was still chuckling when he caught up to her. But, true to her declaration, she ignored his attempt to converse. After a few snubs, he left her to her chosen silence.

Watching her, bent humble and prayerful over the saddle, Will had to shake his head. Madame Lefevre adopted the role of holy brother as quickly and unquestioningly as she had transformed herself from a gentlewoman into an old man into a valet. Will wished his subordinates on his army missions had understood their roles and mastered them as quickly and completely.

Not that she was merely a follower. Had she not astutely observed that travelling in a group offered them the best chance to evade their pursuers and reach Paris undetected, he might never have recognised the potential in that passing group of monks.

He had to appreciate the good Lord's sense of irony. How much better a rebuke to the raging desire that had nearly made him take her by the roadside in the full daylight, where anyone might have discovered them, than to send a band of friars?

But, as that same good Lord knew, even in men's garb, Elodie Lefevre posed enough temptation to break the will of a saint and he was nothing close to that.

All those days telling stories, his gaze continually straying to her soft lips and generous mouth, while eyes blue as the lake at Swynford Court in June focused on him with complete concentration, as if he were the only being in the universe. Wisps of brown hair escaping from under the homespun cap made him itch to slide their silkiness through his fingertips, while his hands ached to cup the softness of those pale, freckled cheeks. Mesmerised by her, he rambled on, recounting by rote stories with which he'd regaled fellow soldiers at camps and billets and dinners from the barren heights of Badajoz to the ballrooms of Brussels, all his will needed to resist the ravaging hunger to taste those lips, invade that soft mouth, pull the essence of her into him, possess her and all her secrets.

It had been worth it, worth everything, to begin the process with that kiss. She tasted of the bread and wine she'd praised, of lavender and woman. He'd hardly begun to penetrate her mystery, to discover the source of that amazing ability to block out all the world's dangers and embrace the joy of a single moment, but he'd learned she was no sensual innocent.

She'd kissed him back with fire and expertise, fanning his passion to an intensity he couldn't remember ever reaching so quickly before. If not for the inextinguishable instinct for survival born of six years living on the streets, he would never have heard the travellers approach—or been able to force himself away from her.

Just then, he spotted the dust cloud in the distance that marked the progress of the monks who'd passed them earlier. Gesturing towards it, he said, 'Time for Act Two to begin.' He checked a smile at the scowl 'Brother Innocent' threw him as he spurred his mount forwards.

Reining in beside the group, Will slid from the saddle and greeted the monks with a nod and the sign of the cross. 'God's peace, good brothers! Where are you bound?'

'His peace to you as well,' replied a monk mounted on a donkey, to whom the others deferred. 'We travel to our abbey at Leonenburg, which we should reach just after nightfall. And you?'

'Returning from Vienna on a mission for our abbot. I'm Brother Francis and this is Brother Innocent—who pledged a vow of silence towards the success of our journey. May we join you?'

'Of course. Anyone doing God's work is welcome.'

As they fell in behind the slow-moving cortège, *madame* gave him a reproachful look from beneath her hood—doubtless again fearing the imminent lightning strike.

But in a sense, they were doing God's work, he reasoned with her silently. Righting the wrong done Max and restoring to the nation the talents of a man who could do great good was a worthy endeavour.

Hauling into danger a woman who he was—grudgingly and much against his will—beginning to think might have been almost as much an innocent victim of the plot as his cousin might not, though, a stab of conscience replied.

Was that the reason, rather than a desire to wash her hands of his blasphemous deception, she'd chosen her name? he wondered.

Maybe the influence of *his* name was affecting his views. Though he'd never been a voluptuary, he'd committed sins enough to stay alive on the streets and to survive years of war.

A little humility and some genuine penance wouldn't come amiss. As they travelled in this herd like docile holy sheep, he appreciated having a divine ally in resisting her allure. As last night's attack chillingly demonstrated, he couldn't afford to let the attraction between them diminish his vigilance.

He didn't even want to think what might have happened, had her assailant been someone other than George. Someone who would have cut her throat without a qualm in the darkness of the hallway while he sat gaming in the taproom.

When he'd slipped from the common room up the stairs, the vision of her seized by an unknown assailant, moonlight glinting off the knife at her throat, had punched all the air from his lungs. Savage rage against her attacker and the urgent imperative to rescue her had refilled them.

George confirmed that the danger her maid feared was very real. The hasty, casual promise he'd given Clara to keep her safe was going to require all his wits and every artifice he'd learned as a young thief and perfected as a soldier. For now, he'd just have to keep a tight rein over his increasingly intense need to possess her.

But once they were safely in Paris… If she thought he'd stand aside and turn her over to some no-surname-Philippe before they settled what raged between them, she knew nothing of the iron resolve of Will Ransleigh.

As predicted, Will and Madame Lefevre had reached the monastery just after dark, were greeted by the abbot and invited to rest from their journey for as long as they liked. Billeted in a common room and eating with the group, he had little opportunity to speak privately with *madame*, stealing just a moment to recommend they remain several days at the monastery, and receiving her nod of agreement in reply.

Madame had mimed her willingness to work in the vegetable garden, while Will joined the monks cutting wood in the forest. Outside the walls of the monastery, he could relax a little; within them, unused to the traditions of a monastic order, he needed all his skill at mimicry to carry off the deception.

Madame, however, must have been raised a good Catholic, or was a better mimic than he, for she followed the order of worship and the prayers as if born to them. Or had she learned them after the fall of the Republic, when Napoleon made his Covenant with the Pope and religion returned to a France which for years had functioned without a church?

After five days with the brethren, who accepted their presence, respected their privacy and asked them no questions, Will approached *madame* to suggest they could move on. Silently she gathered her belongings, Will leaving a handsome gift with the abbot before they left the friendly gates of the abbey and made their way west through the foothills towards Switzerland.

Once they could no longer see the sheltering walls of the abbey in the distance, *madame* pulled down her hood and turned to Will. 'Perhaps we should continue this disguise for the rest of the journey. It's served us well enough thus far.'

Will clapped a hand to his chest theatrically.

'Behold, she speaks! Does this mean you've forgiven me for the deception? Or did you ease your conscience by receiving absolution from the abbot?'

She grinned at him. 'I confessed the truth the very first night. Did you never wonder why the brothers were so discreet?'

'Because they are holy men, above the sin of gossip?'

'They are still human and curious. Besides, that tale of being on a mission wouldn't wash; your ignorance of the ways of holy orders would have shown the moment the abbot questioned you about it, if your performance at Compline the night of our arrival hadn't already made everyone suspicious.'

After a moment's annoyance, Will grinned back. 'And here I thought they'd accepted me as an exemplary monk.'

'They admired how hard you worked, if several had to keep from smiling at your ignorance of the most basic prayers.'

'You broke that vow of silence to discuss me?'

'No, I overheard them talking about you in the refractory. I confessed to the abbot only that I was female, fleeing in disguise under threat of my life, and that you were helping me to reach my family in France.'

'Had you no other sins to confess?' Will teased.

The playful look faded from her face as she stared at him. He felt her gaze roam his face, his mouth, his body and return to focus on his lips. 'Not yet,' she replied.

Her meaning hit him like a punch to the belly, the always-simmering need he worked hard to contain bursting free in a blast of heat that hardened his body and roared through his veins. For a moment he saw only her, felt only the pulse of desire pulling them together.

His mouth dry, his brain scrambled, he couldn't come up with a witty reply. She broke the connection, turning away from him.

'We're still a long way from Paris.' To underscore the point, she urged her mount to a trot.

He didn't dare trust her, but there was no question about the strength of his desire for her. He urged his horse after her, wishing they could gallop all the way.

Chapter Ten

Following their former pattern of hard-riding days and short nights, for almost two weeks Will had led Madame Lefevre around the foothills of the Alps, finally descending to Nancy. Once past that city, they joined a growing stream of travellers headed north-west through the vineyards and fields of the Lorraine towards Paris.

Although in its anti-clerical zeal the Revolution had destroyed or sold off most of France's great abbeys and monasteries, in their guise as monks, they were still able to claim shelter for the night at the re-established churches along their route. Will continued to negotiate for food and fresh horses, joking, to *madame*'s repeated warning about hellfire, that he was fast becoming a model priest.

Allies and collaborators by necessity, they were now an experienced team, able to communicate silently through looks and gestures. Though they'd not encountered any further need for stealth, they maintained their roles diligently. As he'd learned in Seven Dials, one never knew when rats might come pouring out of some unseen hole.

They still took their meals in the open, and Will still spun the tales, *madame* listening with every appearance of fascination. But she never volunteered anything about herself.

He no longer wanted to ask. Instead, foolish as it might be, Will wanted her to open to him willingly, without his having to trick or pry the information from her.

Though this woman had betrayed his cousin and brought scandal upon his name, he was having a harder and harder time reminding himself of the fact. Much as he tried to resist it, the slender sprig of camaraderie that had sprouted in Vienna had grown stouter and stronger through the intrigue and dangers of the road, entwining itself around him until it now threatened to bind him to her as powerfully as the sensual attraction that tempted him with every breath.

Each day, he'd slip into his stories some comment or observation that invited her to reciprocate with a similar experience of her own. At first, he'd wanted to tempt her into talking about herself, eager to use his wits to separate fact from deliberate falsehood.

Each day, as she had remained silent, disappointment grew sharper. He'd long since given up the suspicion that she had any intentions of feeding him false information to gain some advantage; her behaviour upon the road had been absolutely upright and above-board, just as he would have expected of a comrade-in-arms. Increasingly, it pained him that after their shared adventures, he knew nothing more about Madame Lefevre's past than he'd learned before they left Vienna.

In many ways, he felt closer to her than to anyone else in his life save his Ransleigh cousins. He could sense he was nearing the essence of her, the soul of her that danced always just beyond his reach. But she continued to withhold herself from him, in body and in spirit.

Was that a ploy, too? To disarm him by holding herself apart?

Tactic or not, he hungered for both. He wanted her to hunger for him, too. To yield her secrets.

Before he seduced her. For in a day or so, they'd be in Paris and the game would begin again in earnest. Some time before they passed through the city gates, he intended to bind her to him with the silken ties of physical possession. Before she could try to run, or set off to search for the mysterious Philippe.

Before he took her back to England.

Despite their growing closeness, he still meant to carry her there. He just wasn't so sure now, he admitted with a sigh, what he meant to do with her once they arrived.

Having spotted a likely resting spot under a stand of trees near a small river, he motioned her to turn her mount off the road. While she watered the horses, Will removed his saddlebag and extracted their simple meal, his thoughts returning to the conundrum of England.

Maybe he could stash *madame* at some quiet place in the country; he owned several such properties. He'd journey to London alone, feel out some contacts in the Foreign Office.

Maybe there was a way to clear Max's name without incriminating Madame Lefevre.

The idea of giving her up to the gallows was growing more and more unacceptable.

By the time she finished with the horses, he had bread, ham, cheese and wine set out on a saddle blanket on the sun-dappled grass under the trees. This time, hoping to lure her into speaking, as they sat to consume their meal, he did not immediately launch into a story.

It seemed she was content to eat in silence. Just as Will was about to judge his experiment a failure, she said, 'So, are you out of tall tales?'

'Have you not grown tired of my exploits?'

'Not at all. But there is something else I'd like to know about. Won't you describe your childhood? You've spun many stories of your roguish life, but nothing of how you became who you are.'

The whirlpool of the past swirled in memory, threatening to suck him down into its maelstrom of fear, hunger, pain and grief. He shook his head to distance it. 'There's nothing either entertaining or edifying about it.'

'It was…difficult?'

'Yes.'

'I'd still like to know. I've never met a man like you. It's ill bred to be so curious, I realise, but I feel driven to discover how you became who you are.'

He saw an opportunity and grabbed for it. 'I'll tell you about my youth—if you tell me about yours. Over our travels, I've blathered on at length about my misspent life. You've told me nothing.'

After a moment, she nodded. Exultant, he exhaled the breath he'd been holding.

'Very well. But you first. How did you learn all these things you seem to do so instinctively? To move as silently as silence itself. To be so aware of everything, everyone, all the time. The ability to be anyone, mingle with anybody, to converse as an English aristocrat or a Viennese workingman.'

'Silence, so as to move and not be seen. Awareness, in order to snatch purses and not get caught. Pickpockets in England are transported or hung. And to be anyone? Perhaps because I have been almost all those things and had to mimic them to survive until I mastered the roles.'

'How did the nephew of an earl, even an illegitimate one, become a thief, a pickpocket and a working man?'

Will thought of the taunts and hazing at Eton that no amount of bloody-knuckle superiority had stopped. Crude drawings of cuckoos left on his chair, muttered obscenities about his mother issuing from within a gaggle of boys, impossible to identify the speaker. Would this daughter of aristocrats scorn him, too, when she knew the truth?

Somehow, he didn't think so.

'During her come-out in London, my mother, a clergyman's daughter, was bedazzled by my father. The younger son of the Earl of Swynford, he was a rogue, gamester and self-centred bastard of epic proportions. He lured her to his lodgings, a midnight excursion that ruined her reputation. When she refused to slink away to the country in disgrace, her family disowned her. For a time, they lived together at some dismal place just outside Seven Dials, but after losing a fortune at cards one night, he fled to Brussels. His older brother, now the earl, had already warned him he'd pay no more of his debts, and my father wasn't prepared to adapt himself to a debtor's life in Newgate. He left behind my mother, six months gone with child.

Mama managed to eke out a few pennies doing needlework, enough for us to survive.'

Though all he remembered was being hungry. Frightened. Alone. And, later, angry.

'And then?' she prompted softly.

'When I was five years old, the local boss made me a runner and the street lads became my family. For the next six years, I learned the finer points of card sharping, lock-picking, house-breaking, knife-fighting and thievery.'

'Did your father never come back for you?'

'No. I heard he died of a bullet wound, courtesy of a man he'd been trying to cheat at cards in some low dive in Calais. But among his papers, later delivered to the earl, were letters written by my mother, begging him to make provision for their child. The earl set his solicitor to investigate and, once paternity was established, he had me brought to Swynford. Although, over the years, I'm sure he's regretted the decision to turn a second-storey boy into a gentry-mort, my cousins did their best to make me into a proper Ransleigh. Especially Max. Now, your turn.'

He caught her chin, making her face him. 'Who are you, Elodie Lefevre? Because if you're St Arnaud's cousin, I'll eat this tree.'

Before she could deny or dissemble, he rushed on, 'Don't you owe me the truth? I've told you about my ill-begotten youth. I've kept you safe and brought you almost to the gates of Paris. I simply can't believe St Arnaud would have left his own cousin in Vienna. Beaten her, perhaps, but not abandoned her; *someone* in the family would have taken him to account. Who are you, really?'

He held her gaze, implacable, willing her to confess, while his heart pounded, frantic with hope and anticipation.

Finally, she said softly, 'I was born Elodie de Montaigu-Clisson, daughter of Guy de Montaigu-Clisson, Comte de Saint-Georges. Our family home was south of the Loire, near Angers.'

He ran a map of France through his head. 'Isn't that in the Vendée?'

'Yes.'

That fact alone could explain so much. 'Was your family involved in the Royalist rising against the Revolution?'

'My papa joined the Comte de La Rochejaquelein, as did almost all the nobility of the Vendée. I don't know much, I was only a babe when the Republic was declared. But I do remember turmoil. Being snatched from the house in the middle of the night. Fire licking through the windows. Living in a garret in Nantes. Mama weeping. More fighting. Then that day...that awful day by the river.'

She'd lived in Nantes. Suddenly he recalled the event that had outraged all of Europe. 'You witnessed The Noyades?'

'The Republican soldiers herded all the townspeople to the quai beside the river. They marched the priests on to a small boat, locked them below and scuttled the vessel.' He could almost see the rippling surface reflected in the bleakness of her eyes. 'They did it again and again, one boatload of priests and nuns after another. All those holy ones, drowned. I was five years old.'

A child so young, watching that. He put a hand on her shoulder, stricken. 'I'm so sorry.'

'It was terrible. But it was also wonderful. There was no screaming, no pleas, no panic. Just...serenity. Mama said they went to a secret place in their hearts, where no evil could touch them.'

Like you do now, he thought. 'And after? If I'm remembering correctly, the Revolutionary government offered amnesty to all Vendéeans who surrendered and took the oath of allegiance. Did your father?'

'He died in the final battle. We left the garret in the middle of the night, our shoes wrapped in rags to muffle the sound, and boarded a ship. I remember wind shrieking, rain lashing, travellers screaming, thinking we would all drown like the priests and have to swim to heaven. Then…calm, green land, Mama weeping on the shore. We travelled north for many days, around a great city, surrounded by people speaking a language I couldn't understand.'

'You sailed to England, then? A number of *émigrés* went to the north, supported by the Crown.'

She nodded. 'Mama, my elder brother and I settled in a cottage on land owned by Lord Somerville.' She smiled. 'He had a wonderful garden. I used to spend hours there.' The smile faded. 'It was *my* secret place when Mama wept, or food supplies ran low. When the children in the village taunted me for my poor English and tattered clothing, for being a foreigner.'

'If you were living in England, how did you come to the attention of St Arnaud?'

'My brother, Maurice, ten years older than

me, despised the Republicans who seized our land, killed my father and turned Mama into a grief-stricken old woman. When Napoleon abolished the Directoire and made himself First Consul, instituted the Code Napoleon and promised a new France where merit and talent would be rewarded, Maurice was ecstatic. He hated living as a penniless, landless exile, dependent on charity. He determined to enter Napoleon's army, perform great feats of valour and win back our lands. So we returned to France. On his first army leave, he brought home a friend, Jean-Luc Lefevre.' Her expression turned tender. 'I loved him the first moment we met.'

Instinctive, covetous anger rose in him. He squelched it. Devil take it, he wouldn't be jealous of a dead man! 'Whom you married. He was lost in the war?'

Pain shadowed her face. 'He fell at Lützen. He died the day after I reached the billet to which they'd taken him.'

'Is that when you learned to walk like a man? To disguise yourself on the journey?' At her sharp look, he said, 'I was a soldier, remember. I know what happens in the aftermath of battle. It's…dangerous for women.'

Eyes far away, she nodded. 'There'd been another battle at Bautzen, just after I buried Jean-Luc and left for home. Skirting the battlefield, seeking shelter for the night, I came upon a ruined barn. Inside were several soldiers, deserters probably, with a woman. They were…ravishing her.'

He'd seen enough of war to know what happened to some men when the blood-lust faded. Dismay filling him at what he feared he'd hear next, Will seized her arm.

Caught up in memory, she didn't seem to notice. 'I heard her crying, pleading with them.' Tears welled up, and absently she wiped them away. 'I heard her, but I did nothing to help. I was so ashamed.'

'Thank heaven you did nothing!' Will cried, relieved. 'What could you have done, except invite the same treatment?'

'Nothing, probably,' she admitted. 'But I vowed never to be so helpless again. I went back to the field—the burial teams hadn't covered all of it yet—and "borrowed" a uniform from a dead soldier. It was already bloody, so all I needed was a bandage around my head. I wanted to be ready.'

'In case you encountered renegade soldiers?' Will nodded his approval. 'Ingenious, to use the uniform as protection.'

'As protection, and also to be able to intervene if I encountered a…similar situation.'

'Intervene?' he echoed, appalled. 'I trust you never attempted to! Such men are beyond reason or shame; trying to stop them would have gotten you beaten, or worse.'

'I never had the opportunity. If I had, though, I planned to tell them there were willing women in the next town, and ask that they leave the one they had to me, since I was wounded and lacking my usual vigour.'

Will stared at her a moment, astounded. But foolhardy as such an action would have been, he could believe Elodie would have attempted it—and shuddered to think what might have happened.

'Why did you travel to Lützen alone, anyway? Did your husband have no family to accompany you?'

She shook her head. 'His family were *aristos*, like mine. All but he were killed or scattered during the Terror.'

'Had he no friends, then?' When she shook her head, he burst out, 'But to travel among rival armies after a battle, a woman alone? I can't believe you took such a risk!'

'To save the life of someone you love is worth any risk. You, who have done so much for Monsieur Max, must know that is the truth.'

She had him there. He knew without question he'd face any danger to protect his cousins.

'Soon after I got back to Paris,' she continued, 'Maurice came to me. His mentor, St Arnaud, needed a favour.'

'A hostess for Vienna.'

'Yes. My brother met St Arnaud through the army; he approved of us because we were *ancien régime*, part of the old nobility, like he and *his* mentor, Prince Talleyrand. Maurice had become Arnaud's protégé, so, when he needed a hostess, Maurice suggested me.'

'Did you know about the plot?'

'Not until after we arrived.'

'And St Arnaud used this "Philippe" to compel you to participate? Who is he—your lover?'

Even to his own ears, the question sounded sharp. Elodie merely smiled and shrugged.

'Something like. But enough for now; I've

already told you more than you told me and we're losing the light. Besides, as you've said, we will be in Paris soon, perhaps even tomorrow.'

Her eyes on his, she laid her hand on his leg. Every muscle froze.

'In case our pursuers were able to figure out what happened after Karlsruhe, we should refashion ourselves once more. Enter Paris in the early morning with the crowd heading for Les Halles, just another farm couple with something to sell. I still have a simple gown in my pack. I could change here and we could stay at an inn tonight…as man and wife.'

The breath seized in his lungs. There was no question what she offered, with her gaze burning into his and her fingers tracing circles of fire over his thigh.

And no reason not to accept. If this were a trick to impair his vigilance, he'd just have to risk it.

'I thought you would never ask, my dear Brother Innocent. Let me help you change.'

'Not yet. I intend to wash in the river before putting on a clean gown.' She wagged a teasing finger at him. 'You stay here. No peeking!'

But her laughing eyes and caressing fingers told him she wouldn't mind at all if he watched her bathe.

He couldn't have kept himself from following her if the whole of Napoleon's Old Guard stood between him and the river.

Chapter Eleven

The chill of the early summer water shocked her, sending shivers blooming down her skin, but Elodie welcomed its bracing grip. Ah, to be clean, to wear her own clothes again!

Perhaps as soon as late tomorrow, she would find Philippe. As always when she thought of that moment, she felt stirring anew the mingled joy and anxiety that sat like a rock in her belly.

First, she'd have to deal with Will Ransleigh.

She couldn't deny a groundswell of regret that their paths must diverge. He was an amusing companion, a born storyteller, and more skilled at disguise, evasion and subterfuge than anyone she'd ever met.

Dissembling their way across Europe, they'd

made good comrades. Despite the danger, this journey from Vienna had been unique and magical, a gift she would remember and savour, something never to be experienced again.

She would miss him, more keenly than she'd like, but there was no question of a future. Now that Paris loomed and parting was inevitable, best to get on with it as quickly as possible.

She just hoped she'd be able to carry out her plans for that parting without a check, unease fluttering in her gut. Acquainted now with Will's high level of vigilance and excellence of observation, she'd need to be exceptionally careful in order to make her escape.

But before she eluded him, there was one final gift she could give—to him and to herself. Today and tonight, she would send him to the moon and the stars on a farewell journey of pleasure he would never forget.

Steeling herself to the cold, she strode into deeper water, quickly washing herself and her hair with a small bar of soap from the saddlebag. Despite warning him away, she knew he'd be watching from the copse of trees bordering the stream.

She'd start with a show to whet his appetite. Shivering in the chill, she waded back to

knee-deep water. With slow, languorous movements, she smoothed back the wet mane of hair,
knowing it would flow sleekly over her shoulders. She leaned her head back, letting sunlight
play over her breasts, the nipples peaked and
rigid from the cold.

She lathered her skin again, then cupped her
breasts in her hands and caressed the slippery
nipples between her thumb and forefinger.

Sensation sparked in them, hardening them
further, while matching sensation throbbed
below. Half-closing her eyes, she imagined
Will's hands mimicking the action of her
thumbs. Would he bring his tongue to them,
or use that hot, raspy wetness to stroke her
tender, pulsing cleft?

She wanted him to tease her body to madness, as she'd imagined so many nights when
she lay alone, chaste as the church floor they
bedded down upon, acutely conscious of him
sleeping beside her.

Heat crested and flowed outward from the
slippery abrasion at her nipples, the hotter
moisture at her centre. The fire building within
now insulated her from the water's chill, made
her breath uneven, her legs tremble, eager to
part and receive him. She couldn't remember

the last time she'd been so ready for a man, or ever wanting one as badly.

She opened her eyes to a muted splashing, and found Will, already shed of coat, boots and hose, wading out to her. Need blazed in his eyes.

Desire squeezed her breath out, gave it back to her in short, shallow puffs. The sensations at her breasts, between her legs, spiralled tighter, stronger.

'Shall I wash you?' she asked, her throat so dry she could hardly get the words out.

'If you'd be so kind.'

Oh, she wanted to be kind! She tugged at his shirt, impatient for an unimpeded view of the bare chest he'd teased her with so many nights on the road.

The skin was golden, sculpted over broad, muscled shoulders. His flat nipples were peaked, like hers. She couldn't wait to taste them. Couldn't wait a moment longer to see all of him.

Impatiently she tugged open the buttons of his trouser flap, freeing his member, which sprang up before her, proud and erect. Wobbling a bit in the current, he yanked the breeches further down and stepped out of them, tossing them back to the bank.

Her pulse stopped altogether, then stampeded. She could only stand, gaping at this Greek god of a man who'd come to earth to bathe in the stream and steal her heart. Would loving him transform her into some other being, a cow, a tree, as so often happened to unfortunate maidens who tangled with the Olympians? she wondered disjointedly.

Her admiration must have been obvious, for when she forced her gaze from his magnificent physique back up to his face, he was smiling. 'Soap?' he suggested.

She looked for it, then realised she still held it in her hand. After dousing him with water, she applied it to his neck, shoulders and chest. Breath catching in her throat, she massaged the film into a froth, touching, caressing, memorising the hard curve of muscle, the hollows between sinew and bone.

She thought he might break then, seize her and take his pleasure, but to her surprise and delight, he remained completely still, allowing her to touch him as she wished while standing so close she could feel his heat down the whole length of her body.

Lower she scrubbed, over the taut belly, the smooth curve of hip bone, until finally she took him in her hands.

His breath hissed out and he shuddered as she massaged the lather around his glorious hardness. Unable to resist temptation any longer, she leaned in and took one nipple between her teeth.

'Elodie!' he cried with a muffled gasp, then jerked her chin up to kiss her, one strong arm binding her to him. His mouth mastered hers, his tongue probing deep, leaving her senses swimming and giddy.

Still, he did not take her. She knew instinctively that even now, if she pushed him away, he would let her go. Awe and gratitude filled her.

And then, suddenly, she had to feel him there, in that aching, needy place that had been unsatisfied for so long. Her body had been handled and bullied, but not since she was very young, falling in love with the man who'd been so briefly her husband, had she encountered tenderness.

Still revelling in his kiss, she wound her arms around his neck and pulled herself up, so she could wrap her legs around his waist.

Bringing his rigid erection to the hot, moist openness only he could fill.

Groaning, he broke the kiss. 'Are you sure?'

'Yes! Please! Now,' she gasped back, then uttered a long, slow moan of ecstasy as he entered her.

Then, he was walking with her, his hands cupping her bottom to hold her in place as he took them deeper and downstream, beneath the tender summer-green branches of a huge tree that overshadowed the bank. Kissing her again, he balanced her in his hands, using the river's current and the water's buoyancy to augment his thrusts.

It was delicious, floating submerged in coolness yet captured at her very core by urgent, demanding heat. The sensations built and built and built as she rode him, her breath gone to sobbing gasps, her nails digging into the muscles of his shoulders, until finally she shattered and spun apart into dazzling shards of pure delight.

She came to herself, clinging weakly to him, her whole body limp, his hardness still buried deep within her throbbing core. *'Ma petite ange,'* he murmured, kissing her again, light, feathery touches on her eyelids, her brows, her forehead. He licked her throat, the shell of her ear, the edges of her lips, until the spiral within began to rotate again and she rocked her hips against his.

Exquisite sensation shot through her when he put his mouth to her breasts, rolling the tender nipples between his teeth. Desire accelerated, building hotter and faster, making her thrust towards him while the flow of the river magnified every movement. In a rolling, rhythmic motion, they slid together, tugged apart, the liquid friction within and without catapulting her to the waterfall's peak, where this time, they tumbled over together.

Some timeless interval later, Will pulled her with him to the bank. Under the embrace of the overhanging tree's branches, he sat, settling her between his legs, his warmth cradling her from the chill of air and water. 'I really had planned for there to be wooing, fine food and wine, a bed,' he said, planting a kiss on her head.

'I know,' she said on a sigh. 'I just couldn't wait any longer.'

'I'm glad you couldn't. I've wanted that for months.'

'You haven't known me for months,' she pointed out.

'True.' He wrapped his arms around her. 'But I've been looking for you all my life,' he added, so softly she wasn't sure whether she'd heard the words or only imagined them.

So had she been looking, the thought struck deep. Hoping for a lover who would give back rather than demand, who would care about her, rather than simply use her. She'd lived on her own, by her wits, pummelling some small space of existence from a bully prize-fighter of a world for so long, she had to go back into the mists of long-ago childhood to remember when she'd trusted anyone else to keep her safe. When she had last felt so protected. So...not alone.

The realisation was both thrilling and terrifying. Will Ransleigh, who would drag her to the gallows to save his cousin, had no part in her future, and the notion that she could depend on him after tomorrow was madness.

Yes, she'd been touched by his tenderness in seeing to her pleasure. Moved by his respect for her abilities and energised by the excitement of the sleight-of-hand they'd pulled off during their journey. But the sweetness of it was simply the rich dessert at the end of a meal—delectable, but not the sort of whole-some fare it took to sustain life.

Her life was with Philippe and that was an end to it.

She struggled, trying to use logic to disen-tangle her emotions from him, but like pulling at a fraying cloth, ragged threads of connection remained. Giving up, she made herself move away from him, squelching her body's protest at the loss of his warmth.

'It's good you had the foresight to find us a resting place that cannot be observed from the road,' she said, trying for some dispassion-ate comment.

'I know you trust me to keep us safe.'

She wanted to deny it, but had to admit the statement was true. It should frighten her anew to realise she'd fallen into such an instinctive reliance on him…but that reliance remained, tenacious as the river tugging at her ankles.

Which was illogical and dangerous. If she weren't exceedingly careful, this man could stop before it ever began her hunt for Philippe in Paris and she must never forget that.

Pushing her ungovernable emotions aside

in disgust, she said, 'If we don't dress soon, we will freeze.'

'I suppose. But I don't want you dressed.' He skimmed his fingers over her breasts, down between her legs. She sighed and lay back against him, feeling his spent member stir.

'Don't tempt me,' he said with a groan. 'Just the touch of you arouses me and we need to be sensible. We must dress now and ride quickly if we want to reach the village before dark.'

'Yes, sensible,' she agreed. Movement was what she needed. Returning to their travels, like rewinding a stopped clock, would set her emotions back on their proper course and re-animate her purpose, both shocked to a halt by the intensity of this interlude. Remind her that, but for one night of pleasure, their paths *must* diverge.

'We should purchase some livestock, too. Chickens, perhaps? The easier to blend in with the other farmers headed to market.'

'Another good idea. You're quite resourceful.'

She couldn't help feeling warmed by his praise. 'I've had to be.'

He helped her rise, his hands at her waist. 'Posing as man and wife for tonight,' he murmured, bending to kiss her, 'is your best idea yet.'

Ah, yes, she still had tonight, their last night, to savour. Her reward for all her forbearance along the road.

Passion, she could give him, though she could pledge him nothing else. Framing his face in her hands, she murmured, 'Perhaps livestock isn't so essential. All we really need is a room with a bed.'

'I hope that's a promise.'

She skimmed her fingers from his shoulders over his torso and down his body before leaning to snag his breeches and toss them up. 'Count on it.'

Chapter Twelve

Like a man and a maid in love for the first time, they helped each other dress, Will touching, kissing, laughing with Elodie as she donned her simple maid's gown and he changed back into a combination of working man and gentleman's attire that might be worn by a prosperous farmer. He knew that once they reached Paris, she would try to slip away from him, but he felt too light and euphoric to worry about it, happiness fizzing in his chest like a freshly opened bottle of champagne.

He'd had many an adventure, but never one like this. Never with a woman who was as uncomplaining a companion as a man, as resourceful as any of the riding officers with whom he'd crept through the Spanish and Portuguese wilderness, working with partisans and disrupting the French.

Coming together at irreconcilable cross-purposes, their liaison was too fragile to last, but for now, he'd be like his Elodie and suck every iota of joy from an already glorious day that promised, once he'd taken care of provisions for the morrow and found her a room with a bed, to become even more wonderful.

He twined his fingers in hers as they went back to their horses. 'How glad I am to be out of those monk's robes! I've been dying to touch you as we travel.'

'Good thing,' she agreed. 'Since you're grinning like a farmer who's just out-bargained a travelling tinker. I doubt anyone could look at us now and not know we are lovers.'

He stopped to give her a kiss. 'Do you mind?'

'No. I'm grateful for each moment we have together...Will. One never knows how many that may be.'

Happiness bubbled up again as she said his name for the first time, lifting his lips into a smile. He loved how she pronounced it, rolling the 'l's so it was drawn out, like a caress.

He loved her simplicity and directness, her

matter-of-fact approach to life, not fretting over problems incessantly like a shrew with a grievance, but considering them carefully, making the best plan she could and then putting them out of mind. So she was able to draw solace and find joy…in her garden, beside a river.

This time, she'd brought him joy, too. Tonight, in their bed, he would give that back and more, everything, all that was in him.

Only then would he face the dilemma of taking her back to England.

As they approached the village on the outskirts of Paris, they encountered more fellow travellers. After making a circuit of the town, Will chose an inn frequented by respectably dressed men and women—busy enough to indicate its food and service were of good quality, but not elegant enough to attract the wealthy and well connected.

After turning their horses in to a livery, he obtained dinner and a room at the inn he'd selected. It required all his self-discipline, after climbing the stairs and opening the door to a snug chamber with table, chairs and a bed that beckoned, to leave Elodie alone while he went off to purchase a dozen chickens and the cart to haul them in.

Anxious to complete the arrangements, he didn't even bother haggling with the farm woman whose fine fat pullets caught his eye. Settling quickly on a higher price than he'd ordinarily pride himself on getting, he took over the hens, content to leave her thinking she'd struck a good bargain, but not so good that she'd brag to her neighbours about getting the best of a lackwit stranger.

Even this close to Paris, one couldn't be too careful about avoiding notice.

He settled the purchases behind the inn's stables, to the raised eyebrows of the grooms. Farmers, even prosperous ones, didn't usually store their squawking produce at an inn the night before bringing them to market.

But they'd be gone on the morrow before the grooms on duty had a chance to gossip in the taproom, if indeed any watchers had picked up their trail. Will didn't think so; he'd been vigilant—except for a short time at the river—and he'd seen no evidence of their being followed.

Someone would be looking for them in Paris, however. But he'd worry about getting them safely through the city—and out again, Elodie in tow—tomorrow.

Visions of seduction now filling his head, Will hurried back to the inn. For the first time in days, they'd eat a fine dinner and sip wine by their own fire. They'd talk about their adventures, about her life, about Paris.

Maybe she'd even tell him about the mysterious 'Philippe'. Though initially he'd expected during the journey she would try to lull him with lies, when she finally did open up to him, every instinct told him what she'd related was the truth.

Then he'd knead her shoulders, massage her back, take down the honey-brown hair she'd kept hidden and, for the first time, comb his fingers through the long silken strands. Undress her slowly, bit by bit, kissing the newly revealed flesh, as he'd dreamed of for so many solitary nights. Taste the fullness of her breasts, rake the pebbled nipples against his teeth, gauging her arousal by the staccato song of her breath. Finally, he'd taste the honey of her fulfilment on his tongue before he sheathed himself in her and pleasured her again and again.

His body humming with anticipation, he

took the stairs two at a time and knocked at the door to their chamber. 'It's Will,' he said softly before unlocking it.

He entered to find the room in semi-darkness, lit by the flickering fire on the hearth and a single candle on the table. From the shadows of the bed, Elodie held out her hands. 'Come to me, *mon amant.*'

She sat propped against the pillows, the bedclothes at her waist. At the sight of her naked breasts, full and beautiful in the candlelight, his member leapt and all thoughts of dinner vanished.

'Nothing would please me more,' he said, pulling at the knot of his cravat, already impatient for the touch and taste of her.

'No, don't! Come here,' she beckoned. 'Let me undress you. I want to honour you, inch by inch.'

Emotion squeezed his chest while his member hardened to a throbbing intensity. Always a success with the ladies, he had been pleasured by blushing maids, loved by neglected wives, seduced by bored matrons who enjoyed the forbidden thrill of bedding an earl's illegitimate nephew. But no woman had ever vowed to 'honour' him.

'Willingly' was all he could choke from his tight throat.

Swiftly he came to the bed, where she urged him to sit. He kissed her head, finding her hair still damp from a bath, that lavender scent enveloping her again. His mouth watered. 'You smell good enough to eat.'

She smiled. 'We shall both eat our fill tonight.' Tilting down his chin, she leaned up to kiss him, slipping her tongue into his mouth.

Not until his brain registered a sensation of coolness at his chest did he realise she'd unfastened his cravat and opened his shirt. Breaking the kiss, she moved her mouth there, licking and kissing until impeded by the shirt's edges. Murmuring, she urged his arms up and pulled the garment over his head.

'Better.' She trailed nibbling kisses along his collarbone while her fingers shaped and massaged the muscles of his back and shoulders. She kissed from his neck down his chest, flicking her tongue teasingly just to the edge of his nipples, until they burned for her touch. He arched his back, manoeuvring his torso until her lips reached them, shuddering as she suckled them and raked her teeth across the tips.

Meanwhile, her fingers moved lower, beneath the back waistband of his trousers, to cup and squeeze his buttocks. He uttered a strangled groan, his member surging.

She glanced up at the sound. 'You must be tired. Lie down, *mon chevalier,*' she murmured, guiding him back against the pillows.

As he reclined, she removed his boots, giving him a delightful view of her naked back and bottom as she tugged.

The temptation was too great; he seized her and pulled her up to straddle his lap while with the other hand, he undid his trouser flap. She gasped, then uttered a little growling sound as she guided his swollen shaft into her slick passage and rocked her hips to take him deep.

He wrapped an arm around her back to pull her closer. As he branded her neck with his lips and teeth, he slipped the fingers of his free hand between them to caress her soft wet nub while he moved in her.

Panting, she arched against him, pushing him deeper. He moved his lips to her breast while his hand cupped her mound and his fingers played at the entrance, sliding into her to the rhythm of their thrusts.

Sweat coated his body, his neck corded and his arms grew rigid with the effort to hold himself near the peak without going over. And then she came apart in his arms, crying his name. Her tremors set off his own, a pleasure so intense he saw stars exploding against blackness as he spent himself in her.

For some time after, they lay limply in each other's arms. All his life, he'd been impatient, restless, driven by some intangible something to keep moving, searching for a destination he could never quite identify. For the first time, he felt utterly content, filled with an enormous sense of well-being. A deep sense that he belonged here, in this moment, with her.

His suspicions, along with the last bit of the anger he'd harboured against her, both gradually dwindling since they'd left Vienna, vanished completely.

He must have dozed, for he opened his eyes to find Elodie, still deliciously naked, sitting on the edge of the bed, pouring a glass of wine. 'For you, *mon amant*,' she said, handing it to him. 'To keep up your strength. You will need it. Now, where was I before I was so pleasantly interrupted? Ah, here.'

She tugged at the waistband of his unfastened trousers. Obligingly, he lifted himself, letting her pull them free and toss them to the floor. 'That's better. Naked, just as I want you.'

Her eyes gleaming, her expression sultry as a harem concubine intent on enticing a sultan, she gave him a wicked smile. 'Now I may see and taste…everything.

She extracted the wine glass from his fingers and took a sip. 'I'll need my strength also. To make this a night you will never forget.'

Some subtle sound roused him from a fathom's depth of sleep. Will rose slowly to consciousness, the room steeped in darkness, his whole body thrumming from senses wonderfully satisfied, like a chord still vibrating after the last note of a virtuoso's performance. *A night you will never forget.*

He certainly never would.

After that first lovemaking, she'd eased him back against the pillows and straddled him again, taking him within. And then sat chatting of Paris and London as if she were conversing at some diplomatic dinner, all the while moving slowly, rocking him inside her, her breasts bobbing deliciously close to his lips.

It was arousing, erotic, unlike anything he'd ever experienced. At first, he tried to match her aplomb and respond to the conversation, but after several times losing track of his sentences, he gave up the effort and closed his eyes, savouring the sensations.

Breathing itself became nearly impossible when, chatting still, she reached beneath him to where his plump sacks lay hidden, squeezing and massaging them while she urged his cock deeper. Pleasure burst in him, even more intense than the first time.

They dozed, roused to eat their cold dinner, slept again. He woke to find her head pillowed on his thigh. Noting his sudden alertness, she leaned over to trace his length with the tip of her tongue. As his member surged erect, she captured him in the hot velvet depths of her mouth, driving him to another powerfully intense release.

Just thinking about her made him smile. Maybe he could talk her into staying one more day at the inn. What would one more day matter? They'd already spent almost four weeks on a journey envisioned to take just over two. At odd times on the road, he'd considered trying to stretch it out even more, eking out every last second of joy from an experience as unparalleled as it had been unexpected.

Now, for the first time, he was beginning to envision a bond that might last not just a handful of nights, but weeks, months…into the hazy future.

As he stretched languorously, savouring the prospect, suddenly Will realised he was alone in the bed.

He sat bolt upright, his heart hammering. Not the faintest glimmer of dawn showed yet under the curtained windows. Probably she'd gone to the necessary, he thought, trying to force down the alarm and foreboding welling up in his gut.

She'd given him all of her freely, everything, as honestly as he had given it back to her. Stripped bare, with no defences, holding nothing back, they'd created a union of souls as well as bodies. She wouldn't just…leave him without a word.

His anxious, clumsy fingers struggled with flint and candle on the bedside table, but the additional flare of light just confirmed she wasn't in the chamber.

He jumped out of bed. Although the saddlebags he'd given her in exchange for the bandbox she'd packed in Vienna sat against the wall, they were empty; the gown, shift, chemise, stockings and shoes she'd donned after giving him back the monk's robe were gone.

Emptiness chilled him bone-deep as he admitted the unpalatable truth.

Damn her, she'd reduced him to a pudding-like state of completion, not out of tenderness, but so she could escape.

Escape him—and run off to her Philippe.

Nausea climbed up his throat and for a moment, he thought he'd be sick.

Betrayed. Abandoned. An agonising pain, worse than he'd felt after being shot by Spanish banditos, lanced his chest.

He dammed a rising flood of desolation behind a shield of anger. With iron will, he forced back deep within him an anguish and despair he'd not felt since he'd been a small boy sitting beside his dying mother.

It was ridiculous, he told himself furiously, carrying on like a spinster abandoned by the wastrel who had deceived her out of her virtue. The circumstances were nowhere near the same as the tragedy suffered by that five-year-old. He hadn't lost his only love, he'd merely been tricked by a lying jade.

But she'd not got the better of him yet.

Stupid of him to forget one rogue should

know another. He'd forced this journey on her, giving her no real choice. Their adventure had been based on a bargain, each of them getting something they wanted.

She was trying to cheat him out of doing her part.

The sound that had roused him moments ago must have been Elodie, sneaking away. Without the instincts for survival Seven Dials had honed so well, he might never have heard her. It had already been nearing dawn the last time they'd coupled, so she couldn't have got far.

If Elodie Lefevre thought she'd seen the last of him, she was about to discover just how hard it was to dupe Will Ransleigh.

Chapter Thirteen

Her few remaining worldly goods concealed beneath the chickens in one of the baskets she carried on each arm, Elodie hurried in the dim pre-dawn with the press of other farmers heading into Paris. Too impatient to stroll at the crowd's pace, docile as the birds in the dovecote on the pushcart in front of her, she darted around the vehicle, causing the startled doves to flutter. Driven by an irresistible urgency, she only wished their wings beating at the air could fly her into Paris faster.

She had to escape Will, before he woke to find her gone. As skilled as he was at tracking, she must lose herself in the safety of the great rabbit warren of Parisian streets well before he set out after her.

There, as she began her quest, she'd also lose this nagging temptation to go back to him, she reassured herself.

It didn't matter how energised and alive he made her feel. Their time together had been an idyll and, like all idylls, must end. Besides, what they shared was only the bliss of the night, no more permanent or substantial than the lies a man whispered in the ear of a maid he wanted to bed.

A dangerous bliss, though, for it made her wish for things that life had already taught her didn't exist. A world of justice not ruled by cruel and depraved men. A sense of belonging with friends, family…a lover who cherished her. Safety, like she'd felt in Lord Somerville's garden. Illusions that should have vanished long ago with her childhood.

It ought to have been easy to leave him. She knew what he planned for her. She'd allowed herself the reward she'd promised, a spectacular night of passion more fulfilling than any she'd ever experienced.

Up until that very last night, she'd been successful in keeping her emotions, like tiny seeds that might sprout into something deeper than friendship if dropped into the fertile soil of his watchful care, clutched tightly in hand.

Her devotion to Philippe was a mature growth, a sturdy oak planted firmly in the centre of her heart. He was her love, her life, her duty. Returning to him should have shaded out any stray, straggly seedlings of affection germinated by Will Ransleigh.

But it hadn't. Even as she hurried to fulfil the mission that had sustained her for the last year and a half, she ached. A little voice whispered that the wrenching sense of loss hollowing her out inside came from leaving a piece of her soul back in Will Ransleigh's keeping.

Very well, so passion had forged a stronger bond than she'd anticipated. She'd been privileged for one brief night to possess her magnificent Zeus-come-to-earth. But she could no more cling to him than had the maidens in the myths. She'd not been transformed into a cow or a tree; she mustn't let leaving him turn her into a weakling.

She'd just have to blot out the memory of their partnership on the road, forget the sparkle in his eyes and warmth in his smile as he spun tales for her. Obliterate all trace of the feel of him buried in her, catapulting her into ecstasy with skill and tenderness.

She wouldn't have to worry about *him* pining over *her*. When he woke to find her gone, he'd stomp the life out of any tendrils of affection that might have sprouted in *his* heart.

Time to put Will Ransleigh and the last month out of mind, as she always put away troubles about which she could do nothing. Time to look forwards.

The sun just rising in a clear sky promised a lovely summer day. She should be excited, filled with anticipation and purpose. She suppressed, before it could escape from the anxious knot in her gut, the fear that, despite all her scheming, she would not find Philippe.

Losing him was simply unthinkable.

Her agitation stemmed from fatigue, she decided. Certainly it couldn't be pangs of conscience at deceiving Will, she who wouldn't have survived without honing deception to a high art.

Besides, she *had* given him passion—the only honest gift within her keeping. She had no regrets about that.

As she rounded a bend in the road, the walls of Paris towered in the distance, casting an imposing shadow over the west-bound travellers. She forced her spirits to rise upwards like her gaze.

No more time for fear, regret or repining. The most important game of her life was about to begin. After waiting so long and being so close, she was not about to fail now.

Fury and contempt for his own stupidity fuelled Will's flight from the inn, which he quit within minutes of discovering Elodie's deception. Since they'd be entering the city separately, he'd no need to play the farmer. Let the innkeeper roast the fowl for dinner and chop the gig into firewood, he thought, his anger at fever pitch.

Unencumbered by cart and poultry, he was able to move swiftly.

Just a half-hour later, he spotted Elodie as she entered the city gates—his first bit of luck that day, for, once inside, despite her farm-girl disguise, there was no guarantee she'd actually make for Paris's largest market.

Walking quickly, two baskets of squawking chickens on her arm, she did in fact continue towards Les Halles. Camouflaged by the usual early-morning bustle of working men, vendors, cooks, housemaids, farmers, tradesmen, soldiers and rogues returning from their night's revels, he was able to follow her rather closely.

If he hadn't been in such a tearing rage, he might have enjoyed making a game of seeing how close he could approach without being observed. Though anger made him less cautious than he would have normally been, he was still surprised he was able to get so near, once reaching her very elbow as she crossed a crowded alleyway.

Hovering there had been foolish, as if he were almost daring her to discover him.

Maybe he was. With every nerve and sinew, he wanted to take her, shake her, ask her *why*.

Which was more stupidity. He knew why she'd fled, had been expecting it, even. He accepted that she'd outplayed him in the first hand of this game, and in the one tiny objective corner remaining within his incensed mind, he realised it was unusual of him to be so angry about being outmanoeuvred. Normally he would allow himself a moment to admire her skill, learn from the loss and move on.

He would not—*could* not—examine the raw and bleeding emotions just below the surface that contributed to his unprecedented sense of urgency and outrage.

He paused on the edge of the market square, watching as she sold off the chickens and one basket, then moved on to purchase enough oranges to fill the other. He could corner her immediately, but it was probably wiser to wait until he could catch her where there were fewer witnesses who might take her part in the struggle that was sure to follow.

After Elodie left the market area, Will dropped back further, though he was still able to follow much closer than he would have expected, based on how alert and careful she'd been during their escape from Vienna. As consumed as he was by fury, he still wondered why.

Basket of oranges on her arm, she proceeded south-west to the Marais. This area of elegant town houses, so popular during Louis XIV's reign, had been already in decline by the Revolution, and many of the magnificent *hôtels* with their courtyards and gardens looked shabby and neglected. Elodie paused before one of impressive classical grandeur which, unlike its unfortunate fellows, was well tended, its stone walls and windows clean, its iron fences painted, its greenery freshly clipped. After staring at the edifice for a few moments, she turned down the alleyway leading to the garden entrance at the back.

Was this the abode of the mysterious 'Philippe'?

Watching her walk towards the gate, Will pondered his next move. Prudence said to take her before she could disappear within, if that's what she intended.

But if he stopped her now, he might never learn who occupied that house. She had to know he'd be furious if he caught her; if she hadn't revealed the secret of this elegant Marais town house to an accomplice and fellow traveller, there was little chance she'd do so to an angry pursuer.

Curiosity—and, though it pained him to admit it, jealousy—battling logic, Will hesitated. If he waited here, intending to seize her after she came back out, it was possible she might exit by the front door and he would miss her. But in her disguise as a farm girl, it was unlikely she'd be permitted to leave by the grand entrance.

Unless Elodie de Montaigu-Clisson Lefevre had resources he wasn't aware of. During his stay in the city after Waterloo, he'd learned enough about official Paris to know this fine mansion wasn't Prince Talleyrand's home, though it might belong to one of the Prince's spies or associates.

While he dithered, uncharacteristically uncertain, she trotted down the pathway and disappeared through the kitchen entrance and his opportunity to grab her was lost. Exasperated with himself, he retreated down the alleyway bordering the *hôtel* and scrambled up the wall beneath a tree conveniently clothed in thick summer greenery that camouflaged him while allowing him a clear view of the kitchen and garden.

Huddled on the wall against the tree, calmer now, he considered his options. There was no point berating himself for not nabbing her when he'd had the chance. After a night of little sleep, his reflexes and timing were off. It had been a long time since he'd enjoyed a woman so much, longer still since he'd met one who affected him as powerfully as Elodie Lefevre. As the sensual spell she'd created continued to fade, these atypically intense emotions would subside and he'd recover his usual equilibrium.

With that encouraging conclusion, he set himself to evaluating whether to wait where he was, within view of the servants' entry, or move towards the front. Before he could decide, Elodie exited the kitchen.

At the sight of her, his pulses leapt and a stab of pain gashed his chest, giving lie to the premise that his intense emotions were fading. Think, don't react, he told himself as he tried to haul the still-ungovernable feelings under control.

Fortunately, after exiting the back gate, she turned down the tree-bordered alleyway and walked right towards him. This time, he'd grab her at once, before she could elude him again.

Heart rate accelerating, breathing suspended, Will waited until she passed beneath him. He jumped down, landing softly behind her, and seized her arm.

She'd been trained well; rather than yelping or pulling away, she leaned into him, slackening the tension on her wrist while at the same time dropping to her knees, trying to yank her arm downwards out of his grip.

Being better trained, he hung on, saying softly, 'Hand's over, and this time all the tricks are mine.'

At his voice, a tremor ran through her and she stopped struggling. Slowly she rose to her feet and faced him, expressionless.

Will wasn't sure what he'd expected to see on her face: shame? Regret? Grief? But the fact that she could confront him showing no emotion at all while he still writhed and bled inside splintered his frail hold on objectivity with the force of an axe through kindling. Fury erupted anew.

He wanted to crush her in his arms and kiss her senseless, mark her as his, force a response that showed their passion had shaken her to the marrow as it had him.

He wanted to strangle the life from her.

Sucking in a deep breath, he willed himself to calm. He hadn't allowed emotion to affect his actions since he'd been a schoolboy, when Max had taught him channelling anger into coolly calculated response was more effective than raging at his tormentors.

It shook him to discover how deeply she'd rattled him out of practices he'd thought mastered years ago.

But one thing *she* couldn't master. The calm of her countenance might seem to deny he affected her at all, but she couldn't will away the energy that sparked between his hand and her captive arm. An attraction that sizzled and beguiled the longer he held her, making him want to pull her closer as, despite the hurt and anger he refused to acknowledge, his body, remembering only passion between them, urged him to take them once again down the path from desire to fulfilment.

Though he didn't mean to follow that road now, just feeling the force crackling beneath his fingertips was balm to his lacerated emotions. He clutched her tighter, savouring the burn.

'*Bonjour, madame.* I had to hurry to catch up to you. Careless of you to leave me behind.'

'Ineffective, too, I see,' she muttered.

'What of our bargain? Did the heat of the night's activities scorch it from your mind?'

When she winced at that jab, he felt a savage satisfaction. No, she was not as indifferent as she tried to appear.

'I merely wished to begin early to take care of a family matter, just as I told you I would.'

'Here I am, ready to assist.'

'It's better that I do it alone.'

Will shook his head. 'I'll go with you, or you can leave Paris with me now. I move when you move, like lashes on an eyelid, so don't even think of trying to give me the slip again.'

The last time he'd warned her about escaping, he'd talked of crust on bread and she'd licked her lips. A flurry of sensual images from their surrender to passion last night flashed through his mind. In the light of this morning's abandonment, each gouged deep, drawing blood. Cursing silently, Will forced back the memories.

'So, what shall it be?' he asked roughly, giving her arm a jerk. 'Do we head for Calais or…?'

She opened her lips as if to speak, then, shaking her head, closed them. A bleak expression flitted briefly over her face before, with one quick move, she wrenched her arm from his grip and walked off.

In two quick strides he caught back up, grabbing her wrist again to halt her. 'Tell me what we're about to do.'

Freeing her wrist again with another vicious jerk, she said, 'Follow if you must, but try to stop me and, *le bon Dieu me crôit*, I swear I'll take my knife to you, here and now. Observe what I do if you must, but interfere in any way and our bargain is finished. I won't go a step towards England with you, whatever retribution you threaten.'

She delivered the speech in a terse blast of words, like a rattle of hail against a window, never meeting his eyes. Even working with his normally keen instincts diminished, Will was struck by her ferocity and an odd note in her voice he'd never heard before. Something more than anxiety, it was almost…desperation.

Her urgency also shouted of danger, finally giving him the strength he needed to bury emotions back deep within the pit into which he'd banished all loss and anguish since childhood. They weren't in England yet; his first duty to Max was still to protect her so he could get her there.

She resumed walking at a rapid pace, eyes fixed straight ahead, seemingly oblivious to her surroundings. Falling into place beside her, he asked several more questions, but when she continued to ignore him, abandoned the attempt. Instead, he transferred his efforts into assessing all the people and activities in the streets they were traversing, alert for any threat.

While keeping a weather eye out, he was still able to watch Elodie. Her unusual abstraction allowed him to stare at her with greater intensity than she would have otherwise allowed. He tried to keep warmth from welling back up as he studied her striding form and set face, every nuance of the body beneath those garments now familiar to his fingers and tongue.

When his gaze wandered back to her face, he noted it was abnormally pale, her eyes bright, her expression as tense and rigid as her body. She paced rapidly, almost leaning forwards in her haste.

Whatever 'family matter' she was about to address, it was both urgent and vitally important to her.

From the *hôtel*, they passed through the streets of the Marais towards the Seine, south and west until they reached the Queen's gate at the Place Royale. Though some of the houses inside that beautiful enclosure, like those of the Marais, were shuttered and forlorn, even shabbiness couldn't mar its Renaissance beauty.

Rows of lanes, presided over by trees serene in early summer leaf, were well populated by nursemaids with their charges, finely dressed ladies followed by their maids, men with the self-important air of lawyers conversing and a few couples strolling hand in hand. In the distance, on the lawn, several children frolicked.

'Stay here,' she demanded, startling him as she broke her silence. Where her face had been pale before, now hectic colour bloomed in her cheeks. Her eyes blazed, the tension evident in her body ratcheting tighter. Without checking to see if he heeded her directive, she set off.

Neither curiosity nor prudent surveillance permitted him to obey. Will followed at a cautious distance, alertness heightened in him, too, as he sought to identify which of the wandering figures had seized her attention.

As he inspected the several strolling gentlemen, his gaze caught on one who'd paused, leaning over the maid accompanying him. He was too far away to hear their conversation, but the hand the man rested on the girl's shoulder, the juxtaposition of their bodies, nearly rubbing together even in this public space, hinted at intimacy. Had Elodie returned to find the man she loved romancing another woman?

She stopped so abruptly, he had to catch himself before he got too close, though she now seemed so absorbed, he probably could have run right into her without breaking her concentration. Will was scrutinising all the people in the vicinity of her mesmerised gaze, trying to fix upon its object, when a nursemaid nearby called, 'No, no, bring the ball back here, *mon ange*! I'll throw it to you, Philippe.'

A gasp of indrawn breath made him turn back to Elodie. She stood immobile, her gaze riveted on a dark-haired little boy, the basket clutched so tightly in her hand that the knuckles went white. Hope, joy, anxiety blazed in her face.

Philippe. *Philippe.* Comprehension slammed into Will with the force of a runaway carriage, knocking all the preconceived notions out of his head.

A 'family matter', she'd said. It wasn't a lover she'd been so desperate to search for, but a little boy, he realised, even as he recognised her smile, her eyes, in the face of the child. She'd come back to Paris to find her *son*.

Chapter Fourteen

As she neared the children playing in the grass beside the gravelled *allée* in the Place Royale, Elodie picked up her pace. Her heart pounded and her skin prickled as if the mother's love, trapped within her and denied expression for so long, was trying to escape her body and reach him before her feet could get her there.

Discovering from the cook at the Hôtel de la Rocherie that Philippe was, indeed, still in Paris, playing with his nursemaid only a few streets away, had made her desperate to reach him, see him, clasp him once again in her arms. Frantically she raked her gaze from child to child while her thoughts chased one another as quickly as hounds after a fox.

Would his hair still be ebony-black, his eyes

still dark and alive with curiosity? He'd be slimmer now, more like a child than the sturdy toddler she'd left, ready for games and to sit a horse. Would he still love balls, play at soldiers, cajole for sweets?

Then she saw him. Her heart stopped, as did her feet, while everything around her faded to a blur.

He was taller, as she expected, his face more angular, having lost the roundness of babyhood. Pink-cheeked from exertions, his skin glowing with health, his eyes bright, his uninhibited laughter as he chased after his ball with that stubborn lock of hair curling down as always over his forehead, made her heart contract with joy.

As her eyes left his face, she noted that his clothing had been fashioned from quality materials and fit him well. The nursemaid tossing him the ball regarded him with an affectionate eye and a husky footman stood nearby, obviously keeping watch.

One anxiety dissipated. She'd for ever blame herself for not recognising the trap before she walked into it, but at least her instincts about the Comtesse de la Rocherie had been accurate. Philippe was well treated and cared for.

But he was *hers*, she thought with a furious rush of determination. Despite all the odds, she'd survived her ordeal, connived her way back to Paris. She would reclaim her son at last and nothing but death would prevent her.

Another swell of emotion shook her and she almost tossed down the basket to run to him, starved for the feel of him in her arms.

She took a shaky breath, fighting off the urge. He hadn't seen her for eighteen months, an eternity in the life of a young child. She mustn't startle him, but approach quietly, let him notice her, inspect her, rediscover her at his own pace.

Then she would work out how to steal him back.

Hands shaking now on the basket, she strolled down the path, on to the grass near her son.

It took two attempts before she could get the words to come out of her tight throat. 'Would you like an orange, little man?'

He looked over at her, his gaze going from the fruit to her face. Elodie held her breath as he studied her, willing recognition to register in those dark eyes, as lively and energetic as she remembered.

After a moment, he looked away, as if concluding she was of no interest. 'Jean, get me an orange,' he commanded the footman before turning back to the maid. 'Throw the ball again, Marie, harder. I'm a big boy now. See how fast I can run after it?'

Hands raised to catch his ball, he trotted off, all his attention now on the maid. Consternation welling within her, Elodie set down the basket and hurried after him.

'Come back, young gentleman,' she coaxed. 'Let me show you my fine oranges. They'll please you as much as your ball.'

'Not now,' he said with a dismissive wave in her direction, eyes still on the maid.

'No, please, wait,' she cried, catching up to him and seizing an arm.

He tugged away from her, but she held on, desperate for him to look at her again, really *look* at her.

He did indeed look back at her, but instead of recognition, as his gaze travelled from her fingers clutching his shoulder to her face, the puzzlement in his eyes turned to alarm. His chin wobbling, he called out, 'M-Marie!'

He didn't recognise her. Even worse, she'd *frightened* him! Aghast, appalled, she stared at him mutely, while denial and anguish compressed her chest so tightly she couldn't breathe.

The tall footman strode over, menace in his face as he pushed her roughly away from the child. 'What d'ya think yer doing, wench?' he growled, while her son ran from her towards the outstretched arms of his nurse. 'I'll call the gendarme on you.'

Then, somehow, Will Ransleigh was beside her, one hand protectively on her shoulder while he made a placating gesture towards the footman. 'No harm meant, *monsieur*. Just trying to get the gamin a treat, that's all. Gotta make a living, you know.'

'Better she sells her oranges at the market,' the man retorted before walking back to the nursemaid, who handed him the child's ball and hefted the frightened child into her arms. With a wary glance at them, the maid hurried off, the footman trotting beside her.

Philippe, his small hands clutching the maid's arms, didn't look back at all as he buried his head against the nursemaid's shoulder.

Just as he used to nestle into her embrace, Elodie recalled with an agonising stab of loss. Had it been that long? Could the eighteen months of separation have erased from his memory every trace of her three years of tender love and constant care?

She stood, staring after them, heartsick denial rising in her, watching until the small party turned the bend of the *allée* and disappeared out the gate. She couldn't, wouldn't believe it.

Suddenly she felt as if the pressure of all the anguish and anxiety, fear and doubt churning within would make her chest explode. Her feet compelled into motion to try to relieve it, she set off pacing down the pathway, light-headed, nauseated and only dimly aware of Will Ransleigh keeping pace beside her.

How could Philippe have forgotten her? His image was etched into her brain. With her first conscious thought every morning, her last every night, she recalled his face, wondered what he was doing, worried about his welfare.

In the depths of her pain after St Arnaud's savagery, his image burning in her heart had given her the will to struggle out of the soothing darkness of unconsciousness. Determination to return to him kept her from despair and lent her patience and courage during the long slow recovery, through tedious hours of needlework, each completed piece adding one more coin to the total needed to fund her journey back to him.

When she pictured their reunion, she always imagined him fixing on her an intent, assessing gaze that would turn from curious to joyful as he recognised her. Imagined the feel of his slight frame pressed tightly in her arms when he threw himself against her, crying, '*Maman! Maman!*'

Instead, he'd called for Marie. He'd clutched *her* arms, buried his head against *her* shoulder.

But he was only a small boy and she had been missing almost half as many years as they'd had together. It had been unrealistic and probably foolish of her to expect he would remember her after so long.

What under heaven should she do now?

Despite the footman being alerted and the maid alarmed, Elodie knew that with a change of clothing and manner, she could weasel her way close to him again, into the house itself if necessary. She'd always envisioned picking him up, telling him to hush as they played a 'hide-and-seek' game while she stole away with him.

She couldn't do that if he were afraid, crying out, struggling against her to escape.

She couldn't do that to him, even if he didn't struggle. The idea of tearing him from all that was comforting and familiar and carrying him off, alone and terrified, filled her with revulsion.

Yet she couldn't simply give him up.

She walked and walked, circuit after circuit, her thoughts running in circles as unchanging as the perfect geometry of the Place. In continuous motion, but always ending up at the same point.

He was young, he'd recover from the trauma, she argued with herself. He'd adjusted to living with the comtesse; he'd adjust again to living with her…even if he never truly remembered her. He was flesh of her flesh; he belonged with her. No one else alive had as much right to claim him as she did.

But could she live with herself if she put him through such an ordeal? Other than the closest kinship of blood, what could she offer him that might compensate for the terror of being stolen away by a stranger?

As she worked patiently in Vienna, she'd always imagined taking him away to a little village somewhere. Using the funds she'd obtain from selling the last of her jewels to buy a small farm in the countryside, where she could plant a garden, eke out a living selling herbs and doing needlework, watch her son grow to manhood. But now?

She was alone with no friends, no allies and very little money. Somewhere St Arnaud might still lurk, a dangerous enemy who might be the force behind those who'd been trailing them. She'd fallen back into the hands of Will Ransleigh, whose tender care was meant to ensure her delivery to England, where he'd press her into a testimony that might send her all the way to the gallows.

Leaving her son, if she stole him away, an orphan in an alien land.

Was it right to catapult him into poverty, peril and uncertainty? Cut him off from the love, security and comfort of a privileged life in Paris?

If he truly was loved, secure and comfortable.

A sliver of hope surfaced, and she clung to it like a shipwrecked sailor to a floating spar. Perhaps, though his physical needs were being met, he was not well treated by the comtesse.

Perhaps his adoptive mother neglected him, left his upbringing to servants. Kind nursemaids and protective footmen were well enough, but wasn't it best for him to live with the mother who doted on him, who would make his comfort and well-being the focus of her existence?

If St Arnaud's sister, the Comtesse de la Rocherie, was not providing that, wouldn't she be justified in stealing back the son she'd been tricked into leaving, despite the dangers and uncertainty of her present position?

Elodie would never have the funds to provide the luxuries available in the household of a comtesse. But did the comtesse love and treasure Philippe, as she would?

Elodie had to know. She would have to return to the Hôtel de la Rocherie and find out.

And then make her terrible choice.

Watching, as Elodie was, the footman and nursemaid's rapid exit from the square, Will was startled when she suddenly set off down the gravelled path. Quickly he caught up, about to seize her arm and warn her he'd not let her escape again, when the stark, anguished face and hollow eyes staring into the far distance told him she was not trying to elude him; she was barely aware of where she was or who walked beside her.

Knowing he would likely get nothing from her in her current state, Will settled for keeping pace, while he wondered about the story behind Elodie Lefevre—and her *son*.

He couldn't deny a soaring sense of relief that the mysterious Philippe had turned out to be a child of some five summers, rather than a handsome, strapping young buck. Thinking back, her soft laughter and oblique answer—'something like'—to his question about whether Philippe was her lover should have alerted him to the fact that the 'family matter' might not involve the rival he was imagining. He might have realised it, had a foolish jealousy not decimated his usual ability to weave into discernible patterns the information he gathered.

'Something like' a lover. Ah, yes; he knew just how much a small boy could love his mother.

The son in Paris was obviously what St Arnaud had used to compel her co-operation in Vienna. How had he finagled that? A man who'd beat a woman half to death probably would not have many scruples about kidnapping a child.

Had she thought, once she'd got back to Paris, she would give him the slip and then simply go off and steal the boy out from under the noses of the family with whom he'd been living?

Will smiled. Apparently she'd thought exactly that. With her talent for disguise and subterfuge, she probably had in her ingenious head a hundred different schemes to make off with the boy and settle with him somewhere obscure and safe.

Until Will Ransleigh had turned up to spoil those plans. He understood much better now why she'd run.

He wondered which of those hundred schemes she intended to try next. After he gave her time to recover from the shock of seeing her son again, he'd ask her. There was no reason now for her not to confess the whole story to him.

And then he would see how he could help her.

He startled himself with that conclusion. It was no part of his design to drag a small boy back to England. But he had already conceded, despite his anger over her duping him, that he'd moved far beyond his original intention to barter her in whatever manner necessary to win Max's vindication.

Somehow, he'd find a way to achieve that and still keep Elodie safe. Elodie, and her son.

Because, as much as he had initially resisted it, a deep-seated, compulsive desire had grown in him to protect this friendless, desperate woman without family or resources, who with courage and tenacity had fought with every trick and scheme she could devise to reclaim a life with her son. Too late now to try to root that out.

He was beginning to tire of the pacing when, at last, she halted as abruptly as she'd begun and sank on to a bench, infinite weariness on her face. Quickly he seated himself beside her. He tipped her chin up to face him, relieved when she did not flinch or jerk away from his touch.

'Philippe is your son.'

'Yes.'

'St Arnaud used him to make you involve Max in his Vienna scheme.'

'Yes.'

'Why did he choose someone he had to

coerce? Surely he knew other families with Bonapartist sympathies. Why did he not ask one of their ladies to join his plot?'

She sniffed. 'If you were at all acquainted with St Arnaud, you wouldn't need to ask. He thought women useful only for childbearing or pleasure, much too feeble-minded to remain focused upon a course of action for political or intellectual reasons. No, one could only be sure of controlling their behaviour if one threatened something they held dear.'

'How did he get the child into his power?'

'Because I was stupid,' she spat out. 'So dazzled by his promise of a secure life for myself and my son, I fell right into his trap.'

Having been homeless and penniless, he could well understand the appeal security and comfort must have had for a war widow with few friends and almost no family. 'How did it happen?'

'As I told you, my brother, Maurice, suggested to St Arnaud that I serve as his hostess at the Congress of Vienna. I dismissed the possibility, for with all his contacts, why would St Arnaud choose a shabby-genteel widow with little experience of moving in the highest circles?'

'Why indeed,' she continued bitterly. 'What a fool I was! I should have been much more suspicious that he invited a woman with few resources and no other protector but a man already deeply in his debt. Instead, I was surprised and flattered when he confirmed the offer, insisting that my "natural aristocratic grace" would make up for any inexperience. St Arnaud promised if I performed well, in addition to letting me keep the gowns and jewels he would buy me for the role, he would settle an allowance on us. Later, when my son came of age, he'd use his influence to advance my son's career.'

'Inducements hard for any mother to refuse.'

'Yes. At least, until he informed me that Philippe would not accompany us. Upon learning that, I did refuse his offer; there was no way I would leave my precious son behind in Paris.'

She laughed without humour. 'That insistence, I now suspect, probably sealed St Arnaud's conviction that I was the perfect victim for his scheme. Utterly able to be controlled through my son—an easy loss to explain away to the brother who depended on him for the advancement of his career, if something happened to me. In any event, St Arnaud urged me to reconsider. It would only be for a few months, he said. I would be so busy I would hardly have time to miss the child. His sister, the Comtesse de la Rocherie, had recently lost her young son and would be thrilled to look after Philippe.'

She rose and began pacing again, as if propelled by memories too painful to bear. 'When I remained firm in my refusal, he told me he'd promised the comtesse I would bring Philippe to visit her—could we not at least do that? Surely I couldn't be so cruel as to disappoint a grieving mother! And so…we went.'

'He kidnapped the child on the way?'

She shook her head in the negative. 'We did call on her. The comtesse was good with Philippe; he liked her at once, and when she offered to take him up to the nursery to play, he begged me to let him go.'

A sad smile touched her lips. 'She told him she had a toy pony with blue-glass eyes and a mane and tail of real horsehair. What child could resist that? Philippe had grown restless and St Arnaud urged me to send him up to romp while we finished our tea. And the comtesse…there was no disguising the yearning in her eyes as she offered Philippe her hand. So I let him go.'

'I let him go,' she repeated in a whisper, tears welling up in her eyes. 'The next thing I remember, I was in a travelling coach, groggy, nauseated, my hands bound, too weak even to push myself upright. Not until we reached the outskirts of Vienna did St Arnaud allow me to regain consciousness.'

'Vienna!' Will burst out, incredulous that St Arnaud had managed to kidnap, not a child, but a grown woman, and transport her hundreds of miles. 'That's outrageous! Did no one at any of the inns notice anything?'

'I expect it was easy enough for him to spin some story about my being ill. The actions of a man of wealth and authority are unlikely to be questioned by post boys and innkeepers.'

Realising the truth of that, Will nodded grimly. 'Go on.'

'As soon as I was strong enough to stand, I told him I was returning at once to Paris. That was the first time he struck me.'

'Bastard,' Will muttered, wishing St Arnaud would appear on the pathway before them—so he could strangle the life from him.

'He told me if I loved my son and wanted

to see him again, I would do exactly as he instructed. Not to waste my time trying to escape him, for he had swift messengers at his disposal and employees back in Paris. Children, like his sister's son, were so frail, he said. Playing happily one evening, dead of a fever by morning.'

'He threatened to kill your son if you didn't co-operate?' Will said. 'He truly was evil.'

She nodded. 'He said my life, my child's life, was nothing compared to the importance of restoring France to glory under Napoleon. When I asked what assurance I had of ever seeing Philippe again, regardless of what I did, he said he was a "reasonable man". Reasonable! If I did my part to make sure his plot succeeded, he would provide everything he'd promised: clothes, jewels, a handsome financial settlement. I might even be acclaimed in Paris as a heroine of the Empire for helping him restore Napoleon to the throne. But if I refused to play my role...I was finished, and so was Philippe. So I did what he wanted.'

'What about your brother?' Will asked. 'Did he not try to find you when St Arnaud disappeared after the failure of the plot?'

'I don't know. Napoleon escaped Elba within

days of the assassination attempt. Maurice's regiment, like all the French regiments, was called up as soon as the authorities learned Napoleon had landed back in France. He died at Waterloo.'

'I am sorry. Did the comtesse know where St Arnaud went to ground?'

'Perhaps. I don't think she was involved in planning this. We were both just pawns in his game, me in my poverty with a young son to raise, her in her grief and need. When I was reported dead, naturally she would raise Philippe as her own.'

'But you still want him back.'

'Of course I want him back.'

'Very well, I'll help you steal him.'

Her eyes widened, surprise and a desperate hope in their depths. 'You'll help me?'

He shrugged. 'I doubt you'll leave France willingly without him.'

A worried frown creased her brow. 'It won't be easy. He's not a purse you can pick at a Viennese market, but a small boy. He'll feel alone after we grab him. Frightened.'

Remembered anguish twisted in his gut. He knew what it was to be a small child, frightened and alone.

'First, I'll need to get back into the house,' she said. 'Locate the service stairs, find the nursery, manage to see him again.'

'How do you propose to do that? The "orange seller" is unlikely to be welcomed.'

'Probably not,' she admitted.

Thinking rapidly, Will said, 'We'll go as a tinker and his wife. While I keep the staff occupied in the kitchen, distracting them with my wares and wit, you can slip up to the nursery.'

She gave him a wan smile. 'Have you a cart, pots, pans and fripperies in those wondrous saddlebags of yours?'

'No, but I've the blunt to buy some. Have you another gown, one that will make you look like a respectable tinker's wife?'

'I have one more gown in this basket, yes.'

'Good.' Will held out his hand. 'Partners again? No more disappearing at dawn?'

'Partners.' Meeting his steady gaze, Elodie clasped his hand and shook it.

Threading his fingers in hers, Will exulted at the surge of connection, as potent and powerful as ever. It was all he could do to refrain from hugging her, so absurdly grateful was he for this chance to begin again. Abducting a child from the household of a wealthy comtesse was a mere nothing; to keep her beside him, he would have pledged to abscond with the entire French treasury.

His heart lighter than it had been since the terrible moment he'd awakened to find her gone, Will contented himself with kissing her hand. 'We passed a café just outside the entrance to the Place. You can wait for me there.' He offered her his arm.

She took it and he tucked her hand against his body, savouring the feel of her beside him as they walked together. Comrades again, as they'd been on the road.

A few moments later, they reached the small establishment he'd noted. After he'd escorted her to a table, rather than release his arm, she held on, studying him. 'You're a remarkable man, Will Ransleigh,' she said softly.

It wasn't exactly an apology. But it was close enough. 'So I am,' he agreed with a grin. 'Give me about two hours to obtain the necessary items.'

She nodded. 'I'll be ready.'

A spring in his step, Will headed off to the market, running through his mind a list of items to procure. Having spent much time wandering around in markets in his youth, perfecting his skill as a thief, he knew just the sort of shiny objects that would tempt footmen, housemaids, cooks and grooms, and where to obtain them quickly.

He paced through the crowded streets on a wave of renewed energy and purpose, buoyed by the knowledge that Elodie hadn't, after all, abandoned him for another man. She'd been pulled away by a bond he, more than anyone, could appreciate: that between a mother and her son.

That loyalty would no longer stand between them. In fact, her gratitude for his help in rescuing her child would reinforce their powerful physical attraction.

Bit by bit, like a clever spider creating its web, fate and circumstance were adding strand after strand, linking them together. Mastering this last challenge and then completing the voyage to England would take time…time to examine the many subtle threads of connection. Time to sample passion and see if it tasted of a future.

He hadn't solved yet the problem of how to vindicate Max while protecting Elodie from retribution, but he'd figure out something. All in all, he felt more hopeful than at any time since he'd smuggled her out of Vienna.

Chapter Fifteen

Three hours later, in his latest guise as a travelling tinker, Will Ransleigh was putting on his best show for a staff happy for a bit of diversion during the break between the preparation and serving of dinner. After convincing the housekeeper to allow all the employees—including the nursery maid—to come down to the servants' hall, Will's witty repartee, glittering wares and a magic trick or two kept his audience preoccupied enough for Elodie to slip unnoticed to the service stairs.

Before they began their charade, he'd told her he'd give her half an hour to find the nursery, bundle up her son and get him out of the house. He'd then finalise any purchases and meet her with the cart, its contents conveniently configured to hide a small boy, on a side street a short distance away, ready to make all speed out of the city.

She'd nodded agreement. She just hadn't told him that she might not be bringing her son. Her gut twisting at the very thought, she ran up the service stairs, heart pounding in anxiety and anticipation.

As she hurried up, she recalled with perfect clarity every detail of her visit to this house that infamous day eighteen months ago. *Please, Lord*, she begged silently, *let this day not end as that one did, with me leaving without my son.*

The comtesse had told her the nursery was on the third floor. Exiting into the hallway, she peeked behind several doors before, beyond the next, she found a small boy playing with soldiers.

His eyes fixed on the toys he was meticulously placing in assorted groups, Philippe didn't look up as she stealthily opened the door. Taking advantage of his preoccupation, she studied him, her heart contracting painfully with joy at seeing him, with sorrow for the years together that had been stolen from them.

He was a lithe-limbed, handsome little boy

where she had left a toddler just out of baby-hood. He had her eyes, her lips, his now pursed in concentration as he positioned the soldiers just so, Jean-Luc's nose and sable hair that always fell over one brow and his long, graceful fingers.

Just then he looked up, his bright blue eyes curious. 'Who are you? Where is Marie?'

'Down in the kitchen. She asked me to come stay with you while she looked at some fripperies my man is selling.'

'"Fripperies"? Is that something to eat? I hope she brings me some!'

She smiled; Philippe obviously still loved his sweets. 'No biscuits or cakes, I'm afraid. Things like hair ribbons or lace to trim a collar, glass beads for a necklace, or a shiny mirror.'

Suddenly his eyes narrowed and he frowned. 'You were selling oranges in the Place today. You're not going to grab me again, are you? I don't like being grabbed.'

The wariness in his eyes lanced her heart. 'I won't do anything you don't like, I promise.' Trying to buttress her fast-fading hopes, she said, 'What nice soldiers you have! And a pony, too.' She gestured towards the infamous glass-eyed toy horse against the wall behind him.

'I'm too big for it now,' Philippe said, seeming reassured by her pledge. '*Maman* says this summer, she'll get me a real pony. I love horses. I shall be a soldier, like my papa.'

If you only knew, Elodie thought. 'Is your *maman* good to you?'

Philippe shrugged. 'She's *Maman*. Whenever she goes away, she brings me a new toy when she comes back. And reads me a story before bed at night.' He giggled. 'She brings me sweets, too, but you mustn't tell! Nurse says they keep me from going to sleep.'

Elodie pictured the comtesse in her elegant Parisian gown, sitting on the narrow nursery bed, reading to *her* son, ruffling his silken hair, kissing him goodnight. Tears stung her eyes. *It should be me*, her wounded heart whispered.

'I won't tell,' she said.

Philippe nodded. 'Good. I don't like storms. When wind rattles the windows, *Maman* comes and holds me.' His eyes lit with excitement. 'And in summer, when we go to the country house, she lets me catch frogs and worms. And takes me fishing. But she makes Gasconne put the worms on the hook.'

Each smile, each artless confidence, drove another nail into the coffin of her hopes. Anguished, frantic, she said, 'I could take you to the bird market, here in Paris. They have parrots from Africa, with bright feathers of green and blue, yellow and red. Wouldn't you like to see them?' She held a hand out to him.

His smile fading, he scuttled backwards, away from her outstretched hand. 'Thank you, *madame*, but I'd rather go with *Maman*.'

She'd frightened him again, she thought, sick inside. 'Can I ask you one more thing? Will you look very closely and tell me if I remind you of anyone?'

Obviously reluctant, he focused on her briefly. 'You look like the orange lady from the park. Will you go now? I want Marie.'

He scuttled back further, seeming to sense the fierce, barely suppressed instinct screaming at her to seize him and make a run for it. Keeping a wide-eyed, wary gaze on her, he clutched two of his soldiers to his chest…as if hoping they might magically spring to life and defend him from this threatening stranger.

From her. From a desperate need to be together that was *her* desire, not *his* any longer.

Agonising as it was, she couldn't avoid the truth. With her own eyes, she could see her son was healthy, well dressed and well cared for. From his own lips, she'd heard that the comtesse was an attentive, loving mother. One who could afford to give him a pony, who had a country manor probably as elegant as this town house where they could escape the disease and stink of the city in summer.

He was loved. Happy. *Home.*

Her breath a painful rasp in her constricted chest, she stared at him, trying to commit every precious feature to memory.

A patter of approaching footsteps warned her the nursery maid was approaching. Though her mind couldn't comprehend a future beyond this moment, she knew she didn't want to risk being thrown into a Parisian prison.

Even so, only by forcing herself to admit that fear of *her* lurked behind the mistrustful stare of her son, only by repeating silently the plea that had stabbed her through the heart— *will you go now?*—was she able to force her feet into motion.

'Goodbye, Philippe, my darling,' she whispered. With one last glance, she sped from the room.

To Will's surprise, Elodie returned to the kitchen well before the thirty minutes he'd allotted her…and alone. Pale as if she'd seen a ghost, eyes staring sightlessly into the distance, she took a place at the back of the crowd, not meeting his gaze. Wondering what new disaster had befallen her, Will wrapped up his cajolery with a few short words, curbing his impatience as the customers he'd enticed took their time purchasing laces, ribbons and shaving mirrors. At last, he was able to pack up the remaining merchandise and bundle them both back outside.

As soon as they turned on to the small street bordering the Hôtel de la Rocherie, he halted and turned to her. 'What happened? Is the child ill?'

'Oh, no. He's in excellent health.'

'Then why did you not seize him?'

She shook her head. 'I couldn't.'

'Ah, too difficult in full daylight?' he surmised, well understanding her frustration. 'No matter. You know the lay of the house now.

We'll come back tonight. It's clouding over, so the sky will be—'

'No,' she interrupted. 'We won't come back.'

Will frowned at her. 'I don't understand.'

Shivering, she wrapped her arms around herself, as if standing in a cold wind, though the summer afternoon was almost sultry. 'He was playing with soldiers. Very well made, their uniforms exact down to every detail. His own clothing, too, is very fine. He summers at a country manor, where there are streams to fish and ponies to ride.' A ragged sigh escaped her lips. 'I can't give him any of that.'

'What does that matter?' Will asked, his gut wrenching as from the depths of his past rose up the anguished memory of losing his own mother. 'You're his mama!'

'I used to be,' she corrected. 'I'm just the "orange lady" from the park now; it is the comtesse that he calls *Maman*. She dotes on him, reads him stories, even takes him fishing. All I could offer is love, and he already has that, along with so many other things I could never provide.'

'Besides…' she turned to face him, her expression pleading, as if she were trying to convince him—and herself '…bad enough that

stealing him, tearing him away from everything familiar and comforting, would terrify
him. The comtesse married into a powerful
family; she would very likely utilise all her
contacts to track him down and drag him
back, putting him through another round of
terror and uncertainty. He's only four and a
half years old! I can't do that to him.'

'So you're just…giving up?' Will asked, incredulous.

Elodie seemed to shrink into herself. 'He
doesn't need me any more,' she whispered.

Abruptly, she turned and moved away from
him down the street. Not trying to escape him,
he realised at once. There was nothing in her
movements of the purposeful stride that had
taken her from the Hôtel de la Rocherie this
morning into the Place Royale, or even of the
frenzied tramp around the pathways that followed her first rendezvous with her son.

This was the aimless walk, one plodding
foot in front of the other, of someone with no
goal and no place to go.

When he had obtained the cart and goods
necessary for their current reincarnation as tin-
kers, Will had also provisioned them for a rapid
flight to the coast. Avoiding the usual cross-

ing points at Calais or Boulogne, he intended to engage a smuggler's vessel from one of the smaller channel ports to ferry them over to Kent, where several easy days' travel would get them to Denby Lodge, Max's horse-breeding farm.

They had no need for a cart now—and no reason to linger any longer in Paris. With some additional blunt, he could exchange the vehicle and its wares for horses, and they could head for the coast at once.

An instinctive itch between his shoulder blades kept telling him to put as much distance as possible between them and the danger posed by Paris. Philippe, intelligent child that he was, would doubtless have told his nursemaid about the 'orange lady's' return. It wouldn't take any great leap of imagination for that woman and the footman who'd guarded the child in the park to connect the sudden arrival of a tinker and his wife to the man and woman who'd accosted Philippe in the Place Royale. After viewing the sumptuous, well-tended Hôtel, he didn't need Elodie's warning to realise the comtesse had powerful connections who wouldn't hesitate to set the authorities after anyone who threatened her child, an annoyance Will would rather not deal with.

But Elodie looked so limp and exhausted, her face and body drained of the fire and energy that normally animated them, Will wasn't sure she could stand a gallop to the coast now. Perhaps he should settle for obtaining horses and getting them to an inn north of Paris, and start the journey in earnest tomorrow.

Remaining within easy return distance of the city would probably be prudent in any event. Though at the moment Elodie seemed to have lost all the purpose and determination that had driven her to survive St Arnaud's brutality, evade pursuers on the road—and elude *him*—in order to find her son, that might change, once she'd had a chance to rest her exhausted body and spirits. No point getting her halfway to England aboard some smuggling vessel and having her decide she must return to Paris and try again.

He knew only too well the agony of thinking you'd lost the one person you loved most in the world. But unlike a mother claimed by death, Elodie's son was very much alive. Though he understood that love made her put her son's best interests over her own desires, everything within him protested the unfairness of forcing her to make such a sacrifice.

He ached to ease her pain by urging that they return to reclaim her son, but at the moment, he had no reasonable answers to the objections she'd raised to simply stealing him away. By dint of skilful gaming and even more skilful investing, he was no longer the penniless orphan who, at Eton, had taunted the boys into gaming with him to earn a few pence to buy meat pies. But the property and modest wealth he'd thus far accumulated was no match for the resources of a comtesse, even if he could persuade Elodie to accept some.

As for influence, his only elevated connection was his uncle. Not only was the earl highly unlikely to embrace any cause supported by his black-sheep illegitimate nephew, he might well forfeit even the loyalty of his Ransleigh Rogue cousins if, after pledging to restore Max's reputation, he appeared instead to champion the woman who'd ruined it.

He wouldn't suggest they do anything, raise her hopes to no purpose, until he could consider the matter more carefully and come up with a better plan.

An inn north of Paris it must be, Will decided.

* * *

After a quick exchange of cart and contents for horses, Will had got a listless Elodie mounted. For the rest of the day, they had ridden north at a pace he thought easy enough for her to tolerate. Just before dark, they stopped at a village along the coaching road, where Will located a suitable establishment and engaged a room.

For the whole of their journey there, Elodie had neither looked directly at him nor spoken, seemingly lost in an abyss of despair and fatigue too profound for anything to penetrate.

Gently he led her to the room and helped her to the bed. 'Sleep. I'm going to arrange our horses for tomorrow and get some food. I'll be back with your dinner very soon. Men's clothing, too, perhaps, for this last leg of our journey?'

But even that mild jest produced no response. Sighing, Will stripped her down to her chemise and guided her back against the pillows. She was still staring blankly into space when he closed the door.

Darkness had fallen by the time he returned. As he quietly lit a candle, he noted Elodie dozing in the same position in which he'd left her, head thrown back against the pillows like a broken doll, her face pale and her hands limp beside her.

Will considered setting out food and wine and leaving her in solitude with her grief. The last thing he wanted was to witness her pain and be dragged into remembering the anguish of his own youth. Yet, aching for her, he realised he couldn't leave her so alone and vulnerable, even if it meant fending off memories he had no wish to revisit.

Dragging a chair beside the bed, Will settled himself to watch over her.

Suddenly, she shuddered and cried out. 'Hush, sweeting,' he soothed, gathering her in his arms.

Her every muscle tensing, she jerked away before her eyes opened and her hazy gaze fixed on his face. 'Will,' she murmured. Going limp again in his arms, she slumped back.

He plumped up the pillows and eased her up to a sitting position. 'I've brought food and drink,' he said, going over to fetch the supplies from his saddlebag. 'You must eat. It's after dark and you've had nothing but a little wine since before dawn.'

She didn't reply, but when he put the cup to her lips she sipped. After asking how she felt and what she wanted—and receiving no answers—he lapsed into silently feeding her bits of cheese and bread, which she ate mechanically, without seeming aware of him or the nourishment she was consuming.

When she would take no more, Will finished the wine and bread. As he was returning the remaining meat and cheese to the saddlebags, Elodie wrapped her arms around her torso and began rocking back and forth.

Tears welled up in her eyes and, a few moments later, she was weeping in earnest. Tossing down the saddlebags, Will climbed into the bed, gathered her into his arms and held her as deep, racking sobs shuddered through her body.

He cradled her against his chest as she wept out her grief, wishing there was some way he could ease that terrible burden. Finally the sobs grew shallower, slowed, stopped, then she fell asleep in his arms.

He must have dozed, too, for when he woke some time later, the candle had burned out. Too weary himself to light another, he slid far enough away from Elodie to divest himself of his clothing, then rolled back into the bed's inviting warmth.

Gathering her against him, he found her lips in the darkness and kissed her tenderly. 'Sleep, my darling. We've a long journey tomorrow.'

To his surprise, she reached up, pulled his head down and kissed him back.

This was no gentle caress, but a demanding capture of lips, followed by a sweep of her tongue into his mouth that banished grogginess and instantly turned simmering desire into boiling need.

While her tongue probed and demanded, her hands moved up and down his hardness. Still caressing him with one hand, she urged him on to his back and, breaking the kiss, in one swift motion raised her chemise and straddled him, guiding his swollen member to her soft inviting heat.

'Love me, Will,' her urgent voice pleaded in the darkness.

This was anguish seeking the oblivion of pleasure, he knew. But if pleasuring her would keep the pain at bay, he was happy to assist. Grasping her bottom, he thrust hard, sheathing himself in tight, seductive heat.

He would have stilled then, slowed, made it last, but Elodie was having none of it.

Pulling his thumbs to her nipples, she angled her hips and moved to take him deeper still. With him buried within her, she thrust again and again, riding him faster, harder, deeper, her nails scoring his shoulders, her teeth nipping his skin, until she cried out as her pleasure crested.

An instant later, he reached his own release. Wrapping her in his arms, still joined, Will rolled with her to his side and snuggled her there as together, sated, they fell into the boneless sleep of exhaustion.

Chapter Sixteen

Will woke just after dawn the following morning. At the feel of Elodie beside him, her head nestled on his shoulder, a glow of joy and well-being suffused him. The warmth lingered even after his groggy brain, lagging behind his senses, grew alert enough to remember how despondent and grief-stricken she'd been the previous night.

She'd also come alive in his arms, allowing him to sweep her away for a time from the anguish and sorrow. That had to count for something.

As long as her son was alive and well, there was hope. If whoever had been watching Elodie wanted to harm the boy, they could have done so long since, so there was every reason to expect he would continue to be healthy and content, living with the comtesse. Eventually, Will would figure out a way to reclaim him that would place no hardship on the boy. For now, he must get Elodie, who might still be in danger, safely back to England.

She stirred and he kissed her lips, his joy multiplying when she murmured and wrapped her arms around his neck to kiss him back. Desire surged as she fit herself against him and, for a time, the problems awaiting them outside their bedchamber receded as he made love to her, long and sweet and slow.

Eventually, they could avoid them no longer. 'You wanted to leave early for the coast?' Elodie said, sitting up. 'It's long past dawn now. I'd better dress.'

'You're sure you don't want to return to Paris and try again to take your son?'

Her jaw clenched and she closed her eyes briefly, as if reeling from a blow. 'He doesn't even recognise me, Will,' she said softly when she reopened them. 'Even if he did—what was I thinking? I have a few paltry jewels I could sell, enough, perhaps, to buy a small cottage somewhere in the country. But beyond that, I have no money, no family, no resources. Nothing to fall back on, nothing put away to pay for schooling or to assure his future. If Maurice were still alive…but he's not, and there's no one else. Besides, who's to say what will happen after we get to England? How could I drag him into that? No, we should just leave today, as you wished.'

Much as it pained him to see the bleak look back in her eyes, empty platitudes wouldn't comfort her. Until he formulated some intelligent plan that offered real hope, it was better to say nothing.

Apparently taking silence for agreement, she slipped from the bed and picked up her scattered garments. 'So I travel as a woman this time? Or have you yet another disguise in that bag?'

Trying not to be distracted by the arousing vista of Elodie, naked but for the bundle of clothing she held, he forced himself to concentrate on the imperative of getting them quickly to the Channel and on to England, before Talleyrand or whoever else had been following them discovered their current location. Realising now what her objective in Paris had been, any French agent worth his pay must know her story and would have kept the comtesse's house under surveillance. So their pursuers must know they'd made it back to Paris.

'I'm afraid the bag of tricks is rather empty and the funds are running low. We'll travel as we are for now and, as you suggest, go at once.'

Giving him a wan smile—so pale an imitation of the brilliant ones that had warmed his heart during their journey that his chest ached—she dressed quickly. He did the same, then assembled their bags and walked down to pay the landlord. After retrieving their newly hired horses from the stables, with Elodie waiting listlessly beside him, Will fastened their bags on to the saddles.

At first, he paid little attention to the private coach that was progressing slowly down the street, the roadway already filling with the usual early-morning assortment of farmers, maids, vendors, clerks and townspeople going about their business. Until, its driver apparently distracted by an altercation between two tradesmen whose carts had collided, the vehicle began heading almost directly at them.

Will had been about to shout a warning to the driver, when the coach inexplicably began to pick up speed. Preoccupied with controlling their now shying, stamping mounts, he was trying to shift both sets of reins into one hand and pull Elodie back out of harm's way with the other as the coach swayed by them, dangerously close.

Suddenly, the door opened, a man leaned out and grabbed Elodie by the arms. Before Will could finish transferring the reins, the assailant dragged Elodie into the vehicle. Will caught one last glimpse of her struggling figure before the door slammed shut and the driver sprang the horses, scattering people, poultry and produce in its wake.

An hour later, the bruiser who'd muscled Elodie into the closed carriage and bound and gagged her, dragged her from the coach and up the back stairs of an inn. After shoving her into a room, he closed the door behind her. Her anxious ears were relieved to hear no key turn in the lock before his footsteps retreated.

Since the henchman who'd grabbed her had said nothing the entire journey, she still had no idea who had abducted her or why.

Furiously she worked at the bonds, desperate to escape before anyone else arrived to manhandle her. After a few moments, she succeeded in freeing her hands. She'd just ripped off the gag when, her eyes finally adjusting to the dimness of the shuttered room, she realised she was not alone.

Her skin prickled and the sour taste of fear filled her mouth as she recognised the shadowed figure seated at the table of what appeared to be a private parlour. 'St Arnaud!' she gasped.

'Indeed,' he said, giving her a nod. 'You appear to be as delighted to see me as I was to discover you'd apparently come back from the dead. I must admit, I was quite distressed when Prince Talleyrand informed me you'd been sighted in Paris. He advised me to take better care of you this time.'

Fury and loathing coursed through her, swamping the fear. 'You *took care* of me before. You took my son!'

He shook his head. 'Very maladroit of you to be manoeuvred into it. A bit of money, some promises of advancement dangled before you, and it was done. So distastefully predictable. Ah, well, your foolishness has made my dear sister very happy.'

Never in her life had Elodie truly wished to harm someone, but at that moment, she would have bartered her soul for a weapon.

She wanted to pummel St Arnaud, carve the sardonic smile off his face, make him scream with pain. Not for the beatings he'd inflicted on her in Vienna, but for the blow to the heart from which she'd never recover.

'Bastard,' she spat out, her eyes scanning the room for anything she might use against him.

'Not me, my dear! That epithet belongs to the hovel-born Englishman who's been attempting to assist you. And don't bother to agitate yourself searching; I'm not foolish enough to leave lying about anything you might use to defend yourself. Now, how shall we dispose of you this time? Something quick and merciful?'

'You mean to do it yourself? You haven't the stomach.'

His gaze hardened. 'You think not?'

'You let others do the difficult work before. What happened to the poor wretch who pulled the trigger on Lord Wellington?'

St Arnaud lifted an elegant brow. 'He was hanged, I suppose. Only what he deserved for being sloppy and inaccurate. Anyway, he was just a means to an end.'

'Like me.'

'Like you. Although unlike Franz, whom

the Austrian authorities took care of long ago, you're much more trouble, turning up again after all this time.'

'Then let me relieve you of her,' said a voice from the doorway.

'Will!' Elodie cried, her fear and anger swamped in a surge of surprise, relief and gladness.

St Arnaud's eyes widened with alarm for an instant before he smoothed his features back to a sardonic calm. 'Ah, the bastard appears.'

'Surely you were expecting me. A horse can easily keep pace with a carriage and, with the driver on the box and only one flunky within, there was no one to prevent my following. It's about time you had to deal with someone more up to your weight. And after I do, we'll go.'

'You think I'll just let her leave with you?' St Arnaud laughed. 'How quaint, that you survived soldiering and a childhood in Seven Dials with such naïve notions intact. I would have thought you'd expect me to go for the kill.'

'She's no threat to you.'

'Is she not? What about the testimony you want her to give in London? Dredging up that old scandal could cause a great deal of unpleasantness, just as I'm re-establishing my career.'

'Re-establishing?' Will echoed. 'There's a king on France's throne now. What of your love for Napoleon?'

St Arnaud shrugged. 'He'll never escape from that speck of rock in the Atlantic. I don't deny I regret that France has been saddled with fat old King Louis, but one must adapt to changing circumstances, as Prince Talleyrand always says. I'm a St Arnaud; I belong at the centre of France's political affairs. Now, *monsieur*, I don't know how you convinced Raoul to let you in, but I've no quarrel with you. Leave now and I'll not call the gendarmes and have you thrown in jail.'

'Magnanimous of you,' Will said, showing his teeth.

'Quite. I doubt your uncle would bestir himself on behalf of the bastard branch of family and French prisons are so unpleasant.'

'At least I earned that title by birth. Being a bastard, though, don't you think I would have taken care of such small details as a few retainers? As you said, I was breeched in Seven Dials. It's not wise to leave loose knives lying about that might get thrown at your back.'

Had he really eliminated St Arnaud's hench-men, or was he bluffing? Elodie wondered, shooting him a glance. He gave her a wink.

After weeks on the road from Vienna, wit-nessing all his skill and ingenuity, she'd bet on Will against odds much higher than these.

St Arnaud wasn't sure, either. His arrogant confidence wavering a bit, he stepped towards the door.

Will stationed himself in front of it, his gaze challenging. 'Let her leave with me now and I might consider letting you live.' He moved his hand so quickly even Elodie didn't follow it and extracted a knife from his pocket.

Making no attempt now to disguise his alarm, St Arnaud reached into his own pocket, uttering an oath when he found it empty.

'Didn't bring a weapon with you? How careless!' Will taunted. 'But then, against a slip of a woman, I suppose you thought your fists would be sufficient.' His eyes narrowing to slits, his expression so murderous the hair raised on the back of Elodie's neck just watch-ing him, Will stepped towards St Arnaud.

Swallowing hard, St Arnaud retreated be-hind the table. 'Raoul!' he called. 'Etienne! *Venez immediatement!*'

Will laughed and took a step closer. 'Bellow all you want. Your watchdogs are "taking a nap" and the landlord's gone deaf. I outbid you, you see.'

Looking around wildly, St Arnaud fixed his gaze on Elodie. 'Do you really want to go with him? Hanging's an ugly death. I'm sure we can settle our little misunderstanding after all.'

'She knows better than to trust a miscreant like you. Elodie, step behind me, please.' He gave her a quick, pleading glance, as if he weren't sure she would choose him over St Arnaud.

How could he have any doubt? Swiftly she crossed the room. He gave her arm a reassuring squeeze as she passed him, then tucked her behind him. 'His men are tied up, unconscious,' he murmured in an undertone. 'Our horses are at the back. As soon as I deal with this abomination, we'll go.'

Twirling the knife between his fingers, Will looked back at St Arnaud and sighed. 'This is awkward, isn't it? Whatever am I to do with you now? Should I upset my uncle by committing murder? Ah, well, he's upset with me most of the time anyway.' He stepped purposefully closer to St Arnaud.

As he advanced, St Arnaud put his hands out in front of him. 'I'll pay whatever you want! Talleyrand told me the earl never settled on you the sum he promised. I can have a handsome amount transferred to any bank you like.'

'Can you?' Will halted, as if he were considering the offer. Before St Arnaud, looking relieved, could say another word, Will extracted a pistol from his pocket. 'Perhaps I should make it look like you shot yourself instead? Crazed by worry that the old scandal might compromise your new position? I'm sure Elodie could write quite a convincing suicide note.'

'No, please!' St Arnaud wailed. '*Monsieur*, reconsider! What benefit to you if I die? Let me live and I can—'

'Silence, vermin,' Will spat out. 'I've never met a man more deserving of murder, but I'd not soil my blade. However, I might just work the itchiness out of my fists by beating you into the carpet...like you beat her in Vienna.'

'Will, if you're not going to kill him, don't beat him,' Elodie urged, unsure she didn't prefer murder as an option. 'He might hurt my son. He couldn't best you, but he could handle a little boy.'

'Ah, yes, your son.' Will frowned. 'That does present a dilemma. If I let him live, what assurance do we have that he won't harm the boy after we've gone?'

'Of course I wouldn't harm him!' St Arnaud cried with a show of indignation. 'My sister has claimed him as her own, which makes him nearly a St Arnaud. Prince Talleyrand himself dotes upon the boy.'

'I don't know,' Will said, twirling the blade again. 'It would be simpler to gut you and be done with it.'

Elodie didn't know what to think. Much as she detested St Arnaud, she wasn't sure she could live with her conscience if she allowed Will to murder him. Which she was nearly certain Will would do, coolly, cleanly and efficiently, if she told him to.

She didn't trust St Arnaud one bit, but she'd seen for herself that Philippe was treated as the comtesse's beloved son, and she knew St Arnaud was inordinately proud of family and position. Nor would he be foolish enough to cross a man as powerful as Prince Talleyrand, whom he must have already had to appease after the débâcle in Vienna.

'*Madame*, I swear to you, the boy will come to no harm!' St Arnaud cried, recalling her attention.

Will glanced back at her. 'Elodie?'

While Elodie hesitated, agonised, there was a knock at the door, followed by the entrance of a tall, imperious figure.

He halted inside and surveyed the scene, seeming neither surprised nor perturbed to have come upon a woman clinging to the back of a man who was threatening a second man with a knife. 'Madame Lefevre,' he said, bowing to her. 'And you must be Monsieur Ransleigh.'

Glancing at the knife, he wrinkled his nose in distaste. 'Please, *monsieur*, there is no need for such vulgarities. Allow me to introduce myself. Antoine de Montreuil, Comte de Merlonville, assistant to the Duc de Richelieu, who succeeded Prince Talleyrand last autumn as Prime Minister of France.'

Turning his gaze to St Arnaud, he sighed. 'Thierry, must you ever be rash, acting without thinking? When the Prince learned you had rushed off to…detain this lady, he informed Monsieur le Duc at once, telling him he'd made it quite clear to you that you were to speed her on her way.'

'Speed her on—' St Arnaud echoed. 'He told me to "take care of her"!'

'Precisely. However, though the Prince, ah, advises, it is the Duc who makes policy now. Only your family name and lineage persuaded Talleyrand to retain you after the Vienna fiasco. Monsieur Ransleigh has sought *madame*'s assistance to deal with a matter that is of personal interest solely to his family, and perhaps the British Foreign Office. His Highness the King does not need to be troubled about it, so I suggest that you cease obstructing their progress immediately...or I must warn you, the Duc is likely to be much less forgiving than the Prince.'

Turning from St Arnaud in clear dismissal, de Merlonville addressed Elodie and Will. '*Monsieur* and *madame*, I am so sorry you were inconvenienced. The Duc would be happy to offer you an escort to the coast, to ensure no other...recalcitrants trouble you.'

After studying the Duc's self-professed assistant warily for a moment, Will shook his head. 'Thank you, but I don't think that will be necessary.'

'What of the child?' Elodie cried, needing to be sure about this.

'Child?' de Merlonville repeated.

'Philippe. Philippe...de la Rocherie.'

'What has the Prince Talleyrand's godson have to do with this?' the official asked.

'Philippe is Prince Talleyrand's godson?' Will interjected.

'Well, not officially. But the comtesse's late husband being a close associate of the Prince for many years, he watches over the widow.'

'I see.' Her relief that the comtesse did, in fact, have a powerful protector who would ensure her son's safety faded rapidly when she realised the full implications of the association.

In her wildest imagining, she might envision some day acquiring a settled home and enough coin to challenge the comtesse's control over her son. But never in any imagining could she hope to find Philippe a sponsor who had the wealth, power and influence of Prince Talleyrand, who'd been at the highest level of France's political life through three successive governments.

Will seemed to sense her dismay, for, after

stowing his knife and pistol, he reached over to take her hand. 'Are you ready to leave?'

There seemed nothing further to do or say. 'I suppose so.'

Looking to de Merlonville, Will gestured towards St Arnaud. 'If we might have a moment?'

'Only if you'll promise me not to carve him up once my back is turned. So distressing to the innkeeper and so damaging to the carpet, all that blood.'

'I give you my word.'

De Merlonville nodded. 'Monsieur Ransleigh, you will convey my kind regards to your uncle, the earl? I had occasion to meet him and some other leaders of Parliament when I visited London for the Duc last fall. And, Thierry, I trust you now understand your position? The post to the Caribbean for which the Prince recommended you has not been confirmed…yet. I'm certain you would not wish to compromise your political future by delaying these good people any further.'

'Of—of course not, my dear Comte.'

'Then I suggest you gather up your effects and make ready to return to Paris, while they continue on their way.'

Nodding quickly, St Arnaud pivoted to collect his coat and a snuffbox and some other items strewn about the table. While his back was turned, the comte murmured to them, 'A lovely island, St Lucia. But an area rife with tropical fevers, not to mention the danger of pirates. Many venture there and so few return.'

He gave them a wink, then bowed himself out of the room.

After he departed, Will turned to St Arnaud. Having retrieved his personal items and shrugged on his greatcoat, he was careful to keep the table between himself and Will, while his still-florid face gave evidence of his fury and chagrin.

'Well, vermin, it appears that you'll get to live after all. Though I don't count *your* assurances about the boy worth a ha'penny, I do respect the Prince…and his plans. Still, I want you to know I'll be watching. You'd better pray that Madame Lefevre's son lives a healthy, happy, prosperous life. If I learn he's suffered so much as a sniffle, I'll track you down and snuff out your miserable life.'

Taking Elodie's arm, Will said, 'I believe there's a packet at the coast awaiting us in Calais.'

Chapter Seventeen

Though Will and Elodie had politely declined de Merlonville's offer of an escort, even in her state of diminished awareness, Elodie sensed a subtle presence trailing them during the long days of riding towards the Channel. It wasn't until after dark of the fourth day, when Will hustled her from the room he'd engaged at a Calais inn down narrow back stairs to a pair of waiting horses and rode off with her into the night that she realised he, too, had noted—and mistrusted—whatever force was following them.

Silently he led her horse along narrow back lanes, with only the stars and the distant lights of Calais to guide them, until they reached a small port some miles further south down the coast. Will finally brought them to a halt before a mean-looking inn which boasted only one smoky lantern by its entrance to announce its calling.

Warning her in a low voice to remain outside, he disappeared into the structure. A few moments later, he returned to lead their horses to a lean-to barn at the rear and then escort her up the back stairs to a low-ceilinged room under the eaves whose tiny window overlooked the road and the harbour beyond.

'Sorry to drag you out of your comfortable accommodations for something I fear will be much inferior,' he said as he waved her to the table by the window. 'Not that I don't appreciate the good wishes of the Prime Minister's own man. But I'd rather return to England on transport of my own choosing—and hopefully without the Duc or the Prince's knowledge.'

'On a smuggling vessel? This certainly looks disreputable enough to be a smuggler's inn. You have the most interesting contacts, Monsieur Ransleigh.'

His eyes lit at the gentle barb in her response. 'Are you feeling better?' he asked, pulling a flask of wine from his saddlebags and pouring them a cup.

Better? she asked herself, accepting the mug. She'd gone from agony to numbness, like a recent amputee after the opium took hold. Other than that, she felt…empty, barren as a seashell-dotted beach after a storm had swept it of its treasures, scouring it down to elemental sand.

'I'm feeling…here, I suppose.'

'That's progress. You've been gone quite a while.'

It occurred to her that Will had been unusually taciturn for the whole of their journey north from Paris, trotting steadily beside her with minimal chat, stopping to share bread, cheese and wine at midday without attempting to regale her with any of his stories, settling them in an inn long after dark with only a brief caress before they both fell into the sleep of exhaustion.

Not surprising. In the paralysed state in which she'd existed since emerging from the first shock of leaving Philippe, she'd probably been oblivious to any conversational attempts he might have made. The awful reality of losing her son again had been like staring into the sun, the terrible brilliance blinding her to everyone and everything else around her.

Aside from the vivid encounter with St Arnaud north of Paris, she scarcely remembered anything about the days between walking out of Philippe's bedchamber at the Hôtel de la Rocherie and arriving at the coast tonight. Trying to piece events together now, she could come up with only snippets of memory.

Will, walking beside her across Paris. Settling her into a bed. Feeding her with his own hands. Cradling her against his warmth while grief smashed her like a china doll into shards of misery. And when the anguish had been past bearing, helping her escape into the oblivion of passion.

No friend, companion or lover could have treated her with more gentleness and compassion. A tiny flicker of warmth—affection, gratitude—lit the bleakness within.

'Thank you, sweet Will,' she murmured.

'For rescuing you from St Arnaud? That was my pleasure, though I would have preferred to have beaten him into pudding, if I was not to be allowed to gut him.'

'Would you have gutted him?'

He paused. 'I don't know. Would you have wanted me to?'

'Yes. No. Oh, *je sais pas*! How can I know,

when it would make no difference? Killing him wouldn't get Philippe back.'

'It would have guaranteed Philippe could never fall under his power. Although it does seem both Talleyrand and the Prime Minister have united to send him far away, far enough that your son will be safe—and they will be freed from his scheming. Apparently they've also given us their blessing, or so it seems. What do you make of de Merlonville's appearance?'

Like an old iron wheel gone rusty from disuse, she had to scrape away a clogging coat of apathy to focus her mind on the question.

'Talleyrand has been replaced. I didn't know that.'

'Nor did I, but it seems he retains a good deal of influence.'

Thinking more swiftly now, she ran back through her memory the whole exchange between St Arnaud and de Merlonville in the upstairs parlour. 'De Merlonville said Prince Talleyrand had informed the Duc about St Arnaud snatching me, so he must still have agents trailing us…but apparently the Duc now controls who takes action. St Arnaud is tolerated, but just barely. With his thirst for power, I expect St Arnaud will be very careful not to make any further moves against us—or Philippe—without the Duc's approval.'

'In any event, it appears he will soon be leaving France—permanently, de Merlonville seemed to suggest,' Will said. 'The comte also seemed to want to make clear that the French government had no interest in any testimony you might give.'

She nodded. 'Which seems logical—with the king's throne secure, no one would wish to remind Louis of the unhappy past by bringing to his notice a long-failed Napoleonic plot.'

'That matches what George Armitage told us outside Linz—neither the French nor British governments want to dredge up the old scandal now. Which would leave those de Merlonville called "recalcitrants" as the most likely group looking to harass us.'

'Yes, St Arnaud and any of his remaining associates trying to claw their way back into government would be keen to make sure no embarrassing evidence of their former Bonapartist leanings came to light,' Elodie summed up. '*Eh bien*, de Merlonville was instructed to provide us an escort to prevent them from harrying us.'

'Perhaps. Unless de Merlonville's offer was intended to put us off our guard and we are still in danger from Talleyrand's forces, too. Although, since they could have apprehended us any time during our travel north, that seems unlikely, I prefer to remain wary. Hence, this draughty inn.'

'A precaution of the wisest sort.'

'I hope you continue to think so after you've slept in bedclothes clammy from its dripping eaves.'

She tilted her head at him. 'You have slept under its dripping eaves before, perhaps?'

Will grinned at her. 'Never underestimate the contacts of a former thief, cut-purse and salesman of illegal goods.'

'You were involved in smuggling, too?'

'Smugglers make landfall all along the coast, then use a network of agents to move the goods inland. The boss for whom I worked used to have us distribute lace, silk and brandy that had never had duty paid on it to eager, if clandestine, clients. A profitable business, as long as the revenue agents didn't catch you.'

'You *have* led an adventurous life.'

'No more so than you. *Émigrée* creeping from Nantes in the dead of night, returnee to the "New France", soldier's bride, grieving widow disguised as a wounded soldier passing through the detritus of two armies, Vienna hostess, seamstress in hiding, old man, valet, monk, farm girl, orange seller...' Will ticked them off on his fingers.

She'd been smiling at his list until the last disguise reminded her of Paris and the final resolution of her quest. 'Then back to Elodie again,' she said quietly. 'Without home, without family, without my son.' Her voice breaking on the last word, she slumped back in the chair, despair and weariness suddenly overtaking her.

She felt Will's hand cover her own. 'At least you need no longer worry about St Arnaud's interference.'

'Perhaps not,' she replied with a sigh, looking over at him. 'Praise God, my son is safe. But he is still lost to me.'

'Where there is life, there is hope, so—'

She put her hand to his lips, stopping his words. 'Please, Will, no more schemes!' she cried. 'I can't bear it.'

He must have realised how close she still walked to the precipice of falling apart completely, for when she removed her finger, he let the topic drop. Silently he took her hand again, stroking it, his sympathetic gaze on her face.

'I wish I could help. I know how much you've lost.'

Though her rational mind appreciated his attempt at empathy, the wounded animal in her turned on him.

'You *know*?' she spat back. 'How could you? *Je te jure*, you have no idea what I feel!'

'Swear if you like, but I do. I held my mother's hand and watched her die. I was five years old.'

The expression on Will's face struck her to silence, her anger withering in its wake. No wonder he'd never wanted to talk about his childhood.

Five years old—almost the same age as Philippe! And she had thought stealing her son from his home a trial too great for any child to bear.

Compassion—tinged with shame—filled her.

'I'm so sorry,' she whispered.

'She was the only being in the world who'd ever cared for me or tried to protect me,' he said softly, staring beyond her, seemingly unaware of her presence. The anguish in his eyes said he was reliving the experience. 'Though I was always hungry and ragged, even at that age, I knew she was doing the best she could for me.'

Elodie hesitated, unsure what to say that might bring him back from the emotional abyss into which he'd tumbled. Then he shook his head, as if throwing off the memories, and turned to her with an apologetic smile. 'I told you the tale wasn't edifying.'

'How did you survive?'

'I already knew the street boys, though Mama had tried to keep me from running with them. They found me at the market, going through rubbish piles with another, smaller boy, looking for the bits thrown away by the vendors as too tough or rotten to sell. When two of them tried to take away what the younger lad had gleaned, I fought them off. Their leader, an older boy, stopped us. He probably could have finished me with one fist, but instead, he ordered them to leave me alone. Said he liked my spirit and they could use another fighter. So they took me in, taught me the ways of the street.'

'How to thieve?'

He nodded. 'Thieving, house-breaking,

lock-picking, card-sharking, knife-fighting. Sleight-of-hand and how to do a few magic tricks to beguile the gullible while a mate picked their pockets. The real trick was to become skilled enough to win without using a weighted deck or marked cards.'

'It must have been quite a change, when the earl brought you to Swynford Court.'

Will laughed, a rueful smile on his lips. 'By then, I was in line to become a street leader for the boss, and resisted mightily being dragged into the country by the brother of the toff who had abandoned my mother. Nor was I interested in exchanging my mates for three dandified cousins. Alastair and Dom were as unimpressed by me as I was by them. But Max…for Max, it was different. I was a Ransleigh by blood and that was that: whatever it took, he would turn me into one.'

'What did it take?' she asked, curious. 'I don't imagine you would have made the task easy.'

'I did not. After beating some respect into me, he used a bit of everything—coaxing, challenging, empathising, daring, rewarding. By the end of the summer, much to the chagrin of Alastair and Dom, who had bet him the transformation couldn't be done, he'd instilled in me a sufficient modicum of gentlemanly behaviour that the earl agreed not to return me to Seven Dials.'

Elodie thought about the dangers of a child's existence on the streets and shuddered. '*Grace à Dieu* he didn't send you back!'

'I thank God, too. Max saved my life, plain and simple. But passing muster with the earl was just the first step. In many ways, Eton and Oxford were more difficult, not a single test but a limitless series of them. It was Max who taught me there would never be an end to bullies wanting to pummel me, or better-born snobs trying to shame me, and it was smarter to outwit and outmanoeuvre them rather than fight. A born diplomat, even as a boy, he knew I was too proud to take money from him. Though the earl paid my school fees, I had no allowance; it was Max and my cousins who lured the other boys into playing cards or dice with me, or betting on my magic tricks. I'd always win enough for a meat pasty at Eton, or steak and a pint of ale at Oxford.'

'So that's where you perfected your beguiling pedlar's tricks.'

He cupped her chin in his hands and tilted

her face until she met the intensity of his gaze. 'So you understand why I'm so loyal to Max and my cousins? Why the bond between us is as strong as the one between a mother and her son?'

He wanted her to realise why, despite all they had shared, he was still willing to sacrifice her to redeem his cousin. Though she'd thought by now she was incapable of feeling anything, a sharp, anguished pang stabbed in her gut.

'Seeing all you've done since Vienna, I already understood. I respect Monsieur Max, too. He was kind to me, even tried to protect me as best he could from St Arnaud's abuse. Nothing but the imperative to get my son back would have forced me into tricking one of the very few true gentlemen I've ever met. A gentleman who offered to assist me, not to further some scheme of his own, but out of genuine concern.'

As everything else, that story led back to her loss. Recalling it like a knife slash across her heart, she said, 'Ah, *mon Dieu*, it's even worse, knowing I entrapped him and lost my son anyway. At least now I can attempt to make amends by fulfilling our bargain. I will testify to whatever you wish to vindicate your cousin and clear his reputation.'

Will hesitated. 'That might not be such a good idea.'

'Not a good idea?' she echoed, confused. 'Haven't you just spent the last few weeks dragging me across Europe to do just that?'

'True, but your testimony might have...severe consequences if, instead of viewing this as a personal matter concerning only Max's reputation, the Foreign Office decided to open an official enquiry. The penalty for being judged an accomplice in an attempt to murder the allied commander...' His words trailed off.

Would be a long sojourn in prison, or death, she knew. 'That outcome is always a possibility, although both de Merlonville and Armitage said neither government wants a formal investigation. But if they should, it would be as you told me in Vienna: a life for a life. Not so bad a bargain. Monsieur Max would become a great man, who could do much good. I could do this one thing and then I...I am of no more good to anyone anyway.'

For a long moment he held her gaze. 'You're good for me,' Will whispered.

The tenderness of it made her already-decimated heart ache. 'Sweet Will,' she said, attempting a smile. Their strong mutual attraction didn't change the melancholy facts. The unique, incomparable interlude of their journey from Vienna, wary co-conspirators who'd become mutual admirers, then friends, and then the most passionate of lovers, was almost over.

The silly, battered heart she'd thought was beyond feeling anything contracted in a spasm of grief that she must lose Will, too. She stifled its instinctive demand that she find some way to extend their time together.

But the English coast loomed just beyond a narrow stretch of restless sea and she'd never been one to deny reality. It was time to see the bargain she'd made to its conclusion.

Gently pushing Will's hands away, she took the last sip from her mug. 'I imagine you've conjured a vessel and some good sailing weather for tomorrow. We should rest now, if we're to be away early in the morning.'

Looking troubled, Will opened his lips as if to speak. Elodie stopped him with a hand to his lips. 'There's no more to say. Rest easy, Will. *C'est presque fini.* Your quest is almost done.'

Putting aside her mug, Elodie swiftly disrobed down to her chemise and climbed into the uneven bed, settling back on the pillows with a sigh. In the hollow emptiness within, lit only by the warmth of tenderness for Will, the decision to testify, come what may, sat well.

She wasn't sure when she'd made it. Some time during the long silent hours of moving north from Paris, probably, as the reality of life without Philippe settled into her shredded heart. She could repay the debt she owed Max Ransleigh, even the balance between. Like a person suddenly blinded, she could see no future beyond sitting before a green baize table in a Foreign Office enquiry room.

'May you have a happy, distinguished life, Philippe, *mon ange*,' she whispered, as a rip tide of exhaustion swept her towards sleep.

Bone-weary, Will climbed in bed beside Elodie.

During the last of their discussion, he'd wanted to interrupt her, to disagree, to tell her how unique and beautiful she was. But as he hadn't yet worked out a remedy for her stark assessment of her condition—a woman without home, without family, without her son—

she would have seen any such speech as pretty, empty words.

He wanted to tell her she meant too much for him to let her become a sacrifice to Max's redemption. But how could he expect her to believe him, when every step he'd taken since arriving in Vienna had been directed towards doing just that?

Unable to voice or reconcile the conflicting claims of loyalty clashing within him, he fell back to the only language that wouldn't fail. Gently he turned her pliant body towards him.

She murmured when he kissed her, then encircled his head with her arms and pulled him closer. He took the kiss deeper, moving his hands to caress her, filling her when she opened to him, showing her with his mouth and hands and body how much he cherished her.

Afterwards, as she dozed in his arms, exhausted and satisfied, Will lay awake, unable to find sleep. Tormented by a dilemma with no satisfactory answer, his mind spun fruitlessly round and round the final points of their discussion, like a roulette wheel before the croupier settles the ball.

For all his early years and then his time in the army, his survival had depended on making the correct, lightning-quick decision. But from the beginning of his doubts in Vienna through betrayal and reconciliation in Paris, he'd put off deciding what the final move in his game with Elodie would be. With arrival in England imminent, he could put it off no longer. And he was still not sure what to do.

He owed Max his life. But, he might as well admit it, Elodie now held his heart.

A vagabond all his life, he'd never thought of settling down on any of the small properties he'd been acquiring the last few years. Never thought of finding a wife or begetting children.

No more than she had he a home to offer her, and his only family were his cousins. The earl would sever their tenuous connection in a heartbeat, and if he were to betray his vow to Max to side with the woman who had ruined his cousin's life, he wouldn't have them, either.

He wished Max lived in the far reaches of Northumberland, so he would have longer to figure out what to do.

He would still willingly give his life to save Max's. But he was no longer willing to let Elodie give hers. Though he'd been dodging around the fact since the attack on her outside Karlsruhe, after almost losing her again to St Arnaud, he finally could no longer avoid admitting the truth. He'd fallen in love with Elodie Lefevre.

He wasn't sure what he'd expected love to be, but it wasn't the hearts-and-flowers, bring-her-jewels-to-woo-her-into-bed sort of fancy he'd imagined. More a gut-deep bond that made the air fresher, the sun brighter, the taste of wine sweeter because she shared it with him. A deep hunger to possess her, to be one with her, to satisfy her, that seemed to increase rather than diminish the longer they were together. A sense that losing her would suck all the joy, excitement and pleasure from life, leaving him like a mechanical doll, gears and levers taking it through the motions of life, but dead and empty inside.

He simply couldn't lose her.

Admitting this didn't make the way ahead any clearer. Though Elodie desired him, she'd given no indication that she felt for him anything deeper than fondness. But whether she returned his affection or not, he now had no intention of bringing her to the Foreign Office to testify. Despite what Armitage and de

Merlonville avowed, it was too risky, when her testimony could too easily detour down a path to prison or the gallows.

Instead of leaving Elodie at one of his properties and going first to London to snoop around the Foreign Office and see if he could discover what evidence would be sufficient to clear Max, perhaps they should proceed straight to Max himself. Max, much better attuned to the intricacies of the Foreign Office, would be in a better position to know if there were a means for Elodie to absolve him without her having to testify in person. By means of a sworn deposition, perhaps, which he could have delivered after he'd gotten her safely out of England.

His heart quickened at that solution, then slowed and he frowned. But if Max thought there was no way to clear his name but for Elodie to appear before a tribunal in London, he might press Will to take her there. And Elodie, in her current state, would agree to go.

Perhaps it would be better to sail around the south coast to Falmouth and catch a ship to the Americas…except he didn't have sufficient funds with him for such a trip; he'd need to visit his bankers in London first.

Maybe he should just go to Max, explain to him privately why he was breaking his solemn vow. Max had never been vindictive; even if Will's betrayal meant Max would lose for ever the life that should have been his, he knew Max wouldn't force him to risk the life of the woman Will now realised he loved.

But at the thought of facing the man to whom he owed more than anyone else on earth and admitting he was reneging on his pledge, his gut churned. The earl would say that Will had no honour to lose. But Max had always believed in him.

So, if he was prepared to betray Max, and it seemed that he was, he might as well make a clean break. Travel through Kent without stopping to see Max, go to London, obtain funds and head at once to Cornwall to take ship. He could write to Max later, when Elodie was safe in America, beyond the reach of French or English law.

His heart torn with anguish at the thought of leaving behind the only family he'd known—and losing the respect of the one man whose good opinion he valued more than any other—Will sprang up and paced the small room. After several circuits, as he gazed down again at Elodie's sleeping form, he knew if he must choose between Max and Elodie—between cousins, friendship, family, honour and Elodie—he would choose her.

They would go straight to London, obtain funds and leave for the Americas.

Then, the thought of betrayal bitter in his mouth, it struck him that leaving England immediately would only compound the dishonour. Max had believed in him, counselled him and championed him since they were boys. He couldn't just disappear without facing him. If he was going to break his pledge and for ever doom his cousin's government aspirations, he owed it to Max to tell him face to face.

He'd not add the white feather of cowardice to his disgrace.

Max might try to change his mind, but Will knew, on the bond they shared, that Max would never try to prevent him from leaving, or put Elodie in danger by sending the authorities after them.

So tomorrow they would sail in the smuggler's cutter to the Kentish coast and make their way to Max's farm. He'd confess his intentions to Max, receive his curses or farewells, then take Elodie to the safety of the Americas.

In her present despairing and listless state, Elodie might not agree to go with him. Well, he'd figure out a way to persuade her. She'd probably end up liking it, with new adventures to share and a whole continent to explore, not a town or river or meadow in it tarnished by anguished memories of the past. Maybe they could end up at the French-speaking colony at Nouvelle Orléans. He could contact his friend Hal Waterman, investigate the possibilities of investing in this new land.

Some of the terrible burden lifted from his chest, leaving lightness and a peace that testified to the rightness of the decision. Though the agony of abandoning Max still hollowed his gut, Will returned to the bed, took Elodie in his arms and slept at last.

Chapter Eighteen

On a drizzly grey afternoon three days later, mud-spattered and weary, Will and Elodie pulled up their tired mounts before a set of elaborate wrought-iron gates with the image of a running horse in the centre. 'This must be it—Denby Lodge,' Will said, dismounting to knock on the gatehouse door. 'I have to say, I'll be glad of a bath and a good dinner.'

'I still think we should have engaged a room for me at the inn in the last village,' Elodie said. Now that the moment to confront Max Ransleigh had almost arrived, anxiety was filtering through the fog of lethargy that had cocooned her through their Channel crossing—Will having managed to order up fair seas and a swift passage—and the two days of hard riding since. 'I'm sure Monsieur Max will be happy to offer you hospitality. I'm not so sure he'll be willing to offer it to me.'

'You needn't worry,' Will told her as an elderly man trotted from the brick house to unlock the tall gates. 'Max is a diplomat, remember; he'll receive you with such perfect courtesy, you'll never be able to tell what he's really feeling.'

Turning to the gatekeeper, Will asked, 'Is the Lodge straight on?'

'Aye, sir,' the man replied, bowing. 'Follow the drive past the barns and paddocks. The manor will be to your right once the drive rounds the parkland.'

After handing the gatekeeper a coin and acknowledging his thanks, Will ushered Elodie through the entry gates, then remounted and proceeded with her down the gravelled drive.

'The Denby Stud is quite famous,' Will told her as they trotted past lush, fenced meadows. 'Several army comrades purchased their cavalry horses from Sir Martin and swore by their quality. Swift, strong-boned, long on stamina and well mannered.' He laughed. 'Though I can't imagine what Max finds to keep himself busy here, I am curious to meet his wife, Caroline. My cousin Alastair says she's nothing in his usual style. Max always preferred ladies of stunning beauty and alluring charm. A horse breeder is definitely a departure.'

Surprised by Will's sudden loquaciousness, when they had travelled mostly in silence the last few days, Elodie was about to question him when she realised that, so attuned had he become to her, he must have sensed her uneasiness. His commentary was meant to inform her about the farm and the owner she was about to meet—but also to distract her from worrying about Max.

Once again, his thoughtfulness warmed the bleakness within her. How she wished they might have met years ago, when she was young and heart-whole, when she believed the future bright with possibilities.

She would just have to appreciate each moment of the very few she had left with him.

And if he was kind enough to try to cheer her, she could rouse herself to reply. 'It seems a very handsome property.'

'Yes, the fields and fences are in excellent condition. And look, there on the hill!' He pointed off to the left, where a herd of several dozen horses roamed. 'Mares with their foals.

Beauties all!' he pronounced after studying them for a moment. 'It seems Max's wife is maintaining her father's high standards.'

After riding steadily for thirty minutes past pastures and occasional lanes leading to thatched cottages in the distance without encountering barns or paddocks, Elodie said, 'The farm seems very large.'

'Larger than I expected,' Will agreed. 'I'm glad I asked directions of the gatekeeper, else I would fear we'd taken a wrong turn. Ah, finally—I see a barn over that rise.'

After passing an impressive series of barns surrounded by paddocks used for training the colts, Will told her, at last the lane entered a wood and turned to the right. As the trees thinned, they saw a fine stone manor house crowning the top of a small hill, flanked by oaks and shrubbery.

Trepidation dried her mouth, while the fluttering in her stomach intensified. Would Max Ransleigh receive her—or order her off his property?

Then they were at the entry, a servant trotting out to take their horses, a butler ushering them into the front parlour. Trying to be unobtrusive, Elodie stationed herself behind a wing chair set by the hearth, while Will stood by the mantel, toasting his hands at the welcome warmth of a fire.

With Will poised on the threshold of accomplishing all he'd set out to do, she'd expected he would be excited, impatient to see his cousin again, triumphant to be bringing home the means to redress all Max Ransleigh's wrongs. Oddly enough, he seemed as tense as she was, almost...uncomfortable, Elodie thought.

Before she had time to wonder further about it, the door opened and Max Ransleigh walked in, as handsome and commanding as she remembered. 'Will, you rascal!' he said, striding to the hearth and clasping his cousin in a quick, rough embrace. 'Though I ought to spot you a good round of fisticuffs for returning to England and then leaving again without even the courtesy of coming to meet my bride.'

Just as Elodie thought she'd escaped his notice, Max turned to her. 'And Madame Lefevre,' he said, bowing. 'My cousin Alastair told me Will intended to bring you back to England and I see he has succeeded. Welcome to my home.'

Elodie sank into a deep curtsy, studying Max warily beneath her lashes as she rose. If he was angry, he hid it well; his smile seemed genuine and his greeting sincere. A diplomat, indeed— or far more forgiving then she deserved.

'It is of everything most kind of you to receive me, Monsieur Ransleigh. When you would have every right to spit on me and toss me out of your house.'

He surveyed her with that quick, perceptive gaze she remembered so well. 'To be frank, a year ago, I might have. But everything has changed since then.'

'I deeply regret the disservice I did you. Let me assure you, I'm fully prepared to do whatever it takes to make amends.'

'We'll talk of that later,' Will interposed.

'Yes, later,' Max agreed. 'For now, I'm happy to see you without bruises, *madame*. Will must have been taking good care of you.'

For an instant, she recalled the whole amazing, wonderful journey and how well in truth Will *had* cared for her. Suppressing a sudden urge to weep that their time together was over, she said, 'Ah, yes. Most exceptional care.'

'Good.' Suddenly Max's eyes lit and a smile of joy warmed his face. 'Caro, I didn't know you'd come down! Come, my dear, and meet our guests.'

Elodie turned to see a slender woman enter the parlour, her simple green day dress setting off the auburn tints in the dark hair that crowned her head in a coronet of braids. Eyes the bright green of spring moss glowed when she looked at her husband, who walked over to meet her, wrapping an arm around her shoulders. 'Are you feeling strong enough to be up?'

'I'm fine. When Dulcie told me there were riders approaching, I had to come down. Isolated as we are, Denby Lodge doesn't often receive unexpected guests.' Turning towards the hearth, she said, 'But this gentleman needs no introduction. You must be Will! Alastair told me you and Max favour each other strongly.'

'Guilty as charged,' Will said, giving her a smile and a bow. 'Alastair said you were lovely and talented. An understatement on both accounts; we've just had a most enjoyable ride past your fields and some of the handsomest mares and foals I've seen in a long time.'

'Flatterer! You could find no faster way to my heart than to praise my horses.'

'I warned you he was a rogue, my dear,' Max murmured to his wife.

Will moved to Elodie's side, putting a protective hand on her arm. 'Mrs Ransleigh, may I present Madame Elodie Lefevre.'

'You, too, are very welcome,' Caro said, holding out her hand to Elodie, who, after a moment's hesitation, shook it.

'Caro, why don't you show Madame Lefevre up to a room, while Will and I get reacquainted?'

When Will gave his cousin a look and tightened his grip on her hand, Elodie murmured, her voice pitched for his ears alone, 'Don't worry. I'll not try to run away again.'

'It's not that. I feel...better when you're close.'

Watching their interplay with an appreciative smile, Max said, 'You needn't worry to let her go. Caro will take even better care of her than you do. *Madame*, you look exhausted— why don't you rest before dinner? And if you don't mind my saying so, Will, after a quick chat, you could use a bath.'

'Won't you come with me, *madame*?' Caro said. 'After a hard day's riding, there's nothing so soothing as a long soak in a hot tub. I'll have some tea and biscuits sent up, too, to tide you over until dinner. We'll see you later, gentlemen.'

And so Elodie allowed herself to be shepherded out of the room, down the hall and up the stairs to an airy bedchamber that looked out over the expanse of front lawn to the barns in the far distance.

She found herself instinctively liking Caroline Ransleigh, who offered her hand to shake like a man, dressed simply and whose unassuming, straightforward manner spoke of a self-confidence that had no need to impress.

Upon first seeing Max's wife, she'd been surprised, even though Will had told her his cousin said Caroline Ransleigh was not in Max's 'usual style'. She was certainly different from the beautiful, seductive Juliana Von Stenhoff, who'd been Max's mistress at the Congress of Vienna. That lady would never have deigned to greet guests in so simple a gown—nor would she have passed up an opportunity to try to entice a man as handsome as Will.

With that observation, Elodie liked Caroline Ransleigh even better. Though she doubted her hostess would return the favour, once her husband informed her just who she was harbouring under her roof.

Waving her to a seat on the wing chair near the hearth, Caroline Ransleigh turned to direct the footmen who were bringing in a copper tub, while a kitchen maid started a fire. A moment later, a butler appeared to leave a tea tray on the side table and a freckle-faced maid, carrying Elodie's saddlebags, bowed herself in.

'I'll be happy to wash up your things, ma'am,' she said.

'Excellent idea, Dulcie,' Mrs Ransleigh said. 'Having been travelling so long, you probably don't have any clean garments.' She gave Elodie a quick inspection from head to toe. 'You're a bit slighter than I, but we're of a height. You are very welcome to borrow something of mine while your own things are drying.'

A clean gown, one no doubt newer and in better repair than the well-worn few she still possessed! The idea was almost as welcome as a soak in a tub. 'That is most kind of you, Madame Ransleigh, and you, Dulcie.'

The offer confirmed her suspicion that Max's wife, who appeared to be a straightforward woman with no diplomat's artifices, could not know what role she'd played in

Max's life, else she'd be much less accommo-
dating. Feeling guiltily that she ought to ac-
quaint her with the facts before the woman did
her any more kindnesses, she was wondering
just where to begin as her hostess seated herself and poured them each a steaming cup of
tea.

'Here, this will help warm you. Such a raw
day for midsummer! After riding in the damp,
you must be chilled through.'

Murmuring her thanks, Elodie had just
taken a reviving sip when a knock sounded and
an older woman came in, carrying a wrapped
bundle. 'Dulcie said you was in here, Miss
Caro, and that you'd want to tend the young
master as soon as he woke.'

'Andrew, my love!' Her face lighting, Mrs.
Ransleigh reached out to take the bundle—a
closely wrapped, newborn child.

Elodie gasped, her teacup sliding from her
nerveless fingers to clatter against the saucer,
her gaze transfixed on the baby's face.

In a sweeping vortex of memory, she saw
in rapid succession bright dark eyes, a pink
bow mouth and waving arms as the newborn
Philippe surveyed his world. His drunken-
sailor, wobbling steps as he determined, at

nine months, to walk upright. The restless toddler fixing his intent, curious gaze on every object that caught his attention, asking 'What is it? What it do? Why?'

And then the boy she'd left, that intense gaze focused on the soldiers he meticulously arranged in battle formation.

As if lying in wait to ambush her after she had thought she was safely over the worst, the pain of his loss attacked her with the blunt impact of a footpad's club. She couldn't draw breath, couldn't move, could do nothing but stare at Mrs Ransleigh's beautiful child, the very image of all she had lost.

'What is it, *madame*?' Over the roaring in her ears, Elodie dimly heard Mrs Ransleigh's voice, saw her turn to look at her with concern. 'Are you ill?'

Elodie struggled to pull herself together. 'No, no, I am fine, really.' Her fingers shook as she picked up her cup again and took a determined sip.

'You have children, *madame*?'

Elodie nodded. 'I have a son. Had…a son,' she corrected, biting her lip against the urge to weep.

Mrs Ransleigh's face creased in concern and

she hugged her infant tighter. 'He died? How horrible!'

'No, he is alive. But...living in Paris. Another lady looked after him for some years, while I was away. She is wealthy, from an important family. He is happy with her and she can give him many advantages, so I...left him with her.'

'But you miss him,' Mrs Ransleigh said softly.

'With every breath.' A few traitorous tears forced their way to the corners of her eyes. Determinedly, Elodie wiped them away. 'Your Andrew is a handsome child. How old is he?'

'Three weeks today. A lusty lad. His proud papa is already planning his first pony.'

With a pang, Elodie thought of the traitorous toy horse with the glass eyes. 'He may need to wait a few more weeks for that.'

The magnetic power of the newborn still held her. 'May I?' she asked, extending a hand. At the mother's nod, Elodie reached over to stroke the infant's soft cheek. Immediately he turned his mouth towards her, rooting. She gave him her fingertip to suckle.

'Always hungry, too, just like his papa,' her hostess said.

After vigorously sucking for a moment, the baby spat out her fingertip, giving her a mildly indignant look.

Mrs Ransleigh laughed. 'I know that look. I'd better go feed him, before he demonstrates just what a fine pair of lungs he has. Ah, here's your hot water,' she said, as the kitchen maid and two house boys brought in steaming urns of water to pour into the tub, followed by the lady's maid with clean clothing and a towel.

'Ring for me when you're ready, ma'am, and I'll help you into the gown,' Dulcie said, depositing the garments within reach of the tub.

'We'll leave you to your bath.' Mrs Ransleigh rose, cradling her son.

Elodie put a hand on her hostess's arm. 'Treasure every moment with him.'

'I intend to.' About to walk away, Mrs Ransleigh hesitated. 'He's my miracle child. Nearly all the women of my family died in childbed and I almost did, too. So I take nothing for granted. Not Andrew. Not Max. Not the farm and the horses that are my life's blood. They are all precious gifts.'

Elodie smiled. 'You are very wise.'

'Actually, I'm very grateful to you.' At Elodie's startled look, she said, 'Yes, I know who you are and what happened in Vienna. But you see, if Max hadn't been in disgrace after the assassination attempt, I would never have met him. I wouldn't have now the sweetest love a woman could ever desire and the joy of bearing his child. And Max truly is content here.'

With a wife who obviously adored him and a healthy newborn son, Elodie wasn't about to suggest otherwise, but her hostess continued, 'I did try to resist him, you know. I urged him to return to Vienna, to look for you and do everything he could to clear his name and resume his government career. But as he began to work with me, training horses, he discovered he had a real gift for it. He says he's happy with his life here and, of course, I want to believe him.'

It eased her guilt to think that perhaps she hadn't ruined Max's future after all. That their interaction in Vienna had merely sent him down a different path, perhaps an even more rewarding one.

She still intended to do what she could to restore his reputation. For now, he was content training horses, but some day he might long to rejoin the circles of power for which he'd been born and bred. If that happened, she wanted to make sure nothing from their association in Vienna prevented him.

'With a lovely wife and a handsome son, how could he not be content? But I thank you for telling me.'

As if trying to remind his mama of his presence, the newborn squirmed in her arms and gave a preliminary wail.

'My master calls,' Mrs Ransleigh said with a grin. 'Enjoy your bath. We're very informal here, so we dine early. Dulcie will get you anything you need, and then we'll let you rest until dinner.'

With that, shushing the baby with a kiss on the nose, she put him to her shoulder and walked from the room.

Swiftly divesting herself of her grimy clothes, Elodie climbed into the tub and sank with an ecstatic sigh into the hot scented water. Even in the grimmest of times, one should not fail to savour the wonder of a warm bath.

Tired as she was, the water both soothed and made her drowsy. Perhaps, as his wife suggested, Max was no longer angry at being reduced from a rising star of government to a breeder and trainer of horses. What was it he'd said—'everything has changed'?

For the better, she hoped. But she was too weary and the water too deliciously relaxing to contemplate the matter any more. Doubtless Will and Max were discussing it at this very moment. All she need do was be ready, at last, to fulfil the bargain she'd made with Will.

And then see him walk out of her life.

Chapter Nineteen

❦

Will watched Caroline Ransleigh usher Elodie out the parlour door with a panicky feeling in his gut. There'd been no time to reassure her that he didn't suspect she would try to run away. It was just that, after two attacks against her, he didn't feel comfortable about her safety when she was out of his sight.

He turned from the door to see Max studying him and another layer of dread overlay the first. He'd give anything not to have to say to Max what he was about to say. Anything but Elodie's life.

That thought put matters in perspective, so he swallowed hard and looked for a way to begin. The very idea of cutting himself off from his cousins and losing Max's esteem was so painful he'd not been able to bear thinking about or planning what he meant to say, as he normally would have done before broaching a matter of such gravity.

While he stood there, staring at Max and dithering, his cousin shook his head and laughed. 'I should have known if anyone in the world could have turned up Elodie Lefevre—and I gave it more than a go myself—it would be you. A tremendous, and I fear costly, crusade that Alastair said you insisted on funding and carrying out alone. How can I ever convey the depths of my gratitude and appreciation?'

Wonderful—in his very first speech, Max had made him feel even worse. 'I appreciate your kind reception of Elodie; under the same circumstances, I'm not sure I would have been so forbearing.'

'You always were a hothead, faster with your fists than your tongue,' Max observed with a smile.

'You were responsible for teaching me to use my wits instead.'

'I did my poor best.'

'Whatever improvement there is, I owe to your persistence. As for Madame Lefevre, you know the facts of what she did, but you don't know the "why". I think it's important that you do.' *Maybe then you will understand a little better why I'm about to betray you*, he thought.

'Very well, I'm listening. But something tells me the story would be better heard over a glass of port.'

Will didn't object. He'd need all the re-inforcement he could get to force himself through the next half-hour. At the end of which, he would likely be saying goodbye to the best friend he'd ever had.

After a gulp of the fortified wine that warmed him to his toes, Will launched into a halting recitation of how he'd found Madame Lefevre and how she'd become involved in her cousin's plot. But as he began to describe Elodie and her life, the words flowed faster and faster, the stories tumbling out one after another: her childhood trials as an exile, her struggles as a young soldier's wife and then widow, her courageous tenacity in Vienna, when, abandoned by all but her maid after the attack, she found a way to survive, and finally, the return to Paris and the wrenching second loss of her son.

He finished, his glass untouched since his

first sip, to see Max watching him again, that inscrutable, assessing gaze on his face.

'A remarkable woman,' Max said.

Will nodded. 'Yes, she is.' *Now for the difficult, agonising part.* 'Max, you know better than I how much I owe you. I promised Alastair I would find Elodie, bring her back to England and make her tell the Foreign Office how she'd involved you in the plot, corroborating your account of the affair. So your reputation might be restored at last, along with the possibility of resuming the government career to which you've aspired as long as I've known you. But…but if she goes to London and the authorities open an official investigation, she could well be imprisoned as an accomplice to an attempt on Lord Wellington's life. Maybe even hung. I can't let her do that.'

Max frowned. 'Are you sure? If her testimony cleared my name, I might indeed be able to revive my government career. There would be no limit to my gratitude! I don't know how you mean to get on, now that you've resigned your army commission. Papa should have made you an allowance when you returned, but…' Max grimaced '…no great surprise that he'd conveniently forget his promise. If I'm in London, Caro will need help here. She'd never give up the stud; breeding horses is in her blood. You could take my place as manager, be the go-between at Newmarket, take a percentage of the sales. She raises excellent horses; it would pay well. You could have a comfortable position for life, accumulate enough to buy property of your own, if you wished. Become a "landed Ransleigh" at last.'

'Thereby finally earning your father's respect?' Will said derisively. 'Though I thank you for the offer, as it happens, I've accumulated sufficient funds on my own. And even if I hadn't, I'd never bargain for Elodie's life.'

Max's frown deepened. 'You obviously care for this woman. Does she return the favour?'

Will swallowed hard. 'I'm not sure. She's fond of me, I know. But…losing her son again has devastated her. I don't think she's capable of feeling anything now.'

'She's "fond" of you,' Max repeated, a bit dismissively. 'You would betray your oath to me for a woman who you're not even sure loves you, or has any appreciation of the consequences of your dishonouring your pledge?'

Trust Max to strip fine rhetoric down to

its bare essentials. Unpalatable as it was, that was truth. 'Yes.'

To Will's utter shock, Max gave a crow of laughter. 'So, it's happened at last! Wagering Will's bet was called by a lady with a better hand.'

Sobering quickly, he clapped a hand on Will's shoulder. 'As I said at the outset, I can't begin to express my appreciation and admiration for all you've done, going to Vienna to find *madame* and bringing her back. I'm not sure any man deserves such loyalty. But you needn't risk the life of the woman you've come to love.'

'So, you're…not angry?' Will asked, amazed, too rattled by Max's unexpected response to dare believe it to be true. 'Then why did you try to tempt me with a position here?'

'From the look on your face when you spoke of Madame Lefevre and how protectively you hovered around her, I suspected you loved her. I've never seen you that way with any other woman. But I wanted to discover just how deeply the attachment ran. True, I might not always have felt so forgiving towards her. After Vienna I was angry, dismayed, disbelieving. My world and the future I'd always dreamed of had been destroyed and I didn't think I'd ever be content or fulfilled again. But then I met Caro. Worked with her. Fell in love with her and the farm. I have what I want now, Will. I think, in Elodie Lefevre, you have what you want, too. Am I right?'

'Would I have abandoned my vow for any other reason?'

Max nodded. 'I thought as much. I suppose I recognised the devotion; I feel the same about Caro, as if I'd battle the whole world to keep her safe. Give up the rest of the world, if that were the price of keeping her.'

'Then you do understand. But you know your Caroline loves you. I'm not sure what Elodie feels or wants. I planned to take her away to the Americas, where she'd be safe, but I'm not even sure she'll go with me. When she lost her son after directing all her efforts for nearly two years towards reclaiming him, it was as if she felt her whole life was over.'

'I can appreciate her grief and despair. I thought losing the career I loved the greatest tragedy that could befall me...until Caro had difficulty in childbed and I almost...' his voice broke for a moment '...I almost lost her and my son. I can't imagine how one recovers from such a blow. But as I understand it, Madame Lefevre's son isn't dead, so surely there is some hope of seeing him again?'

'Yes, I'm examining some possibilities, but they'll take time to work out. Grieving as she is, I don't want to propose anything; if the plans went awry, I don't know how she would bear another disappointment.'

'She'll need time to heal. I did, and I lost only the career I thought I wanted, not the persons most dear to me. Teach her there is still beauty and fulfilment in life.' He grinned. 'And that you can provide them.'

'I'm not sure I know where to begin,' Will admitted. I don't even know if she'll agree to stay with me, once she learns we won't be taking her to the Foreign Office. I wouldn't put it past her to disappear in the night, thinking she offers me nothing and I'd be better off starting anew, without her.'

'Is she that elusive?'

Will thought of how she'd loved him to satiation and then slipped away. 'Oh, yes.'

'If you love her that much, surely you're not going to despair of winning her before you've even begun! I've seen you beguile women from blushing dairymaids to bored *ton* beauties. I can't imagine you're not capable of be-guiling a lady you actually love. True, trying to win her is a gamble. But Wagering Will never met a bet he wouldn't take. Comfort her, stand by her and marry her.'

Will sighed. 'I want to, but what do I know about being a husband, creating a family?'

'I thought your cousins taught you a good bit. My father, you remember, wasn't much of a model, either. But then, when you hold your wife's hand while she brings your child into the world, then touch his perfect, tiny hands…' A sense of awe and wonder passed over Max's face. 'I can assure you, the rewards of fight-ing for a life with the woman you love far out-weigh the risks of failing.'

How Will wanted that, too, a life with Elo-die, her lovely face finally freed from the shad-ows of pain and sorrow! He hadn't thought beyond the dread of this interview and the ne-cessity of making all speed to catch a ship to the colonies. Now, buoyed by Max's encour-agement, Will started rapidly examining other alternatives.

Winning Elodie's heart, forging a life here… with his cousins nearby. In time, perhaps, giv-ing her another child to cherish, a complement to the one she'd already borne with whom, if the scheme Will was pondering came to fruition, she would forge a new relationship.

'There is another property I've had my eye on, over in Sussex,' he said, running a vision of it through his mind's eye. 'It has a wonderful garden.'

Max raised his eyebrows. 'Another property? Just how many do you own?'

Will grinned. 'Not as many as Alastair or your family, but several. What, you think I just frittered away all my gambling winnings? You remember Hal Waterman, from Eton?'

'That large, inarticulate lad who'd never be lured into playing cards because, he said, the odds were always in the dealer's favour? A sort of mathematical genius, as I recall.'

'Yes. Two misfits, he and I, who later banded together. I happened to meet him in London after Oxford, when I'd had my first really big win at faro. He said if I liked gambling, he could recommend something for which the odds were as risky as gaming, but the potential rewards much greater. Not just in blunt, but in forging the future of the nation. Turns out he's fascinated by finance and technology, and with that limitless fortune of his, has begun exploring the opportunities to invest in new scientific developments. He talked me into putting almost all the blunt I'd won at faro into a canal-construction project he'd put together. With the earnings from that, I bought my first property. I'm also invested in coal mines, mechanical stoves and what Hal claims will be a system that will revolutionise transport, the railroad.'

Max shook his head. 'Does my father know?'

Will laughed. 'Know that his barely civilised, reprobate nephew has become a man of means without his will or intervention? Certainly not! The shock could probably kill him.'

Max chuckled. 'It might at that.'

'However, manufacturing and commerce are close enough to vulgar middle-class shop-keeping that if he does learn of it, I'm sure he'll manage to maintain his disdain.'

'You could have told the Rogues,' Max reproved.

'I would have, had the war and…other projects not intervened.'

'So you're a man of means.' Max shook his head ruefully. 'It's almost as hard for me as for Papa to think you no longer need my help.'

'I'll always need your friendship.'

'That, you'll always have. So, go buy your manor. Would you like us to watch over your Elodie until you return? I must admit, the story you've told piques my curiosity. I liked her when I knew her in Vienna. I'd very much enjoy becoming better acquainted with the remarkable woman who performed so many amazing feats. Not the least of which was capturing my elusive cousin's heart.'

'Would you let her stay here and watch out for her? Although...' Will hesitated, trying to guess how his complex, devious Elodie might react. 'I know it's not fair to keep the knowledge from her, but could we let her go on believing that a visit to the Foreign Office is forthcoming? Not that you need to tell any deliberate mistruths, just be evasive, if she asks directly. I don't think she will. She's committed enough to making recompense for the harm she did you in Vienna that if she thinks I've left Denby Lodge to make preparations for London, she'll not...wander off before I return. It will also give me a chance to think how best to woo her.'

'I may now be a horse breeder, but I'm still a diplomat at heart; I can finesse anything. Especially if it involves the happiness of my dearest friend. So, if you're not going to linger at Denby—and while you're still muddy and smelling of horse—let me give you a quick tour of the stables and stock. My world now.'

'Do you not miss being involved in government?' Will asked, still finding it hard to believe Max could have abandoned so completely the goal that had driven him for as long as Will had known him.

'The idea that I am working for something larger than myself? A bit. But the back-biting and intrigues of those whose mindless ambition far outweighs their concern for the public good? Not at all. I have considered perhaps some day standing for Parliament. Being elected by the men of the district whose respect I've won, whom I respect in turn, giving voice to their concerns in the halls of power, is a more worthy task than what I would now be doing, had Vienna not intervened. Lurking about the Lords, a lackey for my father.'

'Standing for Parliament is an excellent idea.'

'Well, we shall see. For now, I'm just grateful for the blessings of being able to watch my son grow and spend every day—and night—with my wife.'

'So…' Max raised his glass, motioning Will to pick up his own '…to your safe return. To finding love, and cherishing it. To Ransleigh Rogues.'

Now that he was recovering from the shock of realising he would not lose Max's friendship after all, Will felt a rising euphoria and an eagerness for the future he hadn't known since that moment he'd awakened before Paris, marvelling at the peace he'd found in Elodie's arms.

'To all of that,' he replied. 'And to "Ransleigh Rogues, for ever".'

Chapter Twenty

Two weeks later, on a mild summer afternoon, Elodie sat embroidering her new gown in a beam of sunlight in the front parlour at Denby Lodge. Strange, she thought as she methodically set small, perfect stitches, that she was now marking time awaiting the trip to London as she'd spent the hours before leaving Vienna. But instead of longing and anticipation, she passed her days numb and drifting, the only small joy on her horizon the hope to see Will Ransleigh again before the final resolution.

She did wish Will had taken her with him when he left to consult with the authorities about setting up her interview. After he returned, there would be very little time left to share with him. It would take them a few days at most to travel back to the metropolis before she gave her testimony, that end of the road beyond which she could envision nothing further.

Dull as her spirits still were, she missed him. His acute observations, his teasing eye, his stories…and the surcease from sorrow she found in his arms, when he loved her so sweetly and completely that nothing, not even anguish and loss, could tarnish the bliss. She'd hoped he would come to her some time during the one night he spent at Denby Lodge before leaving for London, but he hadn't.

The day of his departure had dawned all the more dreary for that lack.

Surprised at first that Max Ransleigh had not gone with Will to instigate the proceedings, she'd thought he must want to consult with her about the now-distant events in Vienna, so her account of it, when she at last spoke to the authorities, would reinforce what he'd told them of the affair. But to her bewilderment, he had not sought her out in private to quiz her about her memories, nor had he referred to the matter in any way when in company.

Her host and hostess had insisted she dine with them, and though Max had initiated several discussions of Vienna, their object seemed more to entertain Caro than corroborate what she remembered. He described some of the most notable balls and receptions they'd attended, asking her to share her recollections, or else he traded impressions with her about the colourful array of notables and hangers-on who'd attended the Congress.

Perhaps he didn't wish to distress his wife, who was still recovering from her confinement, by referring to the scandal. Elodie's initial favourable impression of Caroline Ransleigh had quickly deepened to a friendship she would sorely miss when the time came to leave for London. Not since Clara in Vienna had Elodie had a female friend with whom she could converse freely, and growing up an exile with no sisters, she hadn't ever had a confidante from her same level in society.

Though Caro insisted she might borrow any garments she liked, not used to being idle, Elodie had asked Max to sell one of the small pieces of jewellery she'd carried with her, so she might purchase material to make herself some garments. Accompanying Caro to the village, she'd bought several dress lengths, and was now completing the second of two stylish gowns.

In addition to the sewing keeping her occupied, she thought that, if she wished the officials at the enquiry to find it credible that she had been the hostess of a high-ranking French diplomat at the most glittering assemblage of aristocrats and government leaders ever gathered in Europe, she couldn't appear in one of her tattered old gowns, looking like a rag picker.

If prison were the outcome, she might be able to sell the new garments to obtain the coal and candles that would make her existence less miserable. And, if the worst happened, at least she'd have something attractive to be buried in.

At that moment, her hostess entered the parlour with her characteristic, brisk step. 'Elodie, what exquisite work!' she exclaimed, coming over to inspect her embroidery. 'I can easily believe an exclusive Vienna modiste clamoured for you to embellish her gowns.'

'Hardly "clamoured",' Elodie replied. 'But she did pay me promptly and rather well for a seamstress.'

'I'm so hopeless, I can't sew a stitch! I ought to commission you to make some gowns for me. I've never cared two figs what I wore, as long as it was modest and serviceable, but now that I'm regaining my figure…' A blush heated her cheeks. 'I'd like to have something new to intrigue my husband and remind me I'm more than just a mama.'

'Something that shows to advantage that fine mama's bosom,' Elodie teased, smiling when Caro's blush deepened. 'I would be happy to make you something, if I have time enough before I leave.'

A shadow crossed Caro's face. 'I do wish you didn't have to go. But I don't mean to speak of that, for it will only make me melancholy, and heavens, it seems lately the merest nothing has me wanting to burst into tears! Me, who has never in her life been missish,' she finished with disgust.

'It goes with becoming a mama,' Elodie said.

'The nursery maid is just finishing Andrew's bath. Shall I bring him down?'

'Please do! I've been working on a gown for him, too.'

'You're sure? Sometimes I worry that seeing him must make it…more difficult for you.'

'I should miss Philippe every day, even if I

never saw another child. But a baby should be a joy. Not for the world would I want yours to diminish, because of my loss! It lifts my spirits to see you with him and know that such happiness still exists in the world. Besides, who could resist such a handsome charmer as your son?'

Caro beamed. 'He is handsome, isn't he? And demanding. Which is good. If I didn't have him to occupy me, I don't know how I would bear the inactivity. I know the doctor said I must not ride for another two weeks, but I'm feeling perfectly fine and cannot wait to get back to my horses!'

'Go get your son and we'll let him entertain us,' Elodie said.

Smiling, she went back to her stitching. She'd not just reassured her new friend to ease her anxiety; she did enjoy seeing the child. Holding and playing with the infant, recalling as it did memories of happier times with Philippe, always lifted her spirits and eased the dull anxiety that sat like a boulder in her gut, an ever-present worry over a future she didn't want to envision.

What if they only interviewed and then released her? Though she tried to keep herself from contemplating anything beyond that meeting in London, occasionally speculation about a different, better resolution crept into her thoughts.

What was she to do with herself if she did not end up in prison or on the gallows? Though she knew her new friend would invite her to stay indefinitely at Denby Lodge, she didn't wish to be a burden. Perhaps she could get lodgings in London and find employment as a seamstress. Rich women would always need new gowns.

There was no question of returning to Paris. The Ransleigh name might command the attention—and protection—of the Prime Minister and the respect of Prince Talleyrand, but Elodie Lefevre, her brother dead and his rising career with him, was no longer of any importance. Besides, sojourning in the same city that contained her son, but unable to be with him, would be a torment beyond enduring.

So, London it must be. Unless…unless Will wanted her. They had been excellent comrades on the road and passionate lovers. Perhaps he would keep her as his mistress for a while, until he tired of her. Such a handsome, charismatic man would make any woman who set eyes on him try to entice him; it wouldn't take Will Ransleigh long to find another lover to share his bed.

As the door opened, she looked up, expecting to see Caro and her babe. Instead, the object of her imaginings walked in.

'Will, you're back!' she cried, jumping up. Within the dull empty expanse of her chest, her moribund heart gave a small leap of gladness.

She couldn't seem to take her eyes from his face as he approached her, smiling faintly, his sheer physical allure striking her as forcefully as it had that first day.

'Sewing again, I see,' he said. 'Just like when I found you in Vienna.'

Was he thinking of their first meeting, too? 'Although this time, you enter, quite boringly, by the door, rather than thrillingly through a window.'

'I see I am failing in my duty as a rogue. I shall have to redeem myself.'

It seemed the most natural thing in the world to walk into the arms he held out to her, to lift her face for his kiss.

He took her mouth gently, but she met him ardently. With a stifled groan, he clutched her tighter, deepening the kiss. She moulded herself to him, her body fitting his like a puzzle piece sliding into place.

After a moment, he broke the kiss, his turquoise eyes dark. 'Does that mean you've missed me?'

'I have. I feel…' At home? At peace? As content as it was possible for her to be? 'Safe when you're near,' she finished.

His expression grew serious. 'And I mean to keep you that way.'

'Must we leave at once for London? I…I had promised Caro to make her a new gown.'

'She has treated you well?'

'Very well. We so very quickly became friends, I shall miss her when we leave for London.'

'We're not going to London.'

'Not going?' Elodie echoed, puzzled. 'Is the Foreign Office allowing me to give a deposition here, rather than testifying in person?'

'No deposition. No testimony at all. I don't want to risk it.'

She shook her head, more confused than ever. 'But what of Monsieur Max? How is his name to be cleared, if I do not testify? What of his career?'

'Max is quite happy with the career—and the family—he has at Denby Lodge. And if, in future, he has a longing to return to government, he means to go on his own merits, elected to Parliament by the men of this district, not relying on the prestige of his family or the patronage of some high official.'

'This is truth? You are sure?'

'Absolutely sure.'

She would not have to testify. After girding herself for that trial for so long, she could scarcely comprehend she would not be facing the looming spectre of prison or the noose. Dizzy and disoriented with relief, she stumbled to the sofa. 'What is to become of me, then?'

Will seated himself beside her, took her hands and tilted her chin up to face him, his gaze intent. Taking a deep breath, he said, 'I want to take care of you, Elodie. I love you. I want you with me.'

'My sweet Will,' she whispered, freeing a hand to stroke his cheek. 'I want you, too. For as long as you'll have me, I am yours.'

'I want you in my life always, Elodie. I want to marry you.'

'Marry me?' Never in her wildest imaginings had the possibility of marriage occurred to her. 'But that is not at all sensible!' she exclaimed, her practical French mind recoiling from a union of two persons of such dissimilar resources. 'I bring you nothing, no dowry, no family, no influence. You don't have to marry me, Will. I will stay with you as long as you wish.'

'But you can't be sure of that with a mistress. One night, she shows you the moon and the stars, gives you bliss beyond imagining. And the next morning, poof, she is gone, without a word of farewell.'

Feeling a pang of guilt, Elodie looked at him reprovingly. 'That was under very different circumstances, as you well know.'

'What I know is that all my life, I've been missing something, here.' He tapped his chest. 'But in your arms that night outside Paris, I found what I didn't even know I'd been searching for. I felt…complete. I don't want to ever lose that again.'

He stared at her intently, as if waiting for her to reply in kind. She felt a strong bond, something deeper than just the physical, but within her broken and battered heart all was confusion. Better to say nothing than to profess a love she wasn't sure she felt, or wound him by admitting how uncertain she was.

Instead, she shook her head. 'You can have that. It is not necessary, this marriage.'

He drew back a bit, and she knew she'd hurt him, much as she'd wanted to avoid it. 'I know I'm only the illegitimate son of a rogue, while you are the daughter of French aristocracy—'

'Oh, no!' she interrupted him. 'How can you believe I think myself above you? I am the daughter of French aristocrats, yes, but one who has no home, no title, no influential family, no wealth. It is you who are above me, a man linked to a rich and prominent family that still wields great power.'

That seemed to reassure him, for the pain in his eyes receded and he kissed her hands. 'I want to marry you, Elodie de Montaigu-Clisson, whether you can ever love me or not. But don't give me a final answer now. So much has changed since Vienna. You've lost the hope that sustained you for so long and must grieve for that. You need time to reflect, to heal and find consolation, before you can move forwards. I want you to take that time. Will you come with me, let me take care of you? I pledge to keep you safe, so safe that one day you'll stop looking over your shoulder, worried about being followed or threatened. Come with no obligation but friendship. And when you feel ready to begin your life again… if I must, I'll let you go. No force, no bargains.'

Elodie felt tears prick her eyes. She couldn't let him commit the idiocy of tying himself legally to a woman who brought him nothing in worldly advantage, but she would stay with him as long as he'd have her.

'No force, no bargains,' she agreed. 'I go with you willingly and will stay as long as you want me.'

'That would be for ever, then,' Will said and bent to kiss her.

Chapter Twenty-One

On a sunny morning a month later, Elodie strolled through the vast garden at Salmford House. Taking a seat on one of the conveniently located benches with a view of the rose parterre, where the potent, drifting scent of the Autumn Damask 'Quatre Saisons' never failed to soothe her, she smiled.

Her enjoyment of it this morning was just as intense as it had been the afternoon Will first brought her to the property he'd purchased near Firle on the South Downs of Sussex, a lovely land of rolling hills and meadows. After touring her through the snug stone manor and introducing her to the staff, he'd led her out the French doors from the library into the first section of walled garden.

Her reactions of surprise and delight had been repeated many times over as he strolled her through each garden 'room', from the topiary terrace adjoining the library with its precisely clipped boxwood and yew, to the white garden of iris, daisies, sweet alyssum, campanula and snapdragons, the multi-hued perennial border backed by red-leaved berberis, to the artfully arranged herb-and-vegetable knot garden adjoining the kitchen and finally to the central rose parterre, where the 'Old Blush' and damask roses were still blooming after the albas and gallicas had ended their early summer show.

As he'd coaxed her reluctantly to return to the house for an early dinner, saying he, for one, was famished, she'd thrown her arms around him and kissed him soundly. 'What a magnificent garden!' she exclaimed.

'When I was considering where to bring you, I remembered the agent showing me this property. Is it as lovely as the garden of Lord Somerville?'

'Oh, yes, and larger, too! Did you truly choose this house for me?'

'You have had enough of sadness in your

life, Elodie. I want you to be happy.' He tapped her nose. 'Clara made me promise.'

'Oh, thank you, my sweet Will! Only one thing under heaven could make me happier.'

But when she took his arm going back to the house and murmured in his ear that she could show him just how grateful she was, pressing herself against him suggestively, he eased her away from him and primly repeated what he'd told her on the drive to Salmford House; that here, they would be friends only, not lovers.

She hadn't believed him, of course, for the idea of refraining from enjoying the powerful passion they shared made no more sense to her than an English aristocrat from a prominent family marrying a penniless exile.

She was not at all happy to discover he'd not been teasing. 'Why, Will? I give myself freely, for your pleasure and mine. Why do you not want such a gift?'

'Oh, I want you—with every breath. But when I make love to you again, I want it to be with you as my wife.'

She sighed in exasperation. 'Is it not the woman who is supposed to withhold her favours until the man succumbs to marriage?'

'Usually, yes. But you see, I'm enamoured of

a very stubborn, peculiar female—the French are often stubborn and peculiar, I find—and persuading her to marry me calls for desperate measures. Passion can be very persuasive, so why should I not dangle before her one of my most potent weapons in securing her consent?' He sighed, too. 'Though, in truth, this remedy is so desperate, it may kill me. But were we not true friends and companions on the road, without being lovers?'

'Yes, but only at first, when our disguises prevented it. And we are not on the road now, but in a *hôtel* of the most fine, with, I am sure, beds of quite amazing comfort.'

'You are distressed. I can always tell; your speech becomes more French.'

'Of course I am distressed. This…this show of chastity is ridiculous!'

'Well, as long as there's a chance this "ridiculousness" might help convince you to become my wife, I am content to wait.'

'It may convince me you are an *imbécile*. And I am not content to wait!' she declared, stamping her foot, frustrated and furious with him, the surge of emotion seizing her the strongest she'd experienced since the loss of Philippe had paralysed all feeling.

'Calm down, *chérie*!' he soothed. 'You need diversion.'

'Yes, and I know just what sort,' she flashed back.

'So do I. A hand of cards after we've dined should do the trick.'

She'd whacked his arm and stomped away, leaving him to follow her to the dining parlour, chuckling. But she couldn't stay angry, as he coaxed her with fine ham, an assortment of fresh vegetables from the garden, aged cheese, rich wine, followed by strawberries and cream, which he fed her with his own hands, rubbing the ripe berries against her lips and then kissing the flavour from them, until she was certain he was going to relent.

Instead of leading her to a bedchamber—by then she would have been quite content with a sofa or even a soft carpet—he handed her into the parlour and produced a deck of cards.

At first, angry with him again, she'd refused to play. But he'd teased and dared, finally winning her grudging agreement by accusing her of avoiding a hand because she was afraid she'd lose.

Within a few minutes, tantalising her with his skill, he'd drawn her into the game. She'd watched him play enough to know he was not trying to let her win, but challenging her to exercise all her skill, which made her redouble her concentration. Interspersed with the hands, he set her to laughing with outrageous observations about the people and events they'd encountered on their travels. When the clock struck midnight and he gathered up the cards, she was surprised to find the hour so late.

It was the most carefree evening she'd spent in years. And she hadn't thought once of her loss.

The yearning returned as he walked her to a bedchamber. She clung to him, trying to entice him to remain with her.

'Marry me,' he'd whispered against her hair as he held her close. 'Marry me, *mon ange*, and be mine for ever.'

When she'd tremulously replied that she couldn't, he'd sighed and gently set her away from him. And then bid her goodnight.

That same frustrating routine had recurred each night of their stay here.

Though he'd laughed at her anger, teased her, given her deep, thrilling kisses as if he meant to relent, he had not. To her extreme irritation and regret, they continued to live as chastely as brother and sister.

She'd thought about slipping into his chamber and into his bed, pleasuring him with her hands and mouth, when, groggy with sleep and tempted by arousal, he would surely yield to her. For the first few nights, she talked herself out of it, worried about embarrassing herself if she were wrong and he refused her still, even in his bed.

By the time they'd been at the manor for a week, she'd grown too desperate to worry about embarrassment. In the early hours of the morning, unable to sleep, she'd crept through the silent house to his chamber—and found the door locked against her.

The following morning, grumpy from sleeplessness and frustration, she'd sulkily enquired if he thought she were dangerous, that he must lock himself away from her. He'd replied that he was not so much of a fool as to subject himself to a temptation he knew he'd never be able to resist, a reply which mollified her somewhat, though it did nothing to relieve the frustration.

But for that one—and very major—fault, Will had been a perfect companion. He had encouraged her to take him on walks through her beloved garden, telling him the names of all the plants—and later making her laugh by deliberately bungling them. Noticing how she loved to linger in the rose parterre, breathing in the potent scent of the autumn damasks, he had bouquets of the spicy blooms put in every room.

As she gradually began to emerge from the cocoon of grief into which she'd spun herself, it was impossible not to notice his cherishing care of her. Some might have found it suffocating, but Elodie, who had experienced precious little cherishing in her tumultuous life, drank up the attention and concern.

Sitting here now, she recalled all the ways he'd seen to her comfort. Foods she mentioned liking would appear regularly on the table. When she thanked him for a new gown in blue or azure or gold, several more of similar style and hue appeared in her wardrobe.

He even found her, heaven knows where, a little French girl to be her lady's maid. Chatting with the homesick lass in their native French tongue helped ease the sadness within her at the loss of her home and language.

Whatever activity he engaged with her in, whether cards or riding or billiards, he roused her from her recurrent bouts of melancholy by teasing her or cheating her back to attention—or indignation. Sometimes, in the evenings, he read to her, surprising her with the wide-ranging breadth of his knowledge and interests. He talked about his friend, Hal Waterman, and the fascinating new technologies they were investing in that would, he told her, eventually change the way people heated their homes, cooked their food and travelled.

Methodically, slow day by slow day, he was drawing her out of the greyness of grief and death back into the light of his life. Letting her bask in the brilliant warmth of his love.

She hadn't earned such devotion, probably didn't deserve it, but he gave it freely anyway. Wanting, in return, only her happiness.

For the first time in a long time, anticipation stirred in her. What was wrong with her, moping about as if her life were over? Yes, she'd lost her child, a tragedy whose pain would never fully leave her. But along the way, she'd found a matchless lover, who was trying by every means he could devise to woo her and win her love in return.

Almost every day, he repeated his request

that she marry him and share his life. And then, praise heaven, his bed!

Will being normally an intense, restless man, she was astounded that he had managed to content himself staying placidly here, doing nothing more exciting than riding in the countryside and playing cards with her. Surely he was ready to go off exploring new places, investigating new projects. He'd said he longed for her to come with him and share the excitement, companions on the road again.

A sense of wonder and enthusiasm filled her. Salmford House's gardens and Will's tender care had worked their magic. She was, she decided in that moment, now ready to put her losses behind her and start living again—with Will.

Suddenly, she couldn't wait to see him.

Picking up her skirts, she rushed back into the manor, hurrying from room to room until she found him in the library.

He looked up as she entered, his handsome face lighting in a smile, and her healing heart leapt. How could she not flourish in the brightness of that smile? In such tenderness, as she leaned down for his kiss and he caressed her cheek with one gentle finger?

She'd been a fool, not for the first time. It was time to be foolish no longer.

'Are you ready for luncheon, *chérie*?' she said. 'I'm famished.'

Smiling up at Elodie, Will twisted in his hands the letter he'd received in the morning's post. The position he'd discussed with his friend Hal Waterman had been arranged; in the letter was his authorisation to go to Paris and enter discussions with the French Ministry of the Interior about the possibilities of developing railway lines in France.

Hal had pledged considerable financial backing to make the venture happen and tapped his network of influential contacts to persuade the British government to approve Will for the task and to give the endeavour their support. The challenge of persuading the French government to permit the work was exhilarating and Will would need to leave almost immediately.

He wanted Elodie to go with him—as his wife. They'd grown so much closer over the last month. Several times, the tender light in her eyes as she gazed at him had sent his hopes winging to dizzying heights, sure that he'd won her at last and she was about to confess her love.

But thus far, that hadn't happened. And now, if he was to put into motion the scheme he'd been devising ever since they left Paris, he would have to tell her of his plans and propose again, even if he wasn't sure of her love.

He wanted her to marry him because she'd realised she loved him and could not imagine spending the rest of her life without him, not because doing so would allow her to be reunited with her son. Even if she did come to love him later, he would never be able to trust that she loved him for himself, not out of gratitude for his ingenuity in bringing her son back into her life.

But he knew, if he must, he would marry her on those terms. Loving her as he did, he couldn't withhold from her the one thing she wanted most in the world because he hadn't had the good fortune to secure her love in return.

Dropping the letter, he rose to take her arm. She danced around him as she took it, mischief sparkling in her eyes.

His heart turned over to see it, as it always did when she looked happy. He knew a reserve of sadness would always remain with her, but it delighted him to see her look so carefree. It was deeply satisfying to know he'd played a vital part in banishing the shadows from her eyes.

From the naughty glances she was giving him, she was probably plotting to seduce him again. Maybe this time, he'd let her. Heaven knows, resisting her was about to drive him mad.

There wasn't enough cold water in the lake beyond their meadow to cool his ardour for his bewitching Elodie, and he'd been swimming at least twice daily. He'd lasted nearly a month without her managing to break his resolve, far longer than he'd thought he could.

'I'm glad to see you have an appetite, sprite. For so long, you have only toyed with your food.'

'Oh, I have quite an appetite today.' Turning suddenly to push him against the bookshelves, she said, 'Shall I show you how much?'

Anticipation roared through his veins. If tempting her to agree to marriage by withholding passion hadn't worked by now, knowing the proposal he was about to make would contain a temptation she wouldn't be able to resist, why not give up the futile fight and let her have her way with him?

He kissed her hungrily, opening willingly when she slipped her busy tongue inside his mouth. He groaned, pulling her against his hardness.

With a little mewing sound, she reached down to stroke him, and this time he didn't catch her wrists to prevent her. What crack-brained notion had made him deny himself this? he wondered, revelling in her touch.

He returned the favour, caressing her breasts through the fine muslin of her gown and light summer stays, until her breath came in gasps as short as his own.

Picking her up, Will kicked the door closed. It had been too long; desperate for the taste of her, he couldn't possibly wait the few minutes it would take him to carry her up to his bed-chamber. The desk would have to do.

In a few quick strides, he reached it and set her on the solid mahogany surface, kissing her ravenously as he slid her skirts up and peeled her stockings down, smoothing the soft skin as he bared it. After working the muslin up to her waist, he parted her legs and knelt before her.

His thumbs teasing the curls at her hot, wet

centre, he kissed the tender skin of her inner thighs, tracking up the velvet softness until his tongue met his fingers and he applied the rasp of it to the swollen bud within.

Gasping, she writhed under him, until a very few minutes later reaching her peak. His fingers still caressing her, he took her cries of ecstasy on his lips, then carried her, limp and pliant, to the sofa and cradled her on his lap.

'Oh, my sweet Will, how I've missed you!'

'And I you, *ma douce.*'

'My love, I've been such a fool and you've been so patient with me! I am of a slowness quite remarkable, but finally, finally, I understand. Can you forgive me for being so stupid, clinging to my grief like a child with a broken toy, too stubborn to let it go? But I shall be stupid no longer.'

His heart leapt. Could she mean what he hoped she did? Trying to restrain the hope and excitement bubbling up within him, he said, 'What are you trying to tell me, *chérie?*'

'That no one has ever cared for or loved me like you. Why I have been so fortunate to have received this gift of wonder, I do not know, but my heart rejoices and I love you with everything in me. I want to belong to you for always, be your companion on your adventures and in your bed. I want to be your wife, and though I still believe it is most nonsensical of you to throw yourself away on so undeserving a woman, I shall accept quickly now, before you recover and change your mind. So, will you marry me, prince of my heart? *Parce que je t'aime*, Will. *Avec tout mon coeur.*'

He'd dreamed of hearing her say those words for so long, he could scarcely believe she really had. 'Truly, *mon ange*? You love me with all your heart?'

'Well, with my body, too, as soon as you'll let me. And from this position…' she wiggled on his lap, rubbing her soft bottom against his hardness '…I am thinking you are ready for me to do so immediately.'

He knew he was probably grinning like the imbecile she'd once called him, but he didn't care. 'Not just yet, in spite of my need. Perhaps tonight, though, if you'll excuse me so I can collect the special licence I brought back from London with me and go to the village to find the rector. If he's available, he can come back and marry us at once. That is, unless you'd like a new gown, or want to plan a ceremony with Max and Caro—'

She stopped his words with a fingertip. 'They can give us a party later. By all means, find the vicar and bring him back at once. I want to be your wife by tonight.'

'I'll kidnap him, if necessary. We've much to discuss tomorrow, but tonight I want to be in your arms.'

Chapter Twenty-Two

The next morning, Will awoke in his bedchamber at Salmford House tired, well loved
and with a euphoric sense of well-being that
glowed all the brighter when he opened his
eyes to see his wife's silky head pillowed on
his shoulder.

His wife. He grinned, loving the sound of
the words. Fortunately, since he would rather
not have had charges brought against him for
kidnapping on the eve of his departure for
an official mission to France, the vicar had
thought his request to wed them immediately
romantic rather than foolhardy. Gathering his
prayer book, he'd hastened to accompany Will
back to Salmford House, where the staff, along

with the blushing French maid, witnessed the marriage and the signing of the parish register.

He wanted to wake up like this, with Elodie in his arms, for the rest of his days, Will thought, bending to give her a kiss.

Her eyes fluttering open, she smiled sleepily at him. 'Can it be daylight already?'

'It's halfway through the morning, slug-abed.'

'Well, when one has spent hours attending with much concentration to long-delayed and important work, one becomes exhausted.'

He chuckled. 'I think I fell in love with you the moment "Uncle Fritz" limped on his cane into that inn, the night we left Vienna.'

She traced a finger from his shoulders to his chest. 'I lusted after you from the moment you launched yourself from the balcony into my room. But I never appreciated in full measure how wonderful you are until after...after Paris. I thought my life over, that I would never experience joy again. Until with patience, care and tenderness, you taught me I was wrong. You say your cousin Max saved your life; you have given mine back.'

It was a good opening and he took it. 'I'd

like to do more. Are you ready to go travelling?'

She shifted up on the pillows to face him, looking so delectably mussed and seductive that only the gravity of what he must discuss with her kept him from pulling her back into his arms and making love to her all over again.

'You have a trip arranged?' she asked while he curbed his amorous appetites. 'To investigate one of those investments you've been telling me about?'

'Yes. This one will be to Paris.'

The excitement faded from her eyes. 'No, Will, please. Anywhere but Paris. I don't think I could bear it.'

'Nor do I, Elodie. It isn't right that your son was snatched from under your nose and you were prevented from reclaiming him. No, hear me out,' he said, forestalling the protest he could see she was about to make. 'Remember, you are no longer Elodie Lefevre, a woman with no home and no family. Elodie Ransleigh is wife to a man of considerable wealth, whose relations, I have it on respected authority, are rich, prominent and wield a good deal of power.'

Though she still looked troubled, he could

tell she was cautiously weighing his words. 'What do you intend to do?'

'I've been given an official mission, sanctioned by the British Foreign Office and arranged and financed by my friend Hal Waterman, to approach the French government about the possibilities of constructing a railroad. So not only will you return to Paris as the wife of a wealthy, well-connected man, but one who will be entertained at the highest levels of government.'

'And that will benefit me…how?'

'While in Paris discharging the mission, we will call on the Comtesse de la Rocherie and propose a bargain. It is true, as you said before, that Philippe doesn't remember you and considers the comtesse to be his *maman*. So we won't demand that she give him up—yet. For the moment, we will insist only that you are allowed to become reacquainted with him. I expect this business regarding the railroad will take some time; if it should terminate more quickly than expected, I have other interests that can keep me in France.'

She pushed herself to sit upright against the pillows, joy and hope, anguish and doubt warring in her face. 'Are you sure, *mon amant*? You really think it is possible?'

'I do. Once Philippe knows you better and is comfortable in your company, he can come stay with us. When you think he's old enough to understand, you can tell him that you, not the comtesse, are in fact his mother. And then he will be yours once more.'

'Oh, that would be heaven! But what if the comtesse refuses? To be so close and be denied again…'

'She won't refuse. Elodie, I've been planning this for a long time. I didn't want to say anything until every piece was in place. It will work, I absolutely guarantee it. Have I ever lied to you?'

'No. Oh, Will, if you can truly reunite me with my son, I will be grateful to you for ever!'

He smiled at her tenderly. 'You can show me how much, right now. And then we'll get packing for Paris.'

After a flurry of shopping in London to equip Elodie for her role as Madame Ransleigh, wife to the economic envoy blessed by the Court of St James to engage in discussions with the Interior Ministry of His Majesty, King Louis XVIII, Will and Elodie sailed for France. Though Elodie remained calm—as she had been in every crisis they'd faced together, whether fleeing Vienna in the middle of the night disguised as a valet or while being held, a knife to her throat, by a British foreign agent—Will knew that beneath the surface, she was torn between anticipation and anxiety.

Knowing every hour of delay before they visited the Hôtel de la Rocherie would be an agony of suspense for her, Will made only the essential calls to present his credentials to the British Ambassador and King Louis's chief advisors before returning to fetch Elodie from the luxurious hotel in which he'd installed her.

He found her pacing the room, from the gilded mantel to the door to the large windows with their view of the Place de la Republique, like a wild bird frantic to escape a jewelled cage.

As soon as she saw him, she rushed to her dressing table, jammed the stylish bonnet on her head and began dragging on her gloves. So nervous was she, she had difficulty pulling the tight kidskin over her trembling fingers.

He walked over to assist her.

'Quite an improvement over our accommodations the last time we were in Paris,' Will said, nodding towards the view of the Tuilerie Gardens in the distance as he coaxed the soft leather on to her hands. 'Though if it would make you less fretful, I could try obtaining some chickens.'

She tried to smile, but her lips were trembling, too. 'Will, I'm so frightened.'

He took her in his arms, wishing he could make this anxious process easier for her. 'You needn't be, my love! Don't you believe I know how important this is to you? I would never have suggested we attempt it if I were not absolutely convinced we shall succeed.' *Even if Will the Rogue has to make a return engagement to guarantee it*, he added silently to himself.

The concierge knocked to inform them their carriage was ready, and he ushered Elodie outside for the short drive to the Marais.

When they arrived at the Hôtel de la Rocherie, Will sent in his card, telling the lackey who greeted them that though he was a person previously unknown to the comtesse, he was in Paris on important government business and must discuss with her a matter of

utmost urgency. After showing them into a
drawing room elegantly appointed with striped
wallpaper and Louis XVI furniture, the man
withdrew.

Too nervous to sit, Elodie walked about,
trailing her hand over the back of the sofa,
down the edges of the satin window hangings.
'Oh, Will,' she whispered, 'This is where *madame* received us when St Arnaud and I called
on her with Philippe. The last place I saw my
son, before they stole him from me.'

'It's fitting, then,' Will said bracingly, 'that,
in this same room, he will be restored to you.'

A few minutes later, an elaborately gowned
woman Will assumed to be the comtesse entered the room. As he bowed over her hand,
she said, 'Monsieur Ransleigh? I cannot imagine what business you might have with—'

'And Madame Ransleigh, too,' Will interrupted, nodding towards Elodie, who stood
frozen by the mantel.

As the comtesse's gaze followed the direction of his nod, the polite smile faded and her
face went pale. 'Elodie Lefevre?' she gasped,
stumbling towards the Louis XVI fauteuil and
grasping the arm so tightly, Will thought she

might have fallen without its support. 'My brother told me you were dead!'

'Sorry to disappoint,' Elodie replied with some asperity, 'but as you can see, I am still quite alive, *moi*. St Arnaud claimed I'd died, did he? How was I supposed to have met my demise?'

'He—he said you'd been injured during the…the attempt on the Duke's life. He did everything he could for you, but you died in his arms later that night. And then he fled.'

'He got the last part right,' Will said drily. 'Shall we sit, *madame*? This must have been quite a shock. You will need time to recover, before we place our proposal before you.'

'Yes, let me order refreshment. I, for one, could use a glass of wine.'

Even while giving orders to the lackey who responded to her summons, the comtesse kept staring at Elodie, as if unable to believe she had truly survived Vienna. After they'd been served, she drank deeply of her wine, then looked back to Elodie again and asked, 'Are you going to try to take my son?'

'Philippe is not your son,' Will reminded her.

'Perhaps not always, but he is now! For

nearly two years he has known no other mother. You have only to ask him, he will tell you I am his *maman*.'

'I know,' Elodie said. 'I do appreciate the tender care you have taken of him.'

'You know?' the comtesse repeated with a puzzled frown. Then her eyes widened and she gasped, 'Was it you who accosted him in the park, two months ago? The servants said someone with an oddly intent manner had approached him. That they came back again to this house the very next day. I was so alarmed, I considered informing the gendarmes, but Prince Talleyrand advised against it.' Her questioning tone turned accusatory. 'You frightened him! How could you, if you care for him?'

'I'd hoped that if he studied me long enough, he would remember me. Can you imagine how it felt to see him again and realise he did not even recognise me?' she burst out. 'When I had thought of nothing but his welfare, every day, since he was taken from me?'

'Taken from you? My brother said you'd agreed to go to Vienna without him.'

'That report was as accurate as the one about my death!' Elodie retorted. 'I regret to disillusion you about your brother, but the only reason I left this *hôtel* without my son was because St Arnaud drugged my tea and abducted me. Once he had me in Vienna, he used the threat of harming Philippe to force me to participate in his plot. Did you truly not know?'

The comtesse dropped her eyes, not meeting Elodie's gaze. 'I am…aware of my brother's strong convictions, and the sometimes ruthless means he uses to carry them out. I knew there was something…suspect about your leaving Philippe so abruptly. But the child enchanted me from the first moment. When St Arnaud told me that he was setting out for Vienna immediately and that you had returned home to finish your preparations without seeing Philippe again, so you wouldn't have to distress him by telling him goodbye, I was too thrilled at being able to keep him to want to question the arrangement.'

'Was he…distressed when I did not come back for him?' Elodie asked.

The comtesse nodded. 'Of course. But I had a nursery full of toys to distract him and he loved listening to me read stories. When he would ask for you, I would tell you were doing an important task, but you would be back soon. He cried at nights, mostly, so I slept in the nursery with him for the first month. And gradually he stopped asking.'

A sheen of tears glazed Elodie's eyes. 'Thank you for being so kind to him.'

The comtesse shrugged. '*Eh bien*, I love him, too. But what do you mean to do now? It was many weeks after you disappeared before he was happy and comfortable. Surely you won't upset him again, by wrenching him from my care?'

'It was to safeguard his happiness and well-being, and for that reason alone, that I did not take him with me when I had the opportunity two months ago. But as much as I appreciate your care of him, he is *my* son and I want him back.'

The comtesse was shaking her head. 'But you cannot mean to take him *now*, surely! Give him some time! He is too young to understand all of this. You would only confuse and upset him.'

'We don't intend to take him away from you immediately,' Will inserted. 'Right now, he thinks of this as home and of you as his *maman*. What we propose is that my wife be reunited with him, spend time with him, let him become comfortable with her again. Once he is enough at ease with her to agree to it, we will take him to stay with us.'

Tears gathered in the comtesse's eyes. 'And then I will never see him again? Ah, *madame*, if you only knew what it is like to lose your son for ever, you would not be so cruel.'

'Believe me, I know!' Elodie retorted. 'Mine has been lost to me for nearly two years.'

'He wouldn't be far away,' Will said. 'I was sent to Paris on an economic mission to the French government. If negotiations succeed and we proceed to implement the plans, I could remain in Paris for many months. You would be able to see Philippe daily, if you liked.'

'I would like him to remain here,' the comtesse replied wistfully. 'My own son is dead; never in this life will I hold him again. But your son, *madame*, is alive. Though in taking him back you cut out my heart, I...I will not prevent you. Only, I beg you, don't drag him away until he is ready to go willingly.'

'I would take him no other way.' Elodie walked over and put a hand on the comtesse's arm. 'Thank you. I know how difficult it must be for you to agree to let him go. But as my husband said, we will be in Paris for an extended time. It will be weeks yet, probably, before he is willing to leave you, months after that before we would return to England.'

The comtesse shook her head sadly. 'There are not enough months in eternity to reconcile me to losing him.'

'You shall never lose him,' Elodie reassured her. 'Not completely. How could you, when you will always hold a special place in his heart? I promise I will never attempt to erase your image there.'

'Even though I let him forget you?' the comtesse replied. 'But surely you see that was different. I thought you were dead! Why should I remind him of a woman who would never return to him?'

'As long as you both make his welfare your first concern, I don't see why we can't all come to a sensible agreement,' Will said.

'Can I see him now?' Elodie asked.

Knowing her so well, Will could hear the longing in her voice. Knowing, too, that negotiating the terms of Philippe's custody would cause her anxiety—and wanting to make sure, in case the comtesse possessed any of her brother's perfidy, that the woman understood exactly what Will was prepared to do to enforce the agreement—Will said, 'Yes, comtesse, would you please have Philippe sent down now? Elodie, my love, you're too distracted and anxious to think clearly. Why don't you go out—' he gestured towards the French doors leading out to a small, formal garden that stretched between the *hôtel*'s two wings '—and take a stroll while we wait for the boy? The comtesse and I can discuss the particulars.'

Gratitude and relief in her eyes, Elodie said, 'Thank you. I would like that.'

Will kissed her hand. 'Into the garden with you, then.'

After the doors shut behind his wife, Will turned back to the comtesse. 'I'm pleased that you are choosing to be reasonable, *madame*.'

She sighed. 'I don't wish to be. I should like to pack Philippe up and run away with him to a place where you would never find us. But…I do know what it is to lose a son. I'm not sure I could live with myself, if I were to deliberately cause another such pain.'

'I applaud your sentiments. My wife, too, wants only what is best for her son, else I would have snatched the boy for her when we first found him. But I should also warn you, in case your longing to have sole control over the boy should ever triumph over your more noble feelings, that having grown up on the streets of London, I myself possess no tender sensibilities whatsoever. There is nowhere you could run where I would not eventually find you. I'd steal the boy back without a qualm, and he'd be halfway to a Channel port before you even knew he was missing. Once safely with his mother in England, protected by the influence of my family, you truly would never see him again.'

The comtesse gasped. 'You would do that, *monsieur*? But that is monstrous!'

'Perhaps, but there's not need to do anything "monstrous" as long as you are sensible. Considering that Philippe isn't truly your son, the arrangement we propose is quite favourable for you.'

'Favourable or poor, you do not leave me much choice, do you?'

'That was my intention,' Will replied. 'Some day, when he's older, Philippe must be told the truth, preferably before he works it out on his own. Come now, *madame*, let us put away our swords. We need not be opponents. Both you and my wife love Philippe. How could he not benefit from having two mothers to love him? The arrangement will work, I promise you.'

The comtesse sighed. 'It had better. Your wife has you, *monsieur*. Philippe is all I have left.'

'Then you will do everything necessary to make sure you keep him in your life. So we're agreed?'

At the comtesse's reluctant nod, Will said, 'Excellent. The boy should be down soon; I'll go fetch my wife.'

Will went quickly into the garden to find Elodie, who, pale and nervous, was pacing around and around the intricate knot garden.

As always, her distress made his chest ache. 'Have courage, sweeting!' he soothed. 'Philippe will be with you soon and you'll never lose him again.'

'Oh, Will, I know you promised me this would work, but are you sure? The comtesse is not just acquiescing to get us to leave, with no intention of honouring the agreement?'

Wrapping an arm around Elodie, he tilted up her chin and gave her a reassuring kiss. 'Do you really think I would let that happen?'

She gave him a wobbly smile. 'No. If I've learned nothing else since Vienna, I know I can trust you to make happen whatever you promise you will.'

'Then stop worrying, *mon ange*. All you desire will soon be yours.'

Taking her hand, he led her back into the salon.

Hardly daring to believe that she was truly going to have her son back again, Elodie fixed her gaze on the hallway door, hungry for her first glimpse of Philippe. When, a few minutes later, he skipped in, a joy of unimaginable sweetness filled her.

'Are we going visiting, *Maman*?' he asked, trotting over to the comtesse. 'Will there be cakes?'

That lady bent to give him a hug, as if to subtly underscore to Elodie that he still belonged to her. Magnanimous in her happiness, Elodie didn't even resent the gesture.

With the impatience of a little boy, Philippe wiggled free. 'Will we leave now, *Maman*?'

'No, Philippe. This kind lady is a…family connection. She's visiting Paris and wanted to become acquainted with you.'

Philippe looked up at Elodie curiously. Recognition flickering in his eyes, he said, 'I know you. You sold Jean an orange in the park, and you came to the nursery and looked at my soldiers.'

'That's right,' Elodie said with a pang, wishing he could have remembered her as well after Vienna. 'What a clever boy you are!'

'This gown is prettier. Why were you selling oranges?'

'I dressed up to play a game of pretend. You pretend, too, don't you, when you play with your soldiers?'

He nodded. 'I am a great general and win many battles. I have a tall black horse and a long, curved sword and I am brave and fierce, like my papa.'

Elodie's eyes misted. 'I am sure you will be just like your papa. He would be so proud of you.'

'You said you would take me to see the parrots at the market. You said the birds had red and green and blue feathers. Can we go now? *Maman*, will you come, too?'

The comtesse wrinkled her nose in distaste. 'I do not wish to visit the bird market, Philippe.'

'Please, *Maman*? I do so want to go!'

'He seems to have a memory like a poacher's trap now. How unfortunate he didn't develop the skill earlier,' Will murmured, echoing Elodie's thoughts.

'Please, *Maman*, let me go now!' Philippe repeated, focusing with a child's single-mindedness only on the part of the conversation which interested him.

'I suppose, if you take Jean and Marie and don't stay long, you may go,' the comtesse said.

'Do let us go, then,' Elodie said. Longing welling up in her for the touch of him, she held out her hand to the boy.

To her delight, Philippe put his small hand in hers. After closing her eyes briefly to savour the contact, she opened them to see Will smiling at her, love and gladness in his eyes. She mouthed a silent 'thank you'.

'What is your name? Can we not hurry? I know I shall like the red parrots best. Can I bring one home?'

Elodie laughed, revelling in the sorely missed sound of her son's voice. 'You may call me "*Maman* Elodie". Yes, we will hurry. As for the red parrot, you must ask your *Maman* about that.'

'Can I have a red parrot, *Maman*?'

'Not today, Philippe. Perhaps the next time.'

As they nodded a goodbye to the comtesse, who watched them walk away, her expression sad but resigned, Philippe said, '*Maman* Elodie, would *you* like a red parrot?'

Elodie looked up at Will, and he groaned. 'Somehow, I fear by the end of this excursion, I'm going to own a bird.'

Several hours later, having inspected all the colourful flock and narrowly avoided the purchase of the red parrot, they had returned a now-sleepy Philippe and his attendants to the Hôtel de la Rocherie. During the outing, Will had let Elodie take charge, following her indulgently as she wandered through the market hand in hand with Philippe, answering his volley of questions, even purchasing some sweets for him from a market vendor.

In the carriage on the way back to their lodgings, Elodie threw herself into his arms, so euphoric and brimming over with emotion, she wasn't sure whether to laugh or weep.

Hugging her tight, he said, 'Was it all that you wished for, sweeting?'

'Oh, my love, it was wonderful! The blessed angels must have been smiling on me the day you climbed up my balcony in Vienna! I still can scarcely believe you convinced the comtesse to agree to our arrangement—and, no, don't tell me how you managed it. I will sleep better not knowing.'

'My dear, your suspicions wound me,' Will replied, grinning. 'Sheer charm and persuasion, that was all.'

'The charm of a rogue!'

'A rogue whom you've bewitched completely.'

'It is I who am bewitched.' She looked at him wonderingly. 'You arranged all of this for me, didn't you? The mission, the railroads. You could have negotiated investments for your friend anywhere. But you chose Paris.'

He shrugged. 'Paris held the key to your happiness.'

Awed at the magnitude of such selfless love, humbled to be its object, she said, 'I can almost forgive St Arnaud for embroiling me in his scheme, for otherwise, I should never have met you. I thought it already a gift that you brought me from despair back to life. And now, you have given me back my soul. How can I ever repay you for such treasures?'

'Hmm, let's see,' Will said, drawing her on

to his lap. 'You could give *me* a son, I suppose. You, Max, Caro, even the comtesse seem to think having one is so wonderful, it would be rather selfish to keep it all to yourself.'

She smiled, it occurring to her that the only thing as marvellous as having Philippe back in her life would be bearing another son—Will's son.

'Sharing that blessing with you, sweet Will, my husband, my life, would be my greatest pleasure.' Framing his face in her hands, she leaned up to give him a kiss full of passion and promise.

* * * * *

A sneaky peek at next month...

HISTORICAL

IGNITE YOUR IMAGINATION, STEP INTO THE PAST...

My wish list for next month's titles...

In stores from 3rd May 2013:

❑ The Greatest of Sins — Christine Merrill

❑ Tarnished Amongst the Ton — Louise Allen

❑ The Beauty Within — Marguerite Kaye

❑ The Devil Claims a Wife — Helen Dickson

❑ The Scarred Earl — Elizabeth Beacon

❑ Her Hesitant Heart — Carla Kelly

Available at WHSmith, Tesco, Asda, Eason, Amazon and Apple

Just can't wait?

Visit us Online

You can buy our books online a month before they hit the shops! **www.millsandboon.co.uk**

0413

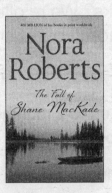
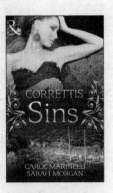